To: Joe Ferbstein

Please enjoy this book as much as I did when writing it.

Mort Kurlander

TEDDY ROOSEVELT

RIDES AGAIN

Published by Lazy K Press Inc.

33 Lafayette Drive

Rancho Mirage, Ca 92270

Printed in the United States of America

Dedication –

To the most important people in my life; my wife, Adrienne Muriel Kurland, is first and foremost in that regard. A close second are our four beautiful, bright and talented daughters. They are chronologically Gabrielle Bear, Abigail Irish, Miriam Burcham, and Jennifer Weiss. They too have children and husbands, but that's for another book.

INTRODUCTION

This is a story about a <u>real person </u>who was the twenty sixth president of the United States, Theodore Roosevelt. Several other individuals involved in this adventure are also real. William Randolph Hearst was the owner and editor-in-chief of the New York Journal and eventually a huge chain of newspapers from coast to coast. Samuel Clemens (Mark Twain was his pen name) lived in Hartford, Connecticut and traveled frequently to New York City. William Barclay "Bat" Masterson was a well known peace officer, gunfighter and "town tamer" in the old west. He was appointed federal marshal for the Southern District of New York by President Roosevelt. Several of Teddy Roosevelt's "Rough Riders" also appear in the text.

T.R. himself is one of the most remarkable presidents ever to hold office. He is one of only four men memorialized on Mount Rushmore. The other three are George Washington, Thomas Jefferson, and Abraham Lincoln. Not bad company. Besides being president, he was the Governor of New York State, the police commissioner of New York City and a state assemblyman in the legislature. He was the first of two American presidents to win the Nobel Peace Prize. He was a bulwark of the conservation movement and at the same time a big game hunter. The peace prize winner was also the man who recruited the cowboys and Ivy League graduates of the "Rough Riders" and then led them on his horse up the slope of San Juan Hill in the decisive battle that freed Cuba from Spanish oppression. For this, he won the Congressional Medal of Honor. The only man in history to win the Nobel Prize AND the Congressional Medal of Honor!

In addition, T.R. was the founder of the U.S. Navy's "Great White Fleet". He also is responsible for building the Panama Canal and the two ocean navy.

The author of twenty eight books, hundreds of magazine articles, the father of six children, the widower of one wife and devoted husband of a second woman, never had a scent of scandal personally nor in his administration.

"Speak softly and carry a big stick" epitomized his demeanor and nationwide administration.

The remainder of the characters in this tale are fictional individuals and, we hope memorable as well. They include Alex Falconer, M.D., another Harvard man and renowned forensic physician, "Gaby" Irish, a journalist for Mr. Hearst, and several other evil and dastardly individuals who aim to destroy Roosevelt and his colleagues.

CHAPTER ONE

The red-headed man with pince-nez glasses balanced on the bridge of his nose spoke with a reedy, high-pitched voice. "The game is five card stud. The ante is one dime, and you are light ten cents, Mr. Masterson. If you'd put down that infernal cigar and look at the table, perhaps we could go on." He spoke with the air of a man comfortable in telling others what to do.

"I know the stogie bothers you, Colonel, when it's lit. But I'm only chewing it now, not smoking it, sir." The erstwhile lawman sounded somewhat cowed.

There were five of them occupying the large parlor room. The house was located on top of a small rise or knoll known as Sagamore Hill, which gave the home its name. They played by gaslight, as electric power lines had not yet been strung to all of the outlying homes in Oyster Bay, that August of the year 1900. Since the midsummer evening air was still warm, the French windows were open and the chirping of crickets underscored the conversation.

The player to the dealer's left would not have been out of place at the tables in Monte Carlo. Alexander Falconer, M.D., displayed the air of self-assurance of a man comfortable in the halls of wealth and power. Although physically tall, the main impression that he conveyed to others was an intellectual aura challenged, at the moment, only by someone of the caliber of the bespectacled master of Sagamore Hill. The doctor was not the kind of man you'd try to bluff out of a winning hand.

"Now that you've replaced the late Mr. Hobart on the ticket, Governor, when do you start campaigning? It looks like you'll do the brunt of it this fall. I expect McKinley prefers to sit on his porch in Ohio and let you battle Bryan."

"That seems to be the way it's playing out, Alex," answered the five foot eight inch barrel-chested man. "Mr. Kane, you have the high card. Do you want to bet on that queen or not?"

"The queen checks, gentlemen." The neatly dressed little man with the razor thin moustache maintained a careful lack of expression as he observed his colleagues around the table.

"My nine'll bet a dime and start some action," offered the fifth player, tall and corpulent, with beads of perspiration popping up on his forehead almost as quickly as he mopped them away with a large, orange bandana. He greedily swallowed half a stein of beer after making his bet. He appeared to be desperately trying to replenish his body fluids as he lost them through the sweat of his brow and body. The rounded angles of his bones and the smooth appearance of his skin showed that the young man kept well ahead of the danger of dehydration and malnutrition.

The man with the pince-nez and the bushy graying moustache was destined to become the twenty-sixth President of the United States. The neatly dressed, small chap with the manicured moustache was "Woodey" Kane, late captain of the Rough Riders and a Harvard graduate. He was the member of Theodore Roosevelt's entourage who planned the vice-presidential campaign. The man chewing the dead cigar was William "Bat" Masterson, already a legendary lawman of the West. A friend of Roosevelt's, he had come to New York to help the former cowboy grasp for national office and also to seek out his own career as a journalist in the nation's largest city.

"Sudsy" Sudberg was Roosevelt's speech writer, press relations man and a general literary presence. Although the governor had written a number of newspaper articles, magazine stories and books, he needed another literary hand to help him with the enormity of paper work of a national campaign. McKinley had no intention of leaving Ohio. It was up to the cowboy hero of the Spanish war to rival the color and charisma of the golden-voiced William Jennings Bryan. Sudberg would be equal to the writing task, as long as he remained sober.

Governor Roosevelt turned to the last, and youngest, member of the poker group. "Alex, why don't you tell us about that medical detection case? The one we read about in the Herald the other day."

There was no question as to who was the leader of this group. When Roosevelt said he wished to hear about Falconer's adventures as a forensic physician, all talk of politics, campaigning, the GOP and the rest went out the open French windows. Falconer was on stage, and as he dealt the next hand he began to tell the story of the Vanderkill murder.

"It all started innocently enough. I gave a lecture at the New York Academy of Science, three or four months ago, concerning the effects of poisonous snakes and their bites on humans. I've been very interested in this lately, especially since the New York Zoological Society decided to accumulate a live collection. Most bites, even those of poisonous snakes, aren't fatal. You have to know what to do and when to do it with each variety to avoid death."

"My talk on the subject was well received. Then, last week, I got a call from one of the people who attended; a physician from New Rochelle. Fortunately, the phone lines are strung all the way up to New Rochelle, even though we don't have them out here." He turned and looked reproachfully at the Governor of the State of New York, whose face reddened as he responded.

"I know, Alex, we've discussed this before. The governor should have a telephone available for emergencies. The telephone people *say* it's expensive to bring a line all the way out here to Sagamore Hill, and I'll be damned if I'm going to pay for it or have the public treasury foot the bill. If we get elected we'll deal with it next summer."

Falconer nodded and shrugged. "As I was saying, this physician called and said he'd been at my lecture and had a case which had just come up that very day."

"George Vanderkill, one of the rich side of the family, had been found dead by one of the servants in the room where he kept his live snake collection."

"Well, my colleague didn't want to sign the death certificate. He had the feeling there was something wrong. Vanderkill was in his early sixties and in good health. A rattlesnake bite should not have killed him that quickly."

"There were two puncture wounds on his left shoulder. The corpse's face was pale, there was foam on his mouth, and his eyes were bulging and glassy. His pupils were dilated. That in itself made the doctor think that this didn't fit the picture of death by a venomous bite."

"In my lecture I had very specifically talked about how to treat snake bites and the fact that because rattlers have what we call hemolytic poisons, their victims tend to present a rather distinctive picture."

"Jest a minute, Doc. Those college boys might know what you're talking about, but I don't. You have to talk plain English to me." Masterson wadded up what appeared to be a piece of tobacco and spit it through the open French window and out into the darkness of the night.

"Hemolytic means that the poison from the rattlesnake, and I'm sure you've seen your share of them, Marshal, causes the blood vessels to explode or dissolve. You then bleed all over inside your body. That's what kills you. When you get a big enough bite, providing enough poison gets into you, time goes by long enough for that to happen. The area where the rattlesnake bites shows swelling and redness under the skin where it bleeds because of breaking up of the blood vessels, you see."

"The problem with this wound was that it was too neat. There was no swelling around the puncture wounds. There wasn't any bleeding where the snake had bitten the dead man. Another thing is that after a rattler's bite, the face becomes kind of bluish. There's a mottled color to the skin, sometimes even a rash. You see a lot of bleeding, and the victim vomits and, excuse me, gentlemen, he moves his bowels. Blood is everywhere."

"None of that was true with George Vanderkill. His doctor was right to call me and ask me to come on up to Westchester right away. He told the family he wasn't going to sign the death certificate until an expert came to see what was going on."

"The presumption was that one of the old man's rattlesnakes had bitten him. The doctor would then sign the death certificate, and the heirs would come into a fortune. When I got there things were a little different."

The game went on as Falconer spoke, and Sudberg, despite what appeared to be his advanced state of inebriation, won two hands in a row.

"I examined the body and discovered that he showed no evidence of hemolytic poisoning at all. I took a sample of tissue and looked at it with my portable microscope and saw no dissolution of the blood vessels. There was nothing to indicate that a rattlesnake toxin had ever been injected into the victim."

"Then I looked at the wound itself. While the two puncture wounds were the same distance apart as a rattlesnake's fangs, the course of the injection into the body indicated that a straight instrument had gone in, rather than the curved fangs of a snake. What had happened, you see, was that the killer made — by then I knew it was a homicide — two injections with a hypodermic needle into the skin. I could follow the track of the wounds from the surface in through the flesh to the muscle where the poison was injected."

"The manner of death indicated the victim had been killed with something both more toxic and rapid than rattlesnake venom. It was the kind of death seen when the nerves that support breathing are paralyzed. The individual dies because his brain stops giving instructions to his body to breathe. It's called a neurotoxic poison. Prussic acid is the most common example of this kind of chemical. It has a distinctive odor. It's the same substance you find in peach or almond pits. Sure enough, right at the wound, I smelled peach blossoms."

"The man was killed by cyanide injection, or prussic acid, as it's commonly called. The next question then was to determine who got the prussic acid, administered it and murdered Vanderkill."

"It sounds simple the way you tell it, Doc," said the now animated Rudy Sudberg. He was looking at his hole card and thrusting forth three dimes. "I'll see your ten cents and raise you twenty. But I heard there was some rough stuff going on there. According to the Herald, you nailed the killer yourself. Isn't that right?"

"I'll see your raise, Sudberg, just to keep you honest. What've you got?"

"Queens over deuces, professor." Rudy smiled, hoping his streak of good luck might have allowed him at least one bluff for the evening.

"Not good enough. Three tens beat you every time." Falconer revealed the hand, and pulled in the winnings.

"It really wasn't that hard. There was only one principal heir. A stepson was the only surviving child. It could be that Harvey Blister, the stepchild, killed the other children too. We'll never know. He had the most to gain by the old man's early death."

"Harvey had suffered big losses in several businesses he'd attempted. One of these was a chemical company in which they were trying to make use of hydrogen cyanide, a by-product of the transformation of coal into coke. They use the poison as an agricultural fumigant to kill rats. Otherwise the stuff doesn't have much value. The new company's idea was to transform the poisonous gas into another product which could be used as a fertilizer. The business failed and the man owed a fortune."

"It seemed clear to me that Blister had motive and means. I wanted to confront him and try for a confession, or at least enough information to trip him up."

Sudberg had gone to the buffet sideboard and created a sandwich of gargantuan proportions. Ham, cheese, tomatoes, lettuce and gobs of mayonnaise and mustard oozed from its sides. The others watched him, awe struck and remarkably he said through full mouth, "This is great food. I'd love to meet your cook, Governor."

"Some other time, Rudy. How did you make contact with the man, Alex?" T.R. asked.

"His firm has an office on Broadway, near Herald Square."

"I had to make an arrangement between the New Rochelle police and those in New York City. The stepson had an office in the city. The New Rochelle police, of course, have no jurisdiction in the city."

He looked directly at Roosevelt, now governor for almost two years, and added, "Because New York does not have a state police force or anyone with jurisdiction from one community to the other."

"The New York City Police Department was very cooperative. They assigned a man to go with me to meet Blister in his office building. I asked the detective to stay in the waiting room while I went in to talk with the suspect. I was afraid if he saw a policeman, he wouldn't talk to me at all."

"I confronted Harvey with the evidence, the nature of his stepfather's death and the fact that it could not have been because of a rattlesnake bite by any stretch of the imagination." He examined his cards in the five-card draw hand that had been dealt by the now seated Sudberg, and was delighted to see that he had a 5 to 9 straight. In a game like this, a likely winner. The six of hearts had a mustard smear above the first red pip.

"I think I'll stick to these. Well, when I confronted the man with all this material, he seemed to lose control. He must have been under a great deal of pressure, hoping he could get away with it but fearing he couldn't. I'm sure you've seen that before, Masterson, in your work as a lawman."

"The man just went off the edge. He started shouting and screaming, running around the office, telling me his stepfather was evil, greedy, and didn't deserve to live."

"And then suddenly Blister came charging at me, holding a syringe filled with what he said was prussic acid. He screamed, saying that if I thought I was going to lock him up, I was badly mistaken and I'd get a dose of the same medicine as the old bastard Vanderkill. He charged straight at me like a cavalry officer brandishing his sabre in front of him."

"Some of you know I spend a lot of time with hand-to-eye coordination and movements, magic tricks, and juggling. I try to be as quick with my hands and feet as I can."

Falconer was preening himself, like a big bird showing his brilliant plumage to those around him. He was verbally showing off his physique and flexing his muscles.

"I stepped aside like a matador, and let the man charge on by me. Unfortunately for him, he slipped on a scatter rug as he rushed past, and fell to the floor. The lunatic actually injected himself with his own lethal poison. The dose was so massive that it was immediately fatal. He showed every characteristic of a man poisoned by cyanide."

"I'd never seen such a vivid reaction before. His skin first looked like ashes and then gray-blue. He foamed at the mouth. His eyes had a glassy glazed look, and started to bulge forward. The pupils dilated. The air had the unmistakable odor of bitter almonds, just the way it's described in the literature, or, more accurately to me, peach blossoms. It was fascinating, almost beautiful, in a grisly way. He was dead in less than a minute."

"The huge dose paralyzed every nerve cell in his body. Even before he died of asphyxiation from non-breathing, his brain must have been dead. The story was in all of the newspapers. It was another example of scientific work coupled with simple awareness and looking for the right thing."

"If you keep your mind open, the answers to what seem to be complex issues come to you without much trouble. The doctor in New Rochelle had an open mind plus the information I gave in a lecture. After he called me, I simply correlated the scientific information at my command. That plus the obvious issues, such as who had the most to gain by the old man's death, and there you are."

Sudberg interrupted, hiccupping, "A regular Sherlock Holmes, Professor Falconer. Your stories are better than the ones in the magazine."

"Actually, Rudy, the Sherlock Holmes stories aren't much different than mine, because they're written by a physician. Arthur Conan Doyle was a practicing physician before he began to write. His theories of deduction are no more than what a working physician puts into practice every day. My work could be compared to a country doctor gathering the facts of an illness and making a diagnosis. In this case, I took the facts of the crime, their relationship to one another, and arrived at the most likely cause. There is a similarity."

"Modesty, if I may say so, doctor, is not one of your faults," the governor offered, and went on. "This hand isn't worth the powder it would take to blow it to hell. I'm out." He folded his cards.

"The doc may not be modest, colonel, but he must have a pretty damned good hand." Sudberg belched and said, "I'll see you, doctor." He thrust three dimes from his rather large pile to the center of the table. "I've got to keep you honest, at least," and suppressed another eructation.

"I've got a straight to the nine," smiled the self-satisfied storyteller. He had entertained the group with a tale of his mental and physical prowess, and at the same time won the biggest pot of the night.

"Not good enough, my friend. Your yarn's a winner, but my flush takes the pot." Sudberg's protuberant belly made it a matter of some physical exertion to lean forward and rake in the silver coins spread across the middle of the felt-covered table. There had to be at least five dollars in the pot, a tidy sum for 1900 when a full-course dinner at the Delmonico's could be bought for less than two.

Bat Masterson was shuffling the cards preparatory to dealing out the next hand. His stack of coins was low. He was one of the big losers of the evening. "All these stories are well and good, and maybe they have something to do with solving crimes, but I don't think we'll need to worry about that kind of scientific stuff in the job we've got in front of us. We're going to elect the colonel vice-president, and later on President of the United States." He pronounced the "U" as if it were the name of a female sheep. "That's what we gotta shoot at now. The game's seven card stud. Ante up, men, this one could be big."

Roosevelt peered at his two hole cards and folded the first up card dealt to him, saying, "These cards aren't even related to each other. I doubt if they've been introduced. I'm out, gentlemen. I do think, Bat, that you should never close off an avenue of interest. Who knows when Dr. Falconer's services might be important to us?"

"We've got three months of hard campaigning ahead of us, and a country to cross doing it. We may need all the help we can get before it's over." Roosevelt played as cautious a game politically as he did poker. His reputation for daring and bold moves was based on the careful planning of every gambit he ever tried. Before Police Commissioner Roosevelt chased the saloon keepers and whoremongers out of downtown Manhattan, he knew he had the backing of the power structure of the city and state. He was a thinker as much as a doer.

Sudberg looked at his hand and offered to open the betting for a dime. "Speaking of pharmacies, gentlemen, did you hear the joke about the duck who walked into a chemist shop in New York last week and asked the druggist for some lip balm? The pharmacist said he had some and offered it to the duck, asking for fifty cents in cash. The duck replied, 'Oh, no, just put it on my bill'." He laughed loudly at his joke. No one else found it amusing.

Masterson, as is the habit with losers, said, "Let's get on with the game. I've had enough of detective stories and medical mysteries and jokes for the night. Deal another hand."

CHAPTER TWO

"Robbie the Robber" Smoot lay quietly in the tall grass beside Sagamore Hill's graveled driveway. The sun had set, and the air was cooling rapidly. It had been an extremely hot summer day, even on Long Island. Robbie, used to the sweltering weather of Manhattan, thought when he took the job that at least he wouldn't have to put up with hot and sticky air out here. He realized how wrong he was after spending the day casing the Oyster Bay estate.

The man who'd hired him had thoroughly described the house, its entrances and windows. But Robbie always liked to see for himself. He was a professional. You could never rely on an amateur.

Smoot had been in the business most of his life. He had gotten his nickname, "the robber," from his schoolmates in Jersey City. At age six, he began stealing small items from the general store up near Journal Square. Later, after they'd put him in the boys' reformatory in Secaucus, he'd stolen extra food and milk even inside that dark, cold place they called 'the block house'.

Robbie never spent time thinking about his life history or future. He was just interested in the job at hand and in life for that moment.

The gas lights were on in all the downstairs rooms. The diminutive thief had no idea who lived there, except it was some rich guy. He didn't care what the swell's name was. Right now he'd been hired to do a job of burglary. Earlier on, a whole bunch of children had run around the house, making lots of noise. Several servants, the owner and his wife and various other people, had come and gone all afternoon until things settled down after sunset.

He'd been warned that the owner was a very active, even a dangerous man who slept with a revolver on his nightstand. He'd also been told about the dogs.

Smoot had a good deal of experience in these matters. It was best to wait at least an hour after everyone went to sleep, including the animals, before moving any closer to the house.

He was prepared for the dogs, bringing enough laudanum to put both of them to sleep for a long time. Tincture of Opium was easily available over the counter in any pharmacy in the country. Robbie had laced two pounds of hamburger meat with the opiate. The beef, in packages wrapped in waxed paper, was ready to hand to the hounds.

This job promised to be a toughie. He never would have considered it if the big dandy with the orange and green cravat hadn't made him such a sweet deal.

"I know this won't be easy, Smoot, but you've been highly recommended to me. I'm willing to make it more than worth your while. I'm going to compensate you famously for the risk you'll be taking." This Fancy Dan even talked funny.

He handed Robbie two twenty dollar gold pieces and added, "There'll be six more of those for you when I receive delivery."

A gold eagle was a month's pay for a laboring man. Robbie, of course, had never done a single day's work in his life, much less a month. But he knew the value of money. Money was the most important thing in life and the only thing he really loved. That included Stella and even their two kids.

He'd never bothered to marry Stella. The two kids had come along a few years ago. He wasn't even sure how old they were. A boy and a girl; Stella took care of them. Every once in a while she'd nag him for money. When he had it, it didn't bother him to give her some. Things had been a little slow lately. The advent of the man with the orange and green tie came "just in the nick of time," as they said in the dime novels.

The man was a neat dresser and had the appearance of a gentleman. He wore a green and black whipcord jacket, even in the hot Manhattan summer. He spoke with one of those college accents, and his shoes were shined. The guy didn't have any calluses on his hands, and his fingernails were short and clean.

He either didn't have to work at all or had the kind of job that relied upon others getting their hands dirty and their shoes scuffed. He was the kind of person that Robbie hated the most. Like the ones that ran the reform school, or the politicians who were far bigger robbers than he ever could have dreamed of becoming. But the man had tempted him.

"What I want you to do, Smoot, is to go into someone's home without being detected. When you get in there, find a framed photograph which I shall describe to you. Take it, bring it to me, and collect your additional six gold pieces."

At least he wouldn't have to carry out a lot of loot. If he got in with no one knowing, he could get out again in two minutes, if he found the photograph where the oversized Mr. Fancy Dan said it would be.

When the stars came out and the lights in the house were extinguished one by one, Robbie carefully took the doctored hamburger out of his pockets. Removing the wax paper, he held a large chunk in each hand. If the hounds were awake, it wouldn't take long for them to smell the meat. He preferred them to *come* to him, not the other way around. He remained very still. Five minutes later the animals moved away from the house in his direction, sniffing and acting more curious than alarmed.

Smoot knew a lot about guard dogs. He'd had to deal with them professionally for twenty years. If you didn't challenge them or show fear, they treated you the way they'd treat anybody. If you weren't afraid of them, they wouldn't attack you. At least they hadn't yet.

He figured the hounds were more like him than anything else. They were greedy, and wanted to get as much as they could. Even though they'd been fed a couple of hours earlier, Robbie knew they'd be ready for some nice juicy hamburger if they got wind of it. They'd eat it all, even though they weren't hungry. He was like that too. He'd grab whatever he could and run away with it if he had the chance.

Which reminded him that Fancy Dan had cautioned him; "Don't take anything at all from the house. I don't want the owner to realize that he's been burglarized, or even that the picture's gone."

"This whole thing is just a practical joke, Smoot. I know it sounds foolish, but this fellow happens to be a particularly bothersome rival of mine. I need to do something to get his attention and to show him I mean business. When the right time comes I'll point out the missing picture. But I don't want him to be forewarned before I'm ready, understand?"

Robbie didn't believe a word of it. Fancy Dan was a very muscular man, and it wasn't the time to argue with him anyway. He had that kind of mean look Smoot had seen before, like the guys in reform school who hurt people. Robbie himself never went in for strong arm stuff. He was just a thief, a sneak thief at that. Besides he was small. Violence scared him. So he agreed to whatever Fancy Dan wanted.

By now, the dogs were coming right up to him, sniffing and whining, acting like they wanted to be his friend. They gobbled up the meat, even licking and tearing up the waxed paper. Then they began to lose their footing. The first one went down, hind legs first, as if he were drunk. It didn't take the other one much longer. Robbie didn't think he'd given them enough to kill them. If so, too bad for them. It was all in a day's work.

Now was the time to make his move. The lights in the house were out. He tiptoed around to the side of the building, avoiding the gravel at the carriage entrance to the mansion.

Robbie had almost been caught once in a break-in, by some damned insomniac. He usually managed to avoid confrontation, relying upon foot speed to stay out of trouble. His size, although an advantage in creeping into windows and coal chutes, made physical encounter a losing proposition for him.

Fancy Dan had given him a plan of the house that showed the location of the room to be entered. "This is the window to use. I'm fairly certain it won't be locked."

"That don't matter much to me, sir. I'm used to working free the little hook and eye locks most people put on their windows, if they use 'em at all. I have this little celluloid collar to help me there. Just a trick of the trade."

Celluloid was a great invention for the burglar trade. It could be cut into small pieces and used as a tool to lift hook and eye locks, slip into spring locks, and when it was thin enough, you could pick a door lock with it. Without this tool, Smoot might have had to go back to stealing fruit and vegetables from pushcarts.

The window was locked after all. Robbie reached into his bag of tricks and slid the scrap of celluloid into the gap between the two French windows. They opened outward. The hook and eye lock was on the inside with its bar in a horizontal position. It was easy to slip the tool under the bar, push it up very slowly, and allow it to fall quietly to the side as he pulled the windows open. They didn't squeak, a piece of luck. A light sleeper might have heard.

The room looked just like Fancy Dan's description. There were animal heads all over the walls. One looked like a mountain lion, or maybe a wildcat, Robbie wasn't sure. He'd never finished the fourth grade. There was a head with horns that looked like a moose or an elk, something like that. The scariest thing of all was in the corner, a big, black bear with his mouth open and giant white teeth glaring at him in the moonlight. If the damned thing were alive, he would have been out of that house in less time than it took to look at it. The dandy had warned him about the stuffed animals and heads, but they looked scary anyway. The other problem was that there were pictures all over the place. In the dark he might get the wrong one. He decided to risk striking a match just briefly to be sure and get the right photo.

"The one you want, Smoot, is of a man in an army uniform with his arm around another chap, in civilian clothes."

There it was on the desk! Two "gentlemen" smiling at the camera, showing off their expensive dental work. The fellow on the left had pretty good choppers at that. He displayed huge teeth and a big, bristly moustache. The man on the right had a round baby face and was younger than the other one. The inscription said: "To Teddy from Winnie, in fond remembrance of Cuba." It was dated July 1898.

By now he was really scared of alerting whoever it was in the house who had shot all of these animals. Anybody who could shoot a big, black grizzly bear along with these horned animals and mountain lions and such was somebody he didn't want to meet, ever. It was probably the guy in the soldier suit. He did look familiar. Guys like that carried guns and used them.

He managed to open the back of the frame, and stuffed the photograph into his pocket. He hardly noticed the paper cut on his hand as he shoved it in. He'd dump the frame in the woods later.

Smoot couldn't quite resist taking something for himself from that rich man's house. Something glimmered on the desk, a round, gold-colored object like a big coin, larger than a silver dollar, probably real gold. He dropped it into a trouser pocket as he left the desk and headed towards the French windows.

He left the way he'd come in, closing the windows carefully, figuring no one would notice that the lock was now open. He'd tell Mr. Fancy Dan, who'd been insistent that he leave no trace that it had been open all along, the way he said, if he asked. It was probably better to lie to him than to risk his anger. He was a mean one. Robbie could tell.

With the dogs asleep, it was easier to depart than to approach. He simply walked in his stocking feet down the dirt pathway till he got to the place near the tree where he'd left his shoes. He put them on, moved through the high grass along the driveway and back onto the road to Oyster Bay.

The rendezvous had been well chosen. A water tank stood by the railroad tracks to replenish the steam engines after their tong haul in from Eastern Long Island to the city. A storage shed adjoined the tank. Together, the two structures cast large dark shadows in the moonlight.

It seemed logical that the college dude wanted to meet there. The guy was so keen no one discovered his part in the "practical joke" that he's made a special point of telling Robbie, "If I learn that you've talked to a single soul about this job, it'll go very hard on you. Be sure of that."

He'd had that mean look when he said it, so Robbie assured Fancy Dan, "I won't tell no one, believe you me!"

And he really didn't. Except Stella, of course. She didn't count. She kept nagging him for money. So when he got the two gold eagles and told her more was coming, she squeezed the story out of him. He'd belatedly remembered Fancy Dan's admonition and instructed her not to breathe a word. He wasn't really afraid that the guy would find out about Stella. When asked if he was married or had family in town, he just lied. Lying came easily to Robbie.

"I'm a lone wolf, sir. My daddy told me if you travel alone you'll travel farther, and I always remember that. I don't have friends, and I don't keep women. When I want milk, I don't have to buy a cow, you know, ha, ha."

He smiled weakly as he remembered telling this to the big dandy. Robbie figured, "What the bastard doesn't know won't hurt him." Besides he'd never see this fellow again.

As for the face in the picture, that did look familiar to Robbie, He felt sure he knew the guy from somewhere. But he'd never had anything to do with rich people who had estates in Oyster Bay and went on hunting trips. Maybe it was somebody he'd run into in New York once.

As Robbie approached the water tower, he didn't see Mr. Fancy Dan. A big guy like that should be easy to spot. Maybe he hadn't got there.

They were to meet an hour before the milk train would arrive to take water. After the payoff, he'd jump on the train and nobody would notice him on his way back to town. His employer would no doubt leave another way. He didn't seem the type to jump on milk trains. He'd have a horse rig somewhere out back of the tracks.

"If things work out," he thought, "I'll be home for breakfast. I'll stash five of the eagles with the two I got before, in the secret place Stella don't know about. I'll turn the sixth one in for greenbacks, and maybe give her a few to keep her mouth shut for awhile. Maybe I'll buy a new outfit." He smiled at the prospect of getting a black and green whipcord suit and becoming a dandy. He was twenty—seven years old and had never worn a new suit of clothes. This was the biggest swag he'd ever scored.

No one seemed to be around at the shed. The swell probably wanted to be sure he wasn't being followed. So Robbie sat down on the tracks and waited. Sure enough, Fancy Dan emerged from the shadow of the water tower.

"You seem to be alone. Did you have any trouble?" The big man wore his black and green coat with black trousers, and black shoes and a black hat. "No wonder I couldn't see him in the dark," thought Robbie. "He just blends in with the shadows." "Did it go well, Smoot? You've got the picture?" Just a trace of anxiety colored the otherwise self—assured and insolent calm of the big bruiser.

"Do you have the gold coins, sir? I'll deliver the picture when you deliver your part of the bargain."

"First, I want to be sure it's the right picture. I'm not going to pay you all this cold, hard cash without making certain." His voice once more had that mean rasp, as when they'd met before. Robbie didn't even want to seem to cross him.

"Oh, it's the right picture, sir. It's got the writing on it like you said," he insisted. "You can see it if I light a match. I've got it right here." He reached into his inside pocket and produced the photograph.

"Let's have a look at it. No matches, Smoot! I think I can make it out by moonlight... .yes, that's the one. Here's your money." Robbie didn't have to count. There were six of them all right. Money was his specialty, when he could get it.

As the dandy peered at the picture, he seemed to relax. He sounded satisfied. "Was anyone disturbed? Did you have any trouble at all?"

"No, sir, it went clean as a whistle. I didn't have a speck of trouble. Nobody knows I was there. Nobody'll ever know it's gone, one picture from so many. The house was just like you said. The French window was open, and I just slipped in there, took the picture, and got away, smooth as a whistle."

"What about the dogs, Robbie, those big dogs? Did they bother you?"

"No, sir, I have a way of dealing with dogs, I told you that. They're fast asleep. They won't wake up till sunrise. They won't know what happened to them, but they'll sure have a real good hangover, you can bet on that." Robbie tried to laugh, but couldn't.

"You didn't harm them, did you? There won't be any dead dogs out there to give us away? That would be totally unacceptable, you know." His voice rose, and he sounded even harsher than before.

"Oh, no sir, don't worry yourself at all about that, sir. They'll be fine. I've done this lots of times before, with never any trouble. I know what to do. Robbie Smoot always delivers. You've got the picture. I've got my pay, and you can be on your way. I'll just wait here for the train to come by." Robbie was feeling more and more apprehensive about Fancy Dan's tone of voice.

"You didn't take anything else, did you, Smoot? You know that would violate our agreement."

"Oh, no sir, nothing else, nothing at all. I just wanted these," and he held his right fist clutching the six twenty dollar gold pieces up in the air. "These are all I wanted. Best night's work I ever done in my life. I wouldn't take no chances in crossing you, sir." Robbie had assumed a hang—dog look, hoping that a show of subservience and passivity would relieve the big suspicions.

It seemed to work. "Yes, Smoot, I do believe that you've done exactly as you've been told. I trust you, Smoot, I have to, of course. There's just one more piece of business to attend to." With that, Mr. D. removed a very large and heavy claw hammer from inside his black and green coat.

In the twinkling of an eye, Robbie knew what was up, and turned to flee. The big guy was going to kill him, take the coins back and get what he wanted for free. It was all so obvious, his insistence on secrecy, the quiet, dark meeting place, the absence of friends, accomplices, anyone to tell about it. It all fit. Robbie realized he'd been had, and as he turned to flit away, the big man's long arm whipped the hammer down with tremendous force and caught him square in the back of the head.

It caved in the rear portion of his skull, just as a tablespoon would crack the top of an egg that had been soft boiled. "Robbie the Robber" had no further thoughts. He fell like a rock. There never was a chance to make his getaway, nor to use his speed to any advantage at all. He'd been had and was quite dead. In fact, he was dead within a moment of hitting the ground. All of his bodily functions ceased and the massive hemorrhage inside of his head squeezed his brain cells into a state of total paralysis and inactivity. His heart stopped and so did his breathing.

Mr. D. didn't waste time. He pried the six coins out of the clenched hand while the hands were still warm and sweaty, and he placed them in his own pocket. Fancy Dan then dragged the small and lifeless body over to the railroad track.

The milk train would be coming along in about thirty minutes, but it never stopped here. Smoot, dressed in his burglar outfit of black, would not be seen by the engineer until the huge wheels were right on top of him. By then it would be too late to stop the train anyway.

Mr. D. thought it would be judicious to make it appear as if the victim had done himself in through the demon rum. He'd brought along a quart bottle of cheap whiskey and liberally poured the fluid into the lifeless mouth of the victim, now getting cold. He sprinkled more, over Robbie's clothing and then placed the empty bottle into the hand that had recently held the gold coins. Dan placed the body across the track so it would a1ppear that the blow which ended Robbie's life had been the result of a tragic accident.

The poor fellow had been drinking, sitting around the tool shed, getting pie-eyed and planning to steal a ride on the milk train back into the city. When the poor sot heard the train coming, he stumbled toward the track, but fell across the tracks. The engineer, of course, couldn't be blamed for being unable to stop quickly enough and had crushed the drunk's head with the wheels of the great locomotive.

It was a shame, but probably what he deserved. After all, he was just a drunk. Since there was no family, he'd be taken to Potter's Field and put away there. There'd be no investigation, and that would be the end of it.

The large man walked away, patting the inside pocket of his black suit which contained the photograph and jingling the six gold coins in his trouser pockets. He had briefly thought about going through Robbie's clothes to see if the original two gold coins were still there, but he decided he didn't want to risk any more time near the body. Besides, two gold coins in exchange for this photograph were the biggest bargain of the new century, and likely to remain so for the rest of the hundred years. What he had now was literally worth an empire. He headed for his horse and buggy with a quiet smile of satisfaction on his face. The large gold coin remained in Robbie's pants pocket.

CHAPTER THREE

Breakfast at Sagamore Hill was a required event. Every family member had to attend. Even the haughty sixteen year old Alice Lee reluctantly broke her fast at 8:00 a.m. promptly. The pater familias presided at the end of a long highly polished oaken table in the dining room.

Theodore III ("Ted"), Kermit, Ethel, Archibald, and three year old Quentin wriggled restlessly in their chairs along the sides of the piece of furniture symbolically representing 'family harmony," as the head of the clan put it. Mrs. Klein (father had always admonished his brood to address all of the servants respectfully as Mr., Mrs., or Miss, "as the situation demands") had stocked the sideboard serving table with a full "American Breakfast." English breakfasts were no different, but Mr. Roosevelt eschewed any reference to foreign appellations when patriotic ones were available.

Atop the groaning sideboard was an array of breakfast food suitable for a squad of Rough Riders. Yellow and white scrambled eggs sat bubbling in a silvery bowl atop a steamer to keep them moist and warm. There had to be at least a dozen in the container. Sliced fried potatoes with sautéed onions and slivers of green bell peppers swam in a butter sauce next to the egg tray. Two other silver trays held thick sliced bacon, and quarter-inch chunks of pink red ham respectively. A small platter held two dozen small white pork sausages, browned on the skillet. A large coffee pot issued the savory odor of the roasted bean and its neighbor, a teapot, did the same with its oriental leaves.

Woven wooden baskets held a full loaf of sliced fresh baked white bread in one, a warm dark brown pumpernickel in another, and a dozen Kaiser rolls in a third.

On the table itself in addition to service for eight, sat a soup bowl size tub of white unsalted butter. Somewhat smaller bowls of orange marmalade, grape jam, brown mustard, and a large bottle of Heinz tomato ketchup added to the colorful array. Salt and pepper shakers and containers of both brown coarse and white refined sugar completed the savories on the table.

Mrs. Klein, the head cook herself, entered brandishing a half full glass pitcher of milk. "Mr. Klein got no milk this morning at the station," she informed the gathered family. "This is all that's left. Go easy boys. I still have plenty of cream for your coffee, Mr. R., and your tea, Mrs. and Alice," she reassured the grown ups.

"No milk? Are the *cows* on strike?" queried the Chief Executive Officer of the State of New York.

"No, sir, Mr. K. says the milk train was held up. They ran over a man on the track a couple of miles up the line, not far from here. Killed him, they say. The track will be clear by now. Mr. Klein will go back and we'll have plenty before noon," she added.

"A body on the tracks, gee! Do you think it was cut in half by the locomotive wheels, dad!" piped up twelve year old Ted, the eldest.

"You mean like the body in Nick Carter in the Northwoods? With blood dripping all over the place and the insides hanging out!" offered eleven year old Kermit.

"Blood is no subject for breakfast talk boys. I will not have it!"

interrupted Edith, clearly offended by tales of minced and maimed bodies and gore interrupting her consumption of the stuffed entrails of the pig.

"Huzzah, blood, hurray, blood!" said the six year old Archie savoring the spicy word which stirred so much excitement. Little Quentin, at two, just laughed.

"Your mother is right young men. A gentleman always considers the welfare of those around him, especially when addressing refined ladies such as your mother and Alice and Mrs. Klein and even young Ethel, who will become a lady soon," admonished T.R.

"Gee whiz, we can't discuss the news without watching our words!" observed Ted.

"Precisely son, a gentleman considers the sensibility of ladies at all times. You young men will be gentlemen all too soon. Believe me, I was your age when I went to Europe with my father and mother. I was ten at the time."

"I'm eleven, dad, Ted's twelve," reminded Kermit. "Tell us about your uncle the blockade runner again."

"Oh yes, tell us, tell us!" added Ted. Even Alice seemed attentive by now.

The "boy governor" smiled broadly revealing his set of even, large, sparkling white teeth which seemed too perfect, too bright, to be real. He wielded half a Kaiser roll, liberally spread with sweet butter and a carpet of orange marmalade in the air to command silence, completed a man size swig of coffee from his twice normal sized cup and began what was clearly a labor of love.

"Your Grandmother Bulloch...."

"That's me! That's me!" screamed the already jelly splattered Archie.

"Yes, son, your middle name is in honor of my mother's distinguished Georgia family, on her father's side. He was a hard working Scotsman named James Bulloch, a distinguished planter and a descendant of Archibald Bulloch, the first President of revolutionary Georgia at the very beginning of the United States of America."

"Archie Bulloch!" shouted the six year old as if he had never heard the tale before. "That's me!"

Their leader went on, nodding his head affirmatively, while grinding half of his confection laden breakfast roll between the already famous teeth. "Yes, a distinguished southern family who were loyal to what they mistakenly believed were the best interests of their country, the Bullochs from Scotland, Ireland, and Germany and on their mother's side a distinguished Gallic family from France. They took up arms. They were Georgians, and they took up arms against the Federal Government led by that great Republican President Abraham Lincoln."

"How could they do that, daddy? If Lincoln was the President of the United States? How could that not be their country?" asked the heretofore quiet nine year old Ethel.

"Aha, Ethel, even at nine you've already seized the core of the problem. Very perspicacious of you," acknowledged her father.

"Purr spacious?" Archie wondered aloud.

"Hush, Archie, it means smart," admonished Alice in her role of omniscient teenager.

"For the people of the Southern Confederacy each state was their country and so a Georgian was loyal to Georgia, a Virginian to Virginia, and so on. They were dead wrong, as Mr. Lincoln demonstrated." He smiled triumphantly with the wisdom available to those who view history forty years down the line.

"The Union forever, hurrah boys hurrah," piped up Kermit, only to be silenced by his father's withering look *as* the governor removed his pince-nez glasses and focused his pale blue eyes on the exuberant balladeer.

"One of your grandmother's brothers, Irvin, "Robbie" Bulloch, decided to leave the plantation near Atlanta, go to Savannah, and become the master of a fast sailing ship to travel back and forth to England and bring big guns back for Georgia and pay for them with cotton, which the English needed for their textile mills. The Federal Navy had a squadron of warships blocking the southern ports to prevent that." Another half roll was washed down with Mrs. Klein's savory Columbian brewed coffee and cream.

"He was a blockade runner, modern buccaneer!" pronounced Ted, the oldest of Roosevelt's second family.

"Perhaps not a pirate, but wanted by the Federal Government nevertheless. And he would have been hung had they captured him, no doubt," affirmed the governor.

"I met him when my dad took us to Europe in 1869. He had remained in England after Sherman had destroyed Atlanta and the Port of Savannah was occupied. He was daring and brave, but no fool. He lived in

Liverpool, no doubt hoping for a resurgence of the Southern cause. An unreconstructed rebel, I'm afraid."

"You mean he never gave up, dad?" asked Ted.

"That's right, and there are others. Some went to Central America and the Caribbean Islands. Many still live in Costa Rica, old men still dreaming that the South will rise again; more than a third of a century after their resounding defeat," he pontificated.

"They still want to have their own country, separate from us?" asked Ted incredulously.

"That's right, Ted. Every once in a while they stir up trouble. A bunch of them called themselves filibusters, tried to set up their own regimes in Cuba, Mexico, and Central America. They and their friends are undoubtedly still up to it now," he intoned.

"And your Uncle Rob? What of him?" asked the now fascinated Alice.

"He was a romantic figure to a little fellow like me. I was only ten and this lean, black haired Gallic looking man with a pronounced southern accent seemed to me to be a knight without armor, a cavalier of the seas. He talked about eluding Union warships in the dark of the night, slipping through fog banks, outracing Men of War, guns blazing on the high seas. He was the kind of man Sir Walter Scott wrote about. Perhaps one of you can research the matter and write his story some day."

"Rob B., the gun runner. The will of the wisp of the Confederacy. Eluding Union cannon and racing for Savannah to the aid of his country. Did he have a wife and family?" asked the now enthralled Alice.

"He was alone in Liverpool. He had married a Georgia woman whose family plantation was burned during Sherman's march to the sea. They had a little girl who died after being thrown from a horse. He never recovered from that and I don't know anything about her life. Perhaps you can travel to Atlanta some day and find out," offered the doting father of his motherless child.

"Well perhaps I will. It would make a great romantic novel and I can write it just like Edith Wharton." Her strong jaw and determined demeanor showed the Roosevelt genes ran strong in Alice's constitution.

Mrs. Klein returned to announce, "Mr. Klein is going back to the station for our milk. Should I have him get anything else, Mrs. R.?"

"I think not, Mrs. K." answered Edith.

"Have him inquire about the railroad accident, if you please. I'm interested in how it happened and why," the governor interrupted. "The legislature has passed, with my prodding, a strong public indemnity act. If their negligence has caused this tragedy, I want to know all about it."

Theodore Roosevelt wanted to know all about everything. Nothing less would do.

CHAPTER FOUR

"May I speak to Dr. Falconer, please? This is Dr. William Weinstein at the Long Island Railroad." The voice on the telephone sounded somewhat officious.

"I'm Alex Falconer, Dr. Weinstein."

"Your name was given to me by Dr. Beck at the College of Physicians and Surgeons. I need a pathology examination of a victim in a recent railroad accident."

"Is this a postmortem examination to determine the cause of death?"

"Yes, it is. One of our trains ran over a man on our right of way the other day. The issue of the cause of his death is important. The Nassau County coroner's preliminary report suggested the man was intoxicated and fell asleep on the tracks. Because of the company's possible legal liability, we need crystal clear post-mortem findings."

"There's some doubt as to whether the train did kill the deceased?"

"As you may be aware, Dr. Falconer, recent legislation requires compensation by the railroad should it cause someone's accidental death, even if he were drunk and took a nap on the track. We wish to be absolutely certain whether we are, in fact, responsible. I'm sure you understand."

"I do indeed. I've had several calls like this since the new laws came into effect. I'll be glad to examine the body and make a report."

"Good. We can offer you a hundred dollars plus your expenses. Will that be satisfactory?"

A hundred dollar fee, a princely sum, might be well worth it considering the possible cost of a verdict against the railroad. Falconer, although he had inherited money from his father, was always a little short. He tended to over spend when it came to his two sons. But he couldn't believe that buying things for his boys spoiled them. He'd been haunted for some time by the feeling that it was his fault they were orphans. He should have been able to prevent his wife's death.

Robbie Smoot's corpse, to all but a pathologist, was thoroughly gruesome. Its head had been caved in, and so was a large portion of the thorax. In fact, the body itself was chopped into two major pieces. One consisted of the head and torso, damaged as noted. The remainder after transection by the wheels was normal. If Smoot had not been dead when he landed on the track, then the cause of his death was certainly obvious.

Alex Falconer examined the upper portion of the torso in minute detail. He'd pause after every ten minutes, carefully wash his hands and write several paragraphs on a clipboard pad. A casual observer might have been shocked to hear him humming a Gilbert and Sullivan tune as he worked.

When he was through, he called the railroad office in New York.

"Dr. Weinstein, this is Falconer. I've completed my examination. I'll send you a written report, of course, but I thought you'd like to hear the conclusion now. I'm also obliged to inform the Nassau County Sheriff."

"The Sheriff? That would suggest some kind of criminal responsibility." The signal of alarm was clear in Weinstein's voice. He'd hired Falconer to get the company off the hook. Now there was a suggestion of criminality in what had happened on the right-of—way.

"Hold your horses, doctor. The crime has nothing to do with your people. It's my opinion that the victim was dead when his body was placed on the track."

The sigh of relief at the other end of the phone was actually audible. Alex reminded Weinstein that alcohol—soaked clothing wasn't evidence that the substance was itself in the victim. The body had very clear skin and showed no evidence of petechiae, little spider-like red *marks* on the skin found in chronic alcoholics.

"Besides, the liver is normal. There are no varicosities anywhere, especially not in the esophagus, where they're commonly found in cirrhotics. Further, there's none of the edema, which we usually see in drunks, nor any abdominal abnormality either.

"It's my impression that the victim was in excellent physical condition, in fact athletic. Just not the kind of man likely to get so drunk that he'd lie down in the path of an oncoming locomotive and not make any move to get away."

"So the Long Island Railroad isn't responsible after all, doctor?" Weinstein was monolithic in pursuit of corporate exculpation.

"No, I'm certain he was done in by a sharp blow to the head, almost instantly. That blow, delivered by a powerful arm, was so hard that it had crushed the skull and caused splinters of bony tissue to be imbedded deep within the brain. Bone fragments severed two major cerebral arteries. The massive subarachnoid bleeding occurred many minutes before the locomotive wheels touched the corpse."

Falconer didn't tell the railroad doctor about his curious discovery in his systematic search of the victim's clothing, which had been bagged by morgue attendants and labeled "Railroad casualty, LIRR." One trouser pocket held an oversized gold coin, apparently a valuable numismatic commemorative, hardly likely to be owned by a vagrant with no money other than a few nickels on his person. The man had probably been a thief. In any event, the coin had somehow been overlooked, both by his killer and by those who had dealt with his body until now.

Alex was pleased with himself, as always after a thorough job of work. He had long since discovered that underlying feelings of anxiety which sometimes plagued him were forgotten with professional activity. As long as he had every variable under control and had left no stone unturned in his investigations, he felt good.

He was an obsessive-compulsive individual. His personality was such that Sigmund Freud would have clapped his hands in joy at examining him. Everything Alex did had to be just so. Every "i" he wrote had to be dotted and every "t" crossed. A friend had once said of him: "If you ask Alex what time it is, he'll tell you how to make a watch." Nothing made him more secure than certainty.

Uncovering criminals and tracking them down, much as a predator hunts his prey, was as much an instinct as a hobby to him.

As Falconer sat in his study that evening, he practiced his hand—to—eye coordination exercises, repeatedly tossing a raw egg up in the air with his left hand and neatly catching it in an egg cup held in his right. The egg never even quivered as it landed.

Alexander Falconer considered that perfection in the pursuit of justice was the only thing worthwhile in life. At least, it was the only thing that made him feel good, ever since that terrible day of Marjorie's death.

He speculated that the killer of the vagrant on the Long Island railroad tracks might resemble Derek Hanley, Marjorie's murderer, known as the Westside Slasher: a man who apparently killed for no reason but who, under close scrutiny, turned out to have a plan and a motive for each and every action. Hanley had killed several other young women before Alex finally caught up with him.

Quite possibly the vagrant's well—planned execution, for there could be little doubt about the nature of that crime, represented only part of a larger scheme. Why else would anyone have gone to so much trouble, making it look like an accident? If the railroad company hadn't been concerned about protecting its interests…..

And what about the big gold coin?

It seemed obvious that the victim had stolen it, but why hadn't the killer taken it? Where did it come from in the first place? Alex picked it up from the blotter on his desk and inspected it more closely, reminding himself to turn it over to the sheriff in the morning. World's Columbian Exposition Chicago. A bust of Christopher Columbus with a picture of the Santa Maria leading the Nina and the Pinta on the obverse. No denomination indicated, hence not a coin but a commemorative medal, intended for dignitaries and important visitors, judging by its size and evident value.

If he were Sherlock Holmes, Dr. Doyle would have provided one or two further clues for his benefit. He began mentally to realign what he did know when young Alex and Gideon banged on his door and burst into his study.

"Dad, we were playing pepper, and Gideon broke Dr. Distelman's window! He missed the old guy's head by an inch. You should've seen how mad old Disty got!" His first-born's face had flushed as bright as the flame of his hair.

His legacy from Marjorie, two motherless boys, both of whom bore the genetic imprint of her fair skin and fiery locks. They were the focal point of his life.

"What's that coin on your desk, Dad?" asked five year old Gideon, two years younger than his brother. "It looks like the one in Lexie's Adventure Magazine. The one with the pirate's curse on it. Is that it, Dad, a Spanish doubloon? Is it responsible for the death of a hundred men, Dad, huh?"

"Men of science like you, Lexie and I don't believe in curses, Gideon." Alex managed a solemn expression for the benefit of the kids. He picked up the coin and scrutinized it again. "This does mean something though, and we're going to find out what. But right now all of us together will visit Dr. Distelman and pay him for his broken window."

As Alex pocketed the coin, Gideon insisted, "I bet it's a clue to some evil, internal plot."

"Infernal, Gid, infernal," said Lex who was more and more like his father every day.

CHAPTER FIVE

The visit to Dr. and Mrs. Distelman's house proved to be traumatic for the boys, but not because of the good doctor's wrath, nor the broken window.

Distelman and his wife lived next door to the Falconer home in the suburban area of the upper west side of Manhattan. The "old man" was in his mid—fifties. A general practitioner, he was especially interested in diseases of the skin so that when he looked at someone, anyone, his gaze was directed at the hands, arms, neck, face, or any other exposed area of that (the largest, as he reminded his colleagues) organ of the body.

Juliette Distelman met the Falconer contingent at the door. "Dr. Falconer, Gideon and Lexie, how nice of you to come by. I expect you want to talk about Dr. D's study window. He's in the back right now preparing some slides of a Greek sailor's skin. He said he's never seen anything like it. Although anything Dr. D. hasn't seen on people's bodies in the past thirty years doesn't exist in my book. It's a good thing the baseball didn't hit his glass slides, he would've had a fit. Thank goodness, there was no damage done, except for the window of course."

A reassuring smile at the two miscreants indicated that the paddy wagon wasn't on its way to take them straight to prison. "Would you young men like some butter cookies? That is, if your father agrees. I made them this afternoon and they're still warm." Indeed the house was filled with the sweet odor of fresh baked goodies.

"I'll get Dr. D. right now. just sit here in the parlor, please. Bitsie will bring in the refreshments," and without awaiting a reply she flew off to both fetch her husband and arrange for an impromptu tea party.

As Mrs. D. guided her mate down the hall from his study, the three Falconers clearly heard her instructing her husband.

"Don't be so fussy, dear. Remember, they are two motherless boys! You must be kind. No one to take the place of that tragic woman. It's been years now .They need a mother's love."

"All right, Julie, shush. I heard you the first two times. I'm not deaf."

The bespectacled, salt and pepper haired man entered the room first, he looked at the hands, neck, and face of each of its occupants and then greeted them.

"Aha, Falconer. I see your two ballplayers have come to retrieve their missile. I'll tell the world, it startled me, but no harm done. Bitsie had to pick up pieces of glass for half an hour."

"Well of course, we will pay for the glazier," Falconer offered. "Please tell him to bill me directly. I've told the boys repeatedly to go to the empty lot down the road to practice, but what can I say?" Alex spread his hands in a display of helplessness at the impracticality of controlling the exuberance of two small boys.

"Certainly, I understand. No mother, lots of energy, summertime, it makes my blood boil to think of the tragedy that took your wife and their loving mother away," Distelman responded.

Before the smell of superheated blood could be detected in the room, a tall black woman entered, pushing a tea cart bearing a tray of cookies. The fragrance of sugar and butter replaced the threatened sanguine odor.

"Cold milk and cookies are just the thing on a summer afternoon for two growing boys," advised Mrs. Distelman. She chucked the two erstwhile ballplayers under their respective chins and ignored their shrinking away from her attempts at affection.

"Have some tea, Dr. Falconer," she commanded. "You'll like the cookies too".

The group broke up after the boys had consumed half a dozen cookies each. The senior Falconer had had a couple as well. Mrs. D. advised them, "I hope we haven't spoiled the boy's supper. But little boys need a lot of energy," in her self—appointed role of surrogate grandparent.

"Thank you so much for your kindness. But we must be off. Mrs. Malone has their supper ready at five thirty every afternoon and it's almost four. Thank you again, both of you. Thank Dr. and Mrs. Distelman, boys, and apologize please," he said.

"We're sorry we broke your window. We won't do it again," promised Lexie, the eldest and therefore the leader.

"The cookies were really good, the best I ever had," added Gid. "Do you ever make cinnamon and raisin cookies? Lexie says our mother made them, but I never had any," he plaintively added.

Mrs. Distelman's eyes welled with tears as she reassured the six year old, "Of course I do, I'll make some tomorrow, Gideon. Be sure and come over at three o'clock and they'll be warm, right out of the oven." She grabbed him bodily and crushed him to her bosom. "You poor little darling."

As the trio walked back home, Lexie observed to his dad, "It's not fair! All of the other kids have a mom. Why did we get cheated?"

"Yeah, me too" chimed in Gid. "I want my mommy. Why did she have to die? Why don't we have a mom like everybody else?" He was crying as he entered their house.

"Let's sit down in the parlor, boys." The two kids knew this was a serious matter.. No one was allowed in the parlor, no one, except Governor Roosevelt when he came to visit and occasionally a couple of their father's doctor friends who came over to talk about college business.

"Your mom was killed by an insane man when you were only two, Gideon, and barely remember....

Gid was bawling copiously and sobbed, "I remember. She smelled sweet and had red hair like Lexie and me. I remember," he insisted.

"Of course you do. A boy never forgets his mother," Alex reassured his motherless son.

"I do too, but not as good as I should," Lexie said. "I can't remember what she looked like even, except in that wedding picture we have on the piano. I think I should remember. I was Gid's age when she died. Why don't I remember? I don't even remember the smell like Giddie does."

"Giddie does," interrupted the pedantic Alex.

"Well, I can't and I should. It's my mother too!" Tears now erupted from his eyes as well. "Why did she have to die?"

"Everyone has to die, son. I'll die someday, so will you and Gid too. Your mother died far too soon, that's true, but it's something that comes to us all sooner or later. If the preachers are right, we'll all meet again in paradise."

"But in the meantime, Giddie and I don't have a mom! Why do we get gypped?" Lexie said in a very loud voice.

"We're not the only ones, son. Governor Roosevelt's first wife died sixteen years ago on the day after their daughter, Alice, was born. Alice never had any memories of her mother at all, not even the color of her hair nor her eyes nor any smell, nothing at all"

"Yeah, dad, but they have a mom! Alice, Ethel, and all the boys, they have a mom. Mr. Roosevelt married another lady and she's Mrs. Roosevelt now, and Alice has a sister and a whole lot of brothers. They have a real family, not like us." Alex Jr. seemed to be accusing his father of malfeasance in the office of father.

"You can't just go out and find someone to take the place of a woman like your mother. Women such as your mother are rare treasures, you can't find them lying on the street like cobblestones!"

Lexie screwed up his face and his courage and said, 'No, you've got to look, father, and you haven't even tried."

CHAPTER SIX

Charles had been sweet on her from the beginning, it was clear that Mr. Majors wanted their relationship to become more than professional. Gaby didn't mind the occasional touch on the shoulder, some hand squeezing, or even a random peck on her cheek in greeting or farewell. After all, this was the beginning of a new era. The world of the oncoming twentieth century would bring a new equality between the sexes. Gaby Irish knew this would be so and she intended to lead the way in every area open to her, including relationships with men.

Of course, you had to overcome your upbringing and background. It might take a while to be as free as she wished. Chuck would have to understand this. Meanwhile, he could settle for friendship with a fellow writer.

But the man wanted more than camaraderie. Even now, as he offered her the biggest break any reporter would be likely to get for years to come, she thought he did so with a trifle too much intimacy. He had his hand on her knee and it was moving in a dangerous direction as he spoke.

"If there's the slightest suspicion that this story came from the Democrats, everyone will discount it as politically inspired. McKinley's got all the advantages of an incumbent and we'd be expected to do anything to defeat him.

"We're deep in the hole as it is, even with Bryan's charisma, it's all uphill for us. Since Hobart had the bad taste to die in office, nominating a war hero nails it down for the G.O.P.

"With the cowboy running, we're in trouble. That's why this information is crucial."

Gaby put her hand atop his to stop its upward progress, but not to remove the stimulating sensations it imparted. She was getting gooseflesh all over.

"Why not read mud for information? Besides, you don't have to give me a lecture on party politics, Chuck. You sound just like my boss. He only tolerates me on the paper because Joe Pulitzer's got a woman reporter too. Otherwise the only job I'd have with the New York Journal would be to come in at midnight with a mop and pail."

"Exactly my point, Gaby. I'm not lecturing you, you luscious sweet meat." He squeezed her thigh with his muscular hand. "I'm offering an opportunity to put Will Hearst in your debt forever."

"Dearest Chuck." Were erotic fantasies clouding her mind? "Why me? Why not release this yourself? You're the official press representative for the Democrats."

"Even though we have sworn statements and an actual photograph as proof, the Republican controlled newspapers are sure to call it a fraud. This story must come straight from an independent journalist. I can't have anything to do with it, neither can the Party.

"But with this story, you'll steal a march on every reporter in the country! This is your big chance, Gaby. This break can make you not only the leading woman reporter in America, but the most famous journalist, male or female, of the twentieth century. I guarantee it!' He even removed his hand from her leg to rap both fists on the restaurant table.

"You're so right. If this allegation were to be proved, it would knock Roosevelt out of the picture entirely and I'd be responsible." As she spoke, Gaby boldly moved his hand back to a somewhat safer position on her right knee.

Chuck raised his eyebrows in surprise, as she went on. "I've got to see the affidavits with my own eyes, and the photograph is a must. The reader, with his own eyes, has to see T.R. in front of his tent with this Negro woman. That, plus the statement of your three witnesses swearing that the old Rough Rider didn't lead the charge on San Juan Hill should blow the lid off this town."

It hadn't been easy for a woman reporter to make it in Manhattan in the nineteenth century, and it didn't seem as if it would be easier in the twentieth. Gaby was fortunate to have any job with the New York Morning Journal. William Randolph Hearst, for all his pretensions of being a twentieth century man, had nineteenth century ideas. He'd hired her on the strength of her college newspaper experience and her famous interview with Teddy Roosevelt in Tampa before the troops sailed for Cuba.

Her coup as a college girl in getting an interview with the organizer and commander of the famous Rough Riders had been unique. She'd traveled alone all the way from Radcliffe to Florida, knowing that the troops were about to embark for Cuba, plotting and scheming to get on the right trains and past checkpoints to gain access to the colonel.

It hadn't been *easy*. Every reporter in the country wanted to talk to Teddy. Well known as Assistant Secretary of the Navy before he was a Rough Rider, he'd personally ordered Commodore Dewey to Manila Bay to sink the Spanish fleet. T.R. was a force to be reckoned with.

She'd taken the train as far south as Richmond without trouble. When she got to Virginia, though, it became impossible to find further transportation, most of it was tied up by the federal people in dispatching troops, supplies and horses to the Tampa Bay embarkation point. There was no room for civilians, especially reporters.

Gaby, then a senior at college, knew how to flutter the large eyelashes fronting her huge brown innocent eyes. She'd perfected the art of throwing her head back and tossing her auburn locks in distress.

Allowed aboard a train with the spurious story that she had to get home to Atlanta to see her dying daddy, her Peekskill, New York origin didn't prevent feigning a southern accent. It worked! Security was hardly air tight on the way to Cuba. Everyone expected a "jolly old time" in a war initiated by Hearst and his yellow journalist rivals in the first place.

"It's like shooting ducks in a barrel, ma'am. You don't need to worry your pretty little head about any of our boys getting hurt. We're going to go down there and beat the, begging your pardon, beat the devil out of them Spics in Cuba." The sergeant ramrodding the troop train exuded confidence from every pore.

In Tampa, Gaby managed to get to see T.R. by dressing up like a bugler boy. It fooled no one as a disguise, but the colonel was unable to resist anything which smacked of daring and innovation.

The interview was printed not only in the Radcliffe paper, but picked up by newspapers from coast to coast. Even Mr. Hearst had been impressed. When she graduated, a job at the New York Morning Journal was assured. It wasn't exactly what she expected. He'd assigned her to the society page.

"You have to make your mark in the big city now, young lady. It isn't enough to run down to Tampa and get an interview with a politician who's hoping to become President by riding his horse to fame. Now you'll have to do some hard work and pay your dues. Take the assignments you get and make the most of them."

The newspaper business was Hearst's whole life. Heir to an enormous mining fortune, he was doing his best to spend it in acquiring papers from coast to coast. Starting successfully in San Francisco, he soon realized that New York was the hub of political and journalistic activity in modern America.

The budding tycoon purchased the New York Morning Journal and made it into the leading penny paper of the day. He wasn't making any money selling the yellow-colored publication every morning for a cent, but planned to get in the black with advertising. He'd already forced old man Pulitzer and other competitors to lower their price to a penny as well. The real fight now was to get circulation high enough so advertisers would be willing to pay the freight and cover the costs of production. The Hearst family fortune made the contest unfair. Pulitzer and the others had to make their money from the newspapers alone. Hearst didn't care.

"All's fair in love and war. And never forget the newspaper game is a war," he once told Gaby. She'd never forgotten that; "The Chief" played for real. He wasn't about to give an inch in any direction. He'd hired her on the strength of a single story. Now she had to prove that she'd be a real journalist.

Hearst papers were called "yellow journals" because of their newsprint color. But soon the term became synonymous with the outrageous things in them. Anything sensational was fair game. Wild and unsubstantiated stories were okay. Chuck's scandal would be a golden opportunity to prove to W.R. and the whole world that she *was* as good as, no, better than, any man reporting in this country. What a chance! If only it were true.

"Just think, the woman who got the interview with Teddy Roosevelt before going to Cuba, now exposes him as a fraud. He never did lead the Rough Riders up San Juan Hill. He was in his tent romancing with a Negro tart. What a story! If you really have the proof, Chuck, I'll show you my gratitude. You can count on that."

Her skin flushed with anticipation of THE BIG STORY, and of the reward she'd bestow upon the handsome man sitting beside her. Her eyes sparkled and, his hand began its upward journey again from knee to thigh and beyond, like a salmon seeking its spawning grounds.

"I'm a free woman, Chuck, but I'm not easy," she snapped and simultaneously impeded Major's escalating fingers.

"I have to see the documents first, and they'd better be the real thing." Her face, beet red with both embarrassment and excitement, Gaby had committed herself to more than one thing.

"They're the real thing all right. Just imagine the son of a Georgia born woman, a man whose uncles fought for the Army of the Confederacy jumping into bed with a Negress and being so drunk that he didn't realize someone took his photograph with the black woman! A man whose great grandfather was a founding Father of the state, the first President of the Republic of Georgia! It's a disgrace. His mother will turn in her grave.' He now seemed more livid with righteous rage than with lust.

"I didn't realize you knew so much about the governor's family history. Did you learn that at Yale?' She facetiously inquired.

"My family are from Mississippi on both sides, old antebellum aristocrats, I'll have you know,' he smiled. "They even sent me to Andover and Yale after The War Between the States to infiltrate the Yankee fortresses of academia and learn their ways. I did, and I never went back."

They had met at Luchow's Restaurant on Fourteenth Street. Despite his apparently oriental name, Luchow was German. He catered to the many affluent German-American families in Manhattan and Brooklyn. Luchow offered them a gastronomic echo of the fatherland. The menu was filled with such items as Knackwurst, Lungen—stew, and Hasenpfeffer. The decor was all dark wood and elaborate brass fixtures, both gleamingly polished. Although there were few windows, the place shined with reflections of the recently installed electric lights on the waxed oak and bright metal.

As they talked, Charles Majors practically inhaled a large piece of sauerbraten, sucking in the marinated fatty beef in its sweet and sour sauce, accompanied by enormous helpings of kartoffel—glace. On the side was an order of red cabbage as large as both of his enormous hands. He sliced a loaf of black pumpernickel into thick pieces and consumed it with almost equally thick slabs of butter.

Gaby reflected that it was a good thing Charles was a large man, otherwise he would surely explode. It amazed her that he'd kept the handsome muscular figure she so greatly admired. He'd told her he'd been on the track and field team at Yale, and kept in shape by working out daily.

Her own eating habits were less inelegant. Even though the prevalent view of feminine attractiveness inclined toward plumpness, Miss Irish felt strongly that being chubby wouldn't present her in the most favorable light. Lillian Russell could get away with being 160 pounds; so could Sylvia Starr, "The American Venus," at 151. Gaby, only 5'1", remained convinced that any scale reading over 105 would be too high for her.

On previous epicurean adventures, Charles had explained that the Party provided him with funds to entertain important people. Therefore, he could afford frequent visits to Sherry's and Delmonico's, where meals cost as much as $2.00 and $3.00 each. His invitations had enabled Gaby to go to places she could otherwise experience only in her dreams.

Charles obviously came from a patrician family, because the money he spent dining out and living "the good life" had to be more than the political party of the laborer and farmer could afford. Of course, it wasn't proper for a young lady to inquire into a young man's finances. That, eventually, was left to one's family. Her relationship with Mr. Majors did not as yet justify such activity.

She rationalized that going out with Charles, aside from his obvious appeal as a man, was useful to her career. It was important to observe the wealthy and famous dining at such places. A society reporter had to travel in the right circles.

Elizabeth Cochrane, famous as Nellie Bly, the globe trotting newshen who had traveled around the world in seventy—two days, also worked for "The Chief." She'd done her globe-girdling stories for Joe Pulitzer's New York World. Hearst stole her away, and Nellie was one of his new "star reporters." There wasn't room for more than one female star on the Journal.

Gaby had long ago decided her personal route to stardom was patience. She'd have to bide her time, wait for the opportunity and seize it, no matter what the cost.

Now it looked very much like this was it! A scandal that would rock the G.O.P. to its very foundation. Theodore Roosevelt was important, not only to the Republicans, but to the whole country: New York City's crusading police commissioner, now Governor of the State, a Vice Presidential nominee, and a war hero to boot! The "Cowboy" was about to be accused of spending the day of the famous charge in his tent with a Negro woman, sporting with her behind canvas flaps while his men won a glorious victory in battle, led by a look-alike.

What a story! What dirt! What a triumph of "yellow journalism"! She was actually salivating, even before the lemon Bavarian cream arrived for dessert.

CHAPTER SEVEN

"The best laid schemes of mice and men aft gang aglay," reflected the man who on certain occasions called himself Mr. D., as he read the Harley note for the third time. It had been a serious mistake giving the photo studio owner his real name and place of business. He'd thought that the man's greed and hope for future business would keep him in line. Here was proof that he'd made an error in judgment, which demanded immediate correction.

The note was short: "I trust that the enclosed will meet your purpose. This has proved to be rather more costly to make up than I had estimated. I shall require additional compensation to cover the difference. I'm sure you understand. Please see me at your earliest convenience."

The bastard was clever as well as greedy. He'd grasped the importance of the picture, and the absolute necessity for it to be kept confidential.

The purloined photograph had been cropped and slickly matched with another one, then rephotographed. Mr. D's inspiration had been that if he could get his hands on a personal picture of T.R. in Cuba and doctor it so that Roosevelt, instead of having his arm about a friend's shoulder, was revealed to be in the embrace of a Negro tart, the man's political career would be forfeited and the course of history changed.

He'd credited divine intervention when he was invited to Sagamore Hill a few weeks ago and the Governor had shown him his study. There was the picture he needed, the great leader, standing in front of his tent, in uniform, warmly greeting a British visitor, who'd autographed the picture with the name "Winnie."

Such a find cried out to be exploited. A remarkable opportunity, it met all of D's requirements. He had to find out who Winnie was and how to prevent him from identifying the picture. He also had to discover whether another copy existed.

It took less than a week to get the information. The transatlantic cable was another godsend. Perhaps the whole mission had actually been ordained by the Almighty. The people who paid him were convinced of this already. It turned out that Winnie was an English aristocrat named Churchill, who had since gone off to the war in South Africa. Fortunately, the Boers had captured him. Even if he had a copy of the photo, he wouldn't even hear about the problems of his American friend for a very long time, much less do anything about them.

The plot looked airtight, steal the picture from Sagamore Hill, find a Black tart and dress her up like a Spanish whore. With the cooperation of a greedy photographer, the picture would provide perfect evidence.

Bill Harley had seemed right for the job. The man had worked for him before when he'd needed some passports forged. He was an excellent craftsman who'd do anything for money. But now he had turned into a blackmailer, one who either knew or guessed too much.

Robbie Smoot, on the other hand, had been a real find because he was a competent burglar who'd performed exactly as he was told. He'd taken the photo as directed, and had been easy to dispose of. Robbie could never compromise the plot.

Harley was another matter. He'd have to be dealt with severely. The important thing was to discover whether the avaricious man had kept a copy of the original picture. If so, he could sell it to the Republicans. Not only would the plot go up the chimney like a puff of smoke, but so might Mr. D. himself, and his associates.

Harley's studio proved to be dimly lit. The fool had agreed to meet after midnight to conduct their private business. He said he didn't want too many lights on to avoid attracting attention. D. couldn't agree more.

"What's all this about more money, Bill? A hundred dollars should be more than fair for your work. It's ten times your customary charge." He was carefully suppressing his anger, preventing it from revealing itself prematurely.

"It's just good business. I've done some pretty chancy things for you before, but this is something else again. People don't mess with Teddy Roosevelt and get away with it."

"I don't know what you're talking about, my good man." D. managed an oleaginously polite smile.

"Don't forget, I've lived in New York a long time, probably longer than you. I remember when T.R. was the police commissioner. He cracked down hard on everything — the crooked cops, the Tammany politicians, even his own party. He don't forget, and he sure don't forgive. He'll know right off the picture was fiddled, and he'll come looking for who done it." Harley's eyes bugged out peering into the dark searching for some unseen enemy.

He continued as his erstwhile employer remained ominously silent. "I'll have to leave town, but I deserve to do it with some style. My business is worth a lot to me. It'll cost a small fortune to set up someplace else. I need your help for that, sir. I know you're well connected. You've got friends."

"When you came to me and asked me to do this job for you, you never mentioned the Governor himself was involved. I don't know I'd have taken it on if you did. A hundred dollars to fool with somebody like T.R. just isn't worth it. The Spanish Army discovered that. The boys at Tammany know it too. That's why I need more money, and right away. I'd say five thousand dollars would be fair."

He had obviously rehearsed this speech, word for word, Mr. D. thought. The man's eyes glittered with avarice, and with the kind of cunning knowledge that a crook shows when he believes he has his victim cornered.

"How do I know you'll be honest with me this time, Bill? You can make other copies of the original picture. You could sell me one and keep the others."

"You can trust me, sir. I know enough not to cross you." The man was beginning to sound a little less sure of himself.

"Five thousand dollars. That's a fortune. I don't carry that kind of money around. I don't even have it in my bank. I'd have to go to my principals for it." D. had to find out if there were other copies of the photograph, and where, before he killed the fellow.

"I guess you have a right to be a bit upset with me, sir. But the governor has a lot of power, and he's smart. My life and my business wouldn't be worth a. plugged nickel in this town if he found out. Five thousand isn't such a lot, considering the stakes in this game."

Harley had started to twitch. He had the nervous habit of picking at his clothing. He would pinch his thumb and forefinger together and pluck at the little fine hairs in the fabric of his trousers. It appeared that he had done this before, for a line ran up and down the outside seam of his left trouser leg, and its twin along the right. Presently he was only doing it with his left hand. Mr. D. got the impression that if Harley became more agitated, he'd start plucking away with both hands.

"How do I know you're not holding out on me, Bill? You must have some kind of insurance, maybe a friend keeping the negatives for you. A clever fellow like you wouldn't take a chance, would he?"

"You're right as ever, sir. I do have some insurance put away. Only I didn't need to bother any of my friends with this. Sure, I've got the negatives and a couple of copies stashed away where you'd never find them. This is a big place, with stacks of pictures stored in all sorts of nooks and crannies."

Mr. D. nodded. He'd heard all he needed to hear, and he observed with detachment that the fellow was now indeed plucking at the hairs on both his trouser legs as he babbled on. "I'm not afraid of you, sir. You're bigger than me, but you couldn't beat it out of me where I've got the goods. You might try, but as soon as I told you that would be the end for me. So I'm never going to tell you where they are. The only way you're going to get rid of me is to pay me five thousand dollars."

"You'd better do it right away too, because if you can't get it by the day after tomorrow, I'm pretty sure I know some people who'll be happy to fork it over to me."

Harley seemed to interpret his employer's silence as a license to increase the boldness of his threats. "Mr. Roosevelt has some wealthy friends, you know that, sir. Old Mayor Grace owns half of South America now. Five thousand dollars is less than a shipload of bananas for him in profit, and well worth it, too, to save his friend. There's other rich Republicans would chip in too. Yes, sir, I know all right where to get that five thousand if you don't come up with it. But I'm a patient man. I can wait forty-eight hours. I don't think you want to wait much longer than that, sir. Am I right?"

Mr. D. nodded again and looked at him. "My God, what a firetrap this place is," he said musingly. "All this old dry wood. All those prints and chemicals. It would go up like a torch, wouldn't it?" As he spoke, Harley's trouser plucking became frantic. He was beginning to get the idea that if the studio burned to a crisp all of his insurance would go, and so would he.

"They tell me that people don't burn to death in fires, Bill. No, they don't burn, it's the smoke that suffocates them. I would imagine that smoke from a place like this would be poisonous, the chemicals you know. Someone would die rather quickly from it, don't you think?" Mr. D. was speaking slowly, carefully and very quietly, well aware that this made him sound all the more frightening to Harley.

"You wouldn't burn me now, you wouldn't kill me, no sir. I didn't mean it about hiding the pictures here, they're elsewhere. They're with a friend. You'll never get them if you kill me."

The big man grabbed him by the shirt front with his left hand and clamped his right over Harley's mouth and nose. "Oh, no, my dear fellow, I wouldn't burn you. That would be heartless. No, I certainly would never do a thing like that.' As he spoke, he pinched the extortionist's nose while holding his hand tightly over the smaller man's face with a grip of steel. Harley tried to claw his assailant, tried to knee him in the crotch as well.

His nails scraped only at his tormentor's overcoat. His knee ineffectively hit his executioner's thigh.

D. wore thin black leather gloves. One now encompassed his victim's entire face, blocking out the air. An arm looped around Harley's chest, pinioning the dying man while his feet kicked out helplessly. Harley fought but his assailant was far too big and strong.

Bill Harley lost consciousness before he died. The killer, perceiving that his prey was purple and showed no sign of life, touched a finger to the man's carotid artery, and felt nothing. He laid the body down on the floor and twisted the arms and legs into a position to suggest that the dying man had been trying to crawl out of the studio towards the front door.

Mr. D. had carefully considered his options in advance. He had taken the precaution of carrying a couple of hip flasks filled with kerosene. His previous visits to the studio suggested it would go up like a bomb, if suitably encouraged.

It was a four-alarm fire. Companies were called in from three other precincts in the city. The fire marshal later advised the Press that all photography studios would become a high priority on the inspection list.

There was hardly anything left when the place finally burned itself out. The main concern of the firemen had been to prevent the neighboring buildings from being consumed. It was fortunate that these adjacent structures were of stone and masonry.

Harley's withered remains were separated with some difficulty from the ashes. The coroner saw little point in ordering an autopsy, but the law required one in such cases. He'd give it to the young loud mouth just out of medical school, Kern.

The fire marshal filed a report of accidental fire caused by the presence of too many volatile chemicals in the area. He recommended that new and stringent rules be established for similar places of business in the future. The marshal pointed out that photography was a growing business, and that many more such establishments would soon open. He suggested that rules concerning the storage of volatile chemicals be established, including the installation of sprinkler systems. This report was later incorporated in an act of the New York State Legislature. Harley thus made a significant contribution to the safety of twentieth century America.

CHAPTER EIGHT

Opening the manila envelope with great anticipation, Gaby perfunctorily read the note: "Enclosed are the photograph and a notarized statement from the man who really led the charge. I hope very much that this will make you the most famous woman reporter in the world. Affectionately, Charles."

There it was, a picture of Teddy Roosevelt, unmistakable in his Rough Rider uniform tailored by Brooks Brothers. Instead of racing up San Juan Hill on his battle horse, he was embracing a lady of the evening; a very black lady at that, and not very attractive. It was dated July 2, 1898, the day of the charge, presumably in the photographer's handwriting. The rogue was smiling, his characteristic big full toothed smile.

A picture is worth a thousand words, she reminded herself. There it is, the picture that can end Roosevelt's career. The attached statement was even more persuasive.

"I, Thomas Renfield, do hereby swear that when serving as a private in the 1st New York Volunteer Cavalry in Cuba, on July 2, 1898, I mounted Lt. Colonel Theodore Roosevelt's charger, Wyoming, and wearing one of the Colonel's uniform blouses, led the attack of our regiment up Kettle Hill, known to the public as San Juan Hill."

"Colonel Roosevelt had instructed me to do so and sworn me to secrecy. He was in his tent with a woman at the time and told me to say that he was overcome with yellow fever. Thinking that I had to do my duty and protect the honor of our regiment, popularly known as the Rough Riders, I obeyed. However, to see to my own protection, I had Private Philip Smith, later killed in action during the battle, to surreptitiously take a photograph of the Colonel and his woman from near the tent. Now my conscience will no longer allow me to remain silent. I do hereby swear and attest that this is true upon my immortal soul. Sworn and dated July 1, 1900, in the city of New York." It was sealed and countersigned by a notary public.

Nothing could be more damning to the Governor, Gaby knew. This was it, enough powder to blow his career and the Grand Old Party to kingdom come. President McKinley's bid for re-election could go up with it, too. T.R. had been hand-picked to replace the deceased Garret Hobart by the old iron major and by Mark Hanna, the party boss, as the vice-presidential candidate. This scandal would come in time to seriously hurt the ticket, even help elect William Jennings Bryan.

McKinley, never much of a campaigner, counted on T.R. to carry the flag. Bryan was running on the platform that once again endorsed free silver, but this time also inveighed against imperialism. He was criticizing American expansion into the Pacific and Caribbean, and claimed that this would be the death of the Republic. The man was a great speaker, and would be certain to exploit the situation to the fullest.

Imagine, Gaby thought as she re-read the statement, what Bryan can do with this. His "Cross of Gold" speech had electrified the country four years ago. What could he do with this one? Maybe another biblical reference; "The Idol with Feet of Clay." But, was it true? Couldn't this be a fake?

Should she go ahead and ask Hearst to publish? Should she get more information? This was the crucial moment of her life. W.R. would have to give her a place ahead of Nellie Bly. The bold thing would be to write the story and charge forward.

Journalists have a responsibility, too, she reflected. Aren't we supposed to check out our stories, see things through? Hearst might not agree, but this was special. She had to consult the chief directly.

He'd probably try to give it to someone else. But she had the inside track. She'd make that clear. It was hers or nobody's. The man was, if nothing else, practical. Well, she decided, I'll soon find out, as she walked up the stairs to his office.

He was, as usual, in conference with two of his editors when she barged in. "Mr. Hearst, sir, I have something here that might turn into the biggest story of the century."

"You mean one of our society matrons has run off with a circus boy?" The tall, bony publisher looked down his long Roman nose at her in evident condescension.

"No, sir, this isn't a society story or a bedroom scandal. It's a lot bigger than that. It's front page. And I need to talk to you alone about it, if I may." Hearst smiled; not quite a leer, and told his companions, "Gentlemen, please excuse us. If the lady wants to discuss a story with me in camera, we must yield to her wish."

They left with smirks and knowing glances. The story couldn't conceivably be good for more than a third-page subhead, but the Chief might make it worth a lot more personally. He'd nursed a fancy for Miss Irish from the day he hired her. She might be a bit skinny, but he favored that kind of dame. After all, he was from California, peculiar in more ways than one.

"A headline story! We have one every day, my dear young lady. We need big ones if we're going to keep ahead of the World. I welcome any really big story. What have you got?"

The "Chief" looked down at Gaby from where he stood behind his desk. His high—pitched nasal voice sounded incongruous coming from a man so tall; he sometimes seemed to see himself as a reincarnated Lincoln. He had political aspirations much like those of the railroad lawyer from Illinois.

"What have you got that causes you to break into one of my editorial meetings, Miss Irish? I expect it's important, or you'd know better than to do that."

"It is important. It's the biggest thing you've seen since the Spanish War, maybe bigger," she assured him with all the courage she could muster. She was terrified of this man who could take her career in his boney hands and crush it in a moment. "I have a document and a photograph that show up Theodore Roosevelt as a fraud, a coward, a whoremonger, and a liar. For a newspaper like ours, it's manna from heaven. Would you like to see it?" She tremulously smiled as she held out to him the manila envelope in her hand.

"Would I like to control the presidential election? Would I like to make the Journal the most important paper in the world? Let's see what you have." He scowled as he looked at the material. Then he began to chuckle as he studied the photograph and, she thought, even salivate as he read Private Renfield's affidavit.

"I've always despised that blowhard Roosevelt," he said musingly. "That phony cowboy and self-made war hero has been more than I could stomach for years. His crusading-police-commissioner charade and his phony attacks on the trusts were bad enough, but those Cuban heroics of his took the cake. We had to exploit them, of course. We had to create a little Caesar. But I hated every minute of it."

Gaby smiled broadly. She had the man hooked. He loved it.

"Where in damnation did you get this stuff? It's dynamite! Enough to blow the cowboy and his gang back to hell where they came from! Where did you get it?" he demanded.

"From a very reliable source. I promised not to tell a soul, not even my publisher. I won't say except the source is a gentleman who cannot afford to be involved in this scandal in any way. And it will be a huge scandal," she insisted.

"To be sure. The scandal of the decade, to say the least. Was it one of his own kind? One of the high and mighty Knickerbockers who control this town? A fellow aristocrat who's fed up with Master Teddy and his populist antics? I'll bet it is, and you met him doing my society column jobs. Isn't that so?" he pushed.

"I can't and I won't say, Chief, I've given my word. That's all we have to trade in our business isn't it? You've said so yourself," she reminded him.

"O.K., hoisted on my own petard. You won't say. But it better be right. I want it to be right. I've waited a long time to nail Mr. High and Mighty." He smiled.

"Well, here's your chance to do him in," said Gaby, greatly heartened by his words.

"You bet your boots. In fact, you can bet the cowboy's boots too. He won't have any when we get through with him. But if this turns out to be a frame-up he's bound to bring suit. The man's a phony and a charlatan, but he's smart, and a clever politician. This stuff has to be carefully checked out. I'll put Ted Grofer on the story to help you. Ted's an experienced man, he knows the ropes. It can be your story together with his."

Hearst was visibly excited as he moved about the room, actually prancing back and forth. Gaby wondered if he was going to leap up and click his heels together in some kind of grotesque ballet movement, such was his evident joy. She knew that Hearst, though interested in her more than professionally, was first and foremost a newspaper man. The idea of a headline story was more important to him than meat and drink, even sex. He always stayed in his office until the wee hours of the morning.

Sometimes he'd not eat unless someone reminded him. The man's lanky frame was sustained on cheese sandwiches and steins of beer throughout the night. Newspapers were his sustenance; everything else was secondary to the son of Senator George Hearst.

His father, the major stockholder in the Comstock Lode, had jollied young Willie along by giving him money to buy the San Francisco Examiner. W.R. had experimented with flamboyant pictures and huge headlines to establish a mass appeal newspaper. It worked. He decided to come to New York to try the big time.

He'd bought the Morning Journal, changed it to an evening paper, and began his war with Joe Pulitzer. He became obsessed with the need to have the best, the biggest and the most notorious paper in Gotham. He hired away Pulitzer's prize reporters, even his top cartoonist.

Hearst claimed personal responsibility for the Spanish War. He called it "my war." W.R. had coined the slogan Remember the Maine after the mysterious 1898 explosion of that battleship in Havana Harbor. He felt sure that he, and he alone, had brought on the conflict.

Gaby held firm. "Mr. Hearst, this is my story. I got it together myself, and I want to keep it as my exclusive. I know Grofer's an excellent reporter and editor. I admire him. But he didn't come up with this story, I did, it's mine."

"Miss Irish, we must make absolutely sure of this. Ted has done this kind of thing before. He can back you up on the verification. It can still be your story." Hearst wasn't used to objections, and he showed it.
"I want to check it out myself. If you assign a photographer to go to Sagamore Hill with me when I talk to the Governor, I'd be very grateful. But it has got to be my story and mine alone, not with Grofer or anyone else. I know you can understand that. I know you won't do anything to compromise my source or my access to the material."

Gaby smiled sweetly as she made this rather bold bid at manipulating the man who controlled a coast—to—coast newspaper dynasty and who promised to become the uncrowned emperor of American journalism. She fought to keep the tremor out of her voice.

Hearst stopped his prancing and looked at her as if he hadn't seen her before.

"Well, my dear young lady, maybe you're right. It is your story, isn't it? And you have gotten this far with it. You certainly have a lot of nerve coming in here, interrupting me, throwing out my editors, and then telling me how to run my business." His nasal voice was rising in pitch to something near a scream.

"You don't want Ted Grofer, you don't have to have him. You don't have to have anyone. You just have to be right. You better nail this down, and crucify Roosevelt!" He suddenly came down in tone to a dramatic whisper. "Or you better find yourself a job in Paducah or in Kokomo, because you'll never work on a major newspaper in this country again."

Gaby knew she had to go for broke. "I'll contact the governor's office right away, if it's okay with you, Chief." She thought it now appropriate to call him Chief, as did most of his trusted friends. "I'll ask for an appointment for tomorrow morning, using your name. I'll tell his people I'm checking out a front-page story. I think that's the best way to approach it, don't you?"

"Wait a minute, wait a minute," Hearst shouted. He strode closer to her and peered down at her. "You've already met Roosevelt, haven't you? That's why I hired you in the first place, back in '98. You were the one that went to Florida and interviewed him there. I wonder if he'll still remember you?"

"Of course, he'll remember me, Chief. A man like that remembers everything about his career. I'm sure he remembers all the details of that story. It was really quite flattering to him, you know. I'll bet he recalls the line I used about the heroic American cowboy coming out of the West to save his country. Not only that, he used some of my material in that article when he ran for governor. Politicians don't forget anything that gets them elected. He'll remember me all right."

Hearst threw up his hands. Roosevelt not only would remember her, but he'd be favorably disposed toward her. She could get in to see the great man and might get him to say something she could quote. Gaby decided to shut up and let Hearst carry the ball at this point. The Chief didn't like others to steal his best ideas, even when they were theirs in the first place.

"I will send you there on your own. You don't need Grofer. Roosevelt might think we are ganging up on him if I sent Ted with you. This could work out well. You go on over there to Oyster Bay and charm that cowboy right out of his boots. Lasso that bronc buster and pull him out of the saddle. I'll make you the most famous reporter since Nellie Bly. No, the most famous who ever lived."

Hearst bestowed a smile upon his diminutive employee and continued, "As a recent naval hero said, you may fire when ready, Irish."

Gaby, flushed with her own triumph, said, "Thank you, Chief. You'll never regret this decision."

If he did, there would always be Peekskill and Mr. Enksten.

CHAPTER NINE

The early morning call was from a former student, now employed by the New York County medical examiner.

"I have a case that might interest you, Professor, a man found burned to death in a downtown fire. Perhaps you read about it in the paper?" Dr. Stanley Kern, had trained under him at the College of Physicians and Surgeons.

"I did read that article. Of course the chemicals used in photo shops are highly inflammable, even explosive. I don't see anything wrong with having a look at the laws regarding businesses using such chemicals. But that, I presume, is not why you called me. There's something unusual about the deceased, is that it, Stan?"

"Well, I'm not sure. Something doesn't quite click. I thought you might like to have a look before I file the case. It's not ordinary smoke asphyxiation. Perhaps you'd better see for yourself before we discuss it further."

Instead of his daily exercise on Riverside Drive, running along the Hudson for an hour, Falconer decided to forego today's effort and engage in mental exercise instead.

"Here's the thing I was talking about, Alex. Look at these lungs. They're as pink and clean as newborn babes. There's not the slightest evidence of smoke inhalation. There isn't even evidence that the heat, enormous a block away, if you can believe the newspapers, scorched any tissue inside his body. As you can see, the skin is burned to a crisp, charred. He looks like a cinder on the outside, but the nasal mucous membranes are clear. There's not even soot on his tongue."

"Well, the answer, of course, is right there in front of us, Stan, isn't it?" Falconer would occasionally sound pedantic, even in conversation with close friends. This time it was as if he were back in class trying to get the reluctant Dr. Kern to come up with the correct answer. Failing to elicit an immediate response, he charged on, "Obviously this man was dead before the fire started. It would be impossible for him, while still alive, to avoid inhaling at least some smoke and soot as well as a great deal of super-heated air to desiccate the tissues of the mouth and nasal passages."

He delicately opened the cut-up cadaver's lips. "It appears, for instance, that his mouth was closed throughout the entire fire. The teeth are unblackened, and as you mentioned the tongue and gingiva are clear! He inspected the open thorax. "Death by asphyxiation, or at least anoxia. He simply didn't have any oxygen. His lungs were filled with carbon dioxide, judging by the considerable congestion of the lung tissue. He was smothered before the fire began, wasn't he? How do you put these facts together, doctor?"

"Alex, you're insufferable. You're trying to get me to come up with answers as if I were still in third year medical school. If I'd been sure, I wouldn't have bothered you in the first place. But at least give me credit for knowing when something's wrong."

Falconer clapped his friend on the shoulder. "I'm sorry, Stan. I slip into playing the professor much too often. I just want to help you put your thoughts together so you don't need to call me in the future with a similar problem. Actually, there's no doubt in my mind that this man was killed before the fire began. Or that the killer started the fire to make it appear as if his victim had died in the blaze."

"What we have here, my dear colleague, is a case of murder. Not only murder, but premeditated, carefully constructed and damned clever. A few years ago, before you and I were on the scene, the killer would have got away with it."

Dr. Kern was pleased. "A murder of a photographer in his shop, made to look like an accident. Right. I'm with you so far." Then he added, "But why? Why would anybody go to all this trouble? Wouldn't it have been just as easy for the killer to knock this fellow on the head and throw him in the river? Do we have a pyromaniac on our hands as well?"

"I've seen several cases involving pyromaniacs, Stan. They're hard to identify because in other respects they're not obvious lunatics," Falconer observed.

"An insane fire starter. We could see more of this. There are thousands of wooden firetraps all over town. Every tenement on the east side is a hazard."

"It's too early to ascribe this particular killing to a lunatic, Stanley. I need more information." Alex always did. "I'll go down to the site of the fire and take a look."

It wasn't until after his return from the gutted building that he even considered breakfast. Peaches were in season, so he stopped on the way home and bought a bag of freshly picked fruit. These, with a quart of milk, made up his meal before he tackled the day's routine.

He spent a couple of hours with Gid and Lexie playing pepper and hitting fungo fly balls on the several empty lots in the still largely undeveloped upper reaches of West Side Manhattan. Although their coloring and hair was a match for their mother's, both had his large bones and were big for their age. He had hopes that they would become athletes too, and perhaps play for Harvard someday as he had.

Lexie had a bruise over his left eye and hadn't said a word about it all afternoon. The boy's concerned single parent could not resist inquiring.

"How did you get that bruise, son?"

"What bruise, dad?"

When his father simply stared at the area about his left eyebrow, Lexie replied, "Oh, you mean this. I got into a fight with a couple of bullies over near Broadway. They made fun of my cap. They said does mama's boy get his head too cold? Does that "H" stand for horseshit, little sissy? Things like that."

Alex had given his oldest son his Harvard baseball cap with a capital H sewn on the front of the crown.

"So he hit you in the eye?" he asked.

"Not until I punched the guy in the nose. I hit him a good one dad, like you said to do. I punched him where it hurts the most and he started bleeding like a water faucet. The blood was pouring all over his shirt. I was surprised, that's when he hit me in the eye. It hurt, but I remembered what you said, always remember that the other guy hurts too when you hit him." The boy was smiling as if to say, I did what you wanted me to and I'm worthy of your love.

"I saw it, dad, he really made that boy bleed." Gideon adoringly affirmed his older brother's prowess.

"Was it right to do that dad? Would you have done that, hit the guy?" Alex Jr. clearly wanted his father's approval.

"Sure I would, Lexie, that's the way to deal with a bully. Show him you can hurt him as much as he can hurt you, or more. I've had my share of scuffles with thugs growing up in Manhattan, all of us kids who grow up in the city like Gid and you and I. Even Governor Roosevelt's had his problems with bullies, even as a grown up. The next time we see him, ask Mr. Roosevelt about the big bully in Albany who teased him about his pea jacket. The guy was twice as big as him. Even so, the governor knocked him down three times before the man cried uncle. He'll tell you all about it, he loves stories where he's the hero."

"Did you ever get a black eye, dad?" asked Gid who had to be part of the discourse.

"I once mixed it up with a chap at Harvard named 'Jake' Weiss. They called him 'Big Jake' because he was big and strong. As strong as a bull. We argued about politics, the poor boob was a Democrat and thought Governor Cleveland was the greatest man in America since Jefferson. I had to dispute that and one thing led to another. Jake gave me a black eye three times the size of yours, Lex. He had quite a temper and so did I. But he was big, every time I looked at him he seemed twice as large as he did at the beginning."

"Dad!" exclaimed Gideon. "Mrs. Distelman promised us cinnamon and raisin cookies. If we go over there now, they'll still be warm."

That night, after retiring, Falconer reviewed the day's events and struggled with their implications. Falling asleep, a dream began. Dreams interested him since he'd studied Sigmund Freud's material in the German literature. Alex Falconer had his own ideas about the subject too.

In this one, he found himself on a Manhattan sidewalk, late at night. The streets were deserted. A ten foot tall giant stood in front of a building. He had never seen any human so large, with legs like tree trunks and matching arms and shoulders.

The fellow carried an oversized steel bucket from which he poured streams of liquid fire onto one building after another. In this dreamy suspension of reality, the giant grew so large that he was able to reach the second floor of most buildings without difficulty, splashing the material on them directly from his bucket which contained never-ending supplies of the incendiary fluid, instantly igniting the wooden structures.

Falconer knew the man was dangerous, not just because of the fires he set but because somehow he was a menace to the whole country. Here was a villain who could destroy the nation from coast to coast unless he was stopped. In the dream, however, Alex also knew that he himself could stop him. He possessed a secret to foil the arsonist and his golden liquid. Moreover, he was ready to use it. Just what that secret was, wasn't clear in the dream. But it would work. It was only a question of implementing it. That's when he awoke.

Falconer was convinced that dreams were the product of the unconscious mind, as Freud had described it. He also believed they were creative. They solved problems while the sleeper was away from the distractions of everyday life. During sleep, the brain was free to work out things that couldn't possibly be accomplished while the dreamer was awake. Dreams had aided him in finding solutions to his problem cases before. This particular dream meant that there was something more to the curious death by strangulation about which Stanley Kern had consulted him. Moreover there was something ominous about the photo studio fire.

At the crime scene, he'd noted that the way the fire had spread was consistent only with flammable material having been poured all about the shop. Not accidental, the blaze had been planned. The goal had been to wipe out everything in the studio.

Falconer was convinced there must have been something specific in the shop that the arsonist wanted to eliminate. For anyone to go to such lengths to destroy what had presumably been a document, a picture or a negative, indicate the individual was either insane or had a great deal at stake; possibly both. Dreams had to be heeded and taken seriously.

CHAPTER TEN

Theodore Roosevelt had a habit of talking slowly and pausing between words when he wanted to make a point. He often pointed out to friends he was not a great speaker, but could drive his point home by emphasizing important passages. He said, "I... may not... know... everything. But... you... will... know... everything.., that... I... have...to... say." Even when not making a speech, he enunciated carefully as if choosing words and evaluating each one.

Teddy had been a young Harvard graduate when he returned to New York and ran for the state legislature in the "silk stocking" district. He'd challenged the incumbent, William Waldorf Astor, for the job. With less money than Astor for his campaign, he went to every public meeting and met as many citizens, one by one, as possible. To the surprise of all, he'd persuaded the elite of the district as well as the tradesmen and laborers to vote for him. He became known as the working man's candidate. T.R. won the election hands down. Astor, defeated in New York, moved to England, became a British subject and a peer of the realm. He married a Gibson girl from Virginia who became renowned as Lady Astor. But that's another story.

"Woody, this appointment with the Journal reporter smells a little funny to me." The governor chopped his fists on the desk. "What in the hell does Willy Hearst have in mind? What good did he ever want to see happen to a Republican? He set up his newspaper as a power base for himself in the future. The man has political aspirations, mark my words. It takes one to know one, you know."

"I'm sure you're right, Ted." The governor hated to be called Teddy. Woody Kane had a clipped New England accent. "Hearst doesn't love you, and he has no affection for the Grand Old Party either."

"He's a sharpie from San Francisco," continued T.R.'s former classmate and present campaign manager. "And he's no gentleman. He doesn't play fair. Sending a woman to talk to us bothers me too. I suggest we deal with her carefully. She works on the society page, you know."

"Where else would she work? I trust and presume she's no Nellie Bly," T.R. said.

"Ted, there's nothing we need to worry about where your family is concerned, is there? I've always been a little troubled about Alice. She's a pistol, of course, but I just hope she hasn't involved herself in anything we can't handle."

"She never knew her mother," T.R. gazed out the window of his study.

"And I've spoiled her beyond belief. I can no more control Alice than the flow of the Hudson River. I'm unable to deal with her flying in the face of society. It's a reaction to her losing her mother and my running away."

"Going off to the Dakota Territory after your mother and your wife died on the same day isn't running away, Ted. For God's sake be reasonable with yourself."

"I try, Woody, I try. But I don't always succeed. I suspect Alice has never accepted my second marriage, although she and Edith get along well. Still my wife can't control her either. When the child started smoking cigarettes, Edith was scandalized. She equates that with Alice drinking alcohol and carrying on with young men. God only knows. This Miss Irish might have something to say about that."

"It's probably something else altogether, Ted."

"The woman's due here for lunch. Mr. Klein went to the station to pick them up. I've asked Al Shaw to join us. Three Harvard men should be enough to deal with a lady journalist, even one from the shop of the shady Mr. Hearst."

"Edith's arranged a buffet", Kane reported. "Some cold potato soup and small sandwiches. We'll take it on the porch, where you can look your *most* vice-presidential. She's bringing a photographer. It would help to show you at home lunching al fresco for the benefit of her readers. It's a rare opportunity to get favorable personal exposure from the politically independent press. If her story is going to be as lightweight as I expect, at least we can score that much off Mr. Hearst."

Gaby Irish and her photographer rode next to Mr. Klein, who was quite hard of hearing. The photographer might have taken pictures of the Civil War, if he'd owned a camera then. Oliver Winterbottom was seventy if he was a day. As far back as anyone could recall he had been known as Windy.

Hearst had made a habit of sending him out when he wanted to be certain that the work was done according to his personal standards. Windy was a strange one. Years ago he must have done some sailing. Even now he dressed the part. He wore tight bell- bottomed breeches mariners had used when they sailed before the mast in the 1850's, topped by a blouse of broad blue and white stripes. His appearance was similar to those seen in pictures of old salts working the clipper ships out of Boston. There hadn't been a clipper around for years.

Sometimes, in addition to his floppy trousers and colorful shirt, he'd sport a sailor hat, the kind that looked like a tam-o'-shanter, flat-topped with a fuzzy red ball in the middle. He wore this costume winter and summer. Windy didn't even wear ordinary shoes. Instead of leather footwear, his was of canvas with gum rubber soles. "So I can grip the deck and not slip on the salty brine." The fact that he hadn't trod the deck of a ship in decades, and spent most of his time on the sidewalks of New York was irrelevant.

But he was a great photographer, or so Mr. Hearst said, and Gaby was glad to have him along.

On a couple of assignments together before, Windy attracted interest away from her. Because she was a female reporter and likely to arouse derision as well as undesirable attention, the old man served as a lightning rod, of sorts. She even hoped the governor might be less angry with her when she produced what she'd have to show him, if **Windy - No**, probably not.

There were some who claimed that Windy had been present at the battle of the Monitor and the Merrimac, and that was when he'd begun to affect his nautical attire. No one could ever prove that. When asked about it, he would talk about something else entirely. He also habitually answered questions with other questions.

On their way to Oyster Bay, Gaby had said, "Windy, do you suppose Governor Roosevelt will take it out on me for bringing up this business about whether or not he really led the charge on San Juan Hill? I know it sounds like a silly question, but I don't have much experience in dealing with politicians. Will he take it coolly or will he become angry and try to shout me down? What do you think? You've been around a long time."

"Think? What do I think? I think a pretty girl like you should be out on a farm someplace, raising children, taking care of a husband. I think the electric light is the greatest invention of the nineteenth century. I think Thomas Edison is a genius. I think Mr. McKinley is President because the people aren't ready to listen to Mr. Bryan's ideas. I think a lot of things."

"But I think the greatest tragedy in the world is that men burn pieces of coal in iron kettles to boil water and move ships across the ocean instead of spreading canvas to the skies and letting God's wind move them the way He intended. That's what I think. What do you think?"

He looked cherubic as he smiled and gazed at the open sky, continuing with the Almighty at every moment of his waking existence.

To say that Windy's attire was too bizarre for presentation to the Governor of the Empire State was an understatement. Gaby, however, was preoccupied with her own appearance. This was the biggest story she'd ever be likely to cover. It was essential to dress properly for the governor. It had to do with what Charles called "credibility."

She had carefully chosen her costume for the day. Appropriate attire for summer dictated white. She'd picked a full-bodiced blouse similar to one she'd seen in Harper's magazine last month. Gaby relied upon Harper's, and in the appearance of people pictured in that publication. She'd spent too much time at college dealing with her studies, and not as much with clothing and appearance as did her contemporaries. As a result, she now had to rely upon the taste of others, as displayed in popular magazines.

Harper's was the only truly national magazine. People like Governor Roosevelt and President McKinley read it. Any woman in its illustrations must be attired properly. The white blouse with cuffed sleeves and a small black bow tie had been in the May issue. She'd complemented it with a white full-length skirt, cumbersome for walking about in the grass at Sagamore Hill, but proper, and sure to be accepted by the governor and his staff.

Her white straw skimmer was designed like men's hats of the day, with a wide black band. In the prim black and white outfit, she looked the part of a young woman of fashion and substance, out to do a job for her employer, the redoubtable William Randolph Hearst.

Gaby thought, "I'm riding out to meet the most powerful politician in the state of New York and all of his aides and officials, people redolent with power and influence. And I am accompanied by a deaf driver and an elderly lunatic."

CHAPTER ELEVEN

The Roosevelt estate was sprawled atop a small, grass covered hill. Gaby's trepidations concerning facing the governor in his home were not allayed by the aspect of the property. Sagamore Hill was a squared, massive and relatively unattractive structure, not unlike a National Guard Armory in appearance.

As they approached the entrance to the fortress, Gaby made a final pocket mirror inspection. Her hair in place and hat primly atop her head, she recalled Mother's advice concerning the dangers of city life.

"Besides keeping your headpiece in place, you can ward off mashers with a sturdy hatpin. You've got to keep them at their distance."

A Victorian girl of virtue threatened by improper approaches *could* reach to her hat, remove the six-inch piece of steel and use it as a stiletto to ward off an ardent suitor.

"Believe you me, any man will think twice before he bothers you with that in your hand."

It was the only sexual advice she had ever gotten from the woman. Everything else was learned from classmates at Radcliffe and during recent occupational travels for the paper. She'd learned an awful lot about things which proper people didn't discuss in 1900.

Windy was, as usual, telling stories. This one was about the gubernatorial election of 1898.

"Teddy came back from Cuba," he wound on, "you weren't with the paper then. This cowboy on his horse, a real war hero, something the people hadn't seen since General Grant, a home town boy from New York. The politicians had to let him run, knew he'd get elected. They got on the bandwagon, and he toured the state. That was a time girl! Torchlight parades in Queens, clambakes in Syracuse, picnics in Rochester. It was something to remember!"

"It wasn't all peaches and cream. One time I was attacked by a butcher while I was taking pictures of Roosevelt. Can you imagine that, physically attacked in his shop. I thought the man'd kill me. He had this big meat cleaver."

Gaby, pulled from her hatpin reverie, made the mistake of asking: "Why did he attack you Windy? For taking a picture?"

"I don't' know, I wasn't doing anything to him. He just came after me with a big axe, had wild staring eyes. I thought he'd froth at the mouth. The lunatic screamed something about killing me. I wasn't doing a thing, just standing there on this side- o- beef taking a picture of the candidate."

The rig stopped at the front portico where the governor and entourage replete in brown trousers, matching waistcoat, and maroon tie, awaited them.

Masterson, who more and more was assuming the role of chief bodyguard and head of security for the upcoming national campaign, eyed Gaby and her eccentrically dressed companion with more than a little suspicion. It was the same look he gave an itinerant tinhorn gambler exiting the stagecoach in Dodge. The former town tamer stood three feet behind the governor and all the while kept his right hand resting on the grip of the six shooter he wore beneath his suit jacket.

T.R, displayed his inimitable electioneering grin. His overlarge teeth gleamed brilliantly beneath his pince-nez glasses. Close to blind without the glasses, it was said that he charged that Cuban hill (if indeed he ever did) waving his sword, astride the war horse, wearing nose spectacles.

"Why, it's you, the little bugler boy. Dee lighted! Now I know why Willy Hearst sent you to talk to me." With this, he enveloped her hand in both of his and energetically pumped it back and forth. His smile broadened. "It's bully to see you, Miss Irish, bully. That was a capital story you did before we left for the Antilles,"

"Thank you, Colonel, excuse me, Governor. Thank you for remembering. It was such a brief interview." Gaby was genuinely pleased that the great man knew her, especially her outfit in the uniform of one of his troopers. She feared it might, in retrospect, seem too bold and unconventional. Of course, the absence of convention was characteristic of the cowboy politician.

"Remember you! I'll never forget. When I first saw you I was convinced Leonard Wood had gone out and gotten himself a bugler boy after all. He wanted one to sound the charge when we moved into battle."

"I told Wood buglers were too exposed in an outfit with smokeless powder ordinance. A boy blowing a brass cornet gleaming in the sun, would have been holed by the enemy in a minute."

"But you did look like a young man dressed in that Rough Rider outfit with your hair piled up underneath the western hat."

"Thank you, governor. I really fooled you didn't I?" she laughed.

"I thought you were small, but we had all sizes in that outfit, men from all over the country and overseas too. Those were the days." Roosevelt herded the group into the house like steers on his Dakota ranch.

The governor held court in the parlor for friends and visiting dignitaries. Sagamore Hill, not the official residence in Albany, was the focus of most of T.R.'s interests and activities.

The room was filled with mementoes of these activities. Stuffed moose, buffalo, and elk heads occupied large areas of the walls. Their horns protruded into the space above the passerby. Innumerable plaques and statuary awarded by all manner of organizations and institutions filled other spaces, plus photographs of the great man chronicling his varied interests over the past twenty years.

One picture showed a young Harvard athlete in boxing attire assuming a classic pugilistic pose. In another a politician stood on a platform, waving his fist in the air making some cogent point. Next was a photograph of a man in buckskin with six-guns strapped to his waist, plus many shots of family, and notables of the day. They crowded the walls and spread over onto the desk and any other available flat surface. The room was crowded with the personae of many people, but dominated by the charismatic presence of the master of Sagamore Hill in his various guises.

After offering morning refreshments, Roosevelt got right down to business. "What is it that Willy Hearst has cooked up now, Miss Irish? It can't be good. Willy Hearst has no love for me or my party, as you well know. Any dirt he can dig up about the Grand Old Party would be, if you'll excuse the expression, mother's milk for him. Tell me straightaway."

Struck by the aura of power around the governor and the man's obvious certitude, Gaby began to disbelieve the allegations of the affidavit and even what she saw in the photograph. Nevertheless, she must pursue her story.

"I received this affidavit from a reliable source, Colonel. *It's* very specific and, could be damaging to your career. Please read it and tell me how you respond to it." She handed him Renfield's statement.

He placed the paper before him, removed a handkerchief from his pocket and slowly polished his pince-nez glasses in preparation for reading. It seemed as if he were thinking through his response to the document even before reading it. Roosevelt scanned the material with no visible sign of emotion. His eyebrows raised once or twice, and at the end, he placed it back on the desk.

"Well, little bugler boy, you've delivered a remarkable document. I remember Renfield very well. I personally recruited the vast majority of the 1st New York Volunteer Cavalry. The outfit was my own idea from the beginning. I couldn't allow myself to remain safe in the Navy Department while brave men were fighting the war I had helped plan."

"And Renfield, sir, you do remember him?" She tried to steer T.R. back on course rather than allow the wily spellbinder to divert her into a history lesson.

"Renfield was one of the Dakota territory volunteers, an Englishman who came West to seek his fortune and never made it. He became a cow man, good with a horse and even better with a gun."

He reminisced. "It was the finest group of men ever recruited for war. We had volunteers from all over the country. There were horsemen from the west, sharpshooters from Kentucky, even some of my fellow alumni from Harvard. You were in Tampa. You saw them!"

"Indeed I did, sir. They were an impressive lot," she recalled. "That makes it even harder to believe some of your own men could betray you. And yet there it is."

"Renfield was a fine rider and a great shot. But he was flawed, no doubt of it, as so many of us are."

"Coincidentally, his initials are the same as my own, T.R. The man began to have the delusion that he was my carbon copy. He once asked me who made my blouses, wanted to hire my tailor. As an enlisted man he was entitled to them free from the government."

"He wanted custom made uniforms?" Gaby scribbled furiously in her note pad.

"Yes, strange isn't it? I always use Brooks Brothers. It would have cost poor Renfield three month's pay just to have a tunic cut. In retrospect, I should have known I was dealing with a mentally crippled man."

"He once told me it was important we have identical clothing so he could impersonate me. When I inquired why I should need a double, he said I'd run again for elective office and an impersonator could prevent assassination. What claptrap!" With this, Roosevelt once more donned his pince-nez and looked at the document signed with Renfield's broad hand.

"Well, he seems to have been somewhat of a prophet, doesn't he, Colonel," Gaby observed. "You have indeed run for office and are running again. Perhaps he's a seer as well as a double, and a lunatic too."

"Prophetic, perhaps, but strange. I remember a conversation we had shortly before going into action. He had come to my tent once more with his notion of acting as my double. He even suggested he go in my place leading the troops. Of course, I had none of it. Where is he now, do you know?"

"Governor, I have no further information aside from the affidavit and this picture. I don't know the whereabouts of Renfield or the three corroborative witnesses." She offered him the photograph.

"Thank you, Ma'am. I must add for the record, that a day prior to our attack on Kettle Hill, Renfield went completely over the edge. I thought he had Yellow Fever. He didn't appear jaundiced, but was feverish and excited. He muttered something about saving me and the regiment and sacrificing himself. I ordered him to go directly to the medical officer, Major Clifton."

"You think this lunatic, as you suggest, in his fevered state, did as you said?" Gaby, impressed by the probity of Roosevelt's personality, still tried to maintain a journalist's open—mindedness.

"Yes, indeed, sick as he was, he was a soldier and followed orders. I'm sure he visited Clifton. We can verify that with the doctor."

"Let's look at your photo. Let's see this damning piece of evidence."

The picture showed the colonel in the embrace of a somewhat overdressed, Negro woman. He took it in his hand, inspected it carefully, held it at a distance, then closer, and said, "Very clever, very, very clever. I wasn't aware that the art of photography had made such leaps in technical advancement. It is well done and looks quite real but, of course, is an outrageous forgery. I can assure you of that."

"Can I quote you on that?" Gaby asked, writing furiously in her note pad.

The bespectacled governor responded with some impatience. "I'd rather you didn't quote me at all at the moment, ma'am. If you can persuade our mutual friend, Mr. Hearst, to hold off, I promise a full statement and complete explanation of this entire matter within a fortnight."

He stroked his moustache with the backside of his right index finger. Had Gaby been more aware of the governor's idiosyncrasies, she would have realized he was extremely angry. Such preening was similar to a bull pawing the ground before his charge.

Roosevelt, furious at what he had just seen, was ready to attack. He didn't want this girl to become the object of his rage, so remained controlled while trying to fend off her zeal for a good story.

"Two weeks will take us too close to September, Governor. My boss will never agree to that long a delay. He lives by the clock, not the calendar. Twenty-four hours is too long for him to wait on most stories." As she spoke, she saw that the Rough Rider *was* equally unlikely to accept compromise.

Maybe she could back them both out of a corner, "But I think, in deference to you, sir, I can persuade him to wait a few days, at least."

She had no real confidence of achieving this. It was akin to asking a ravenous shark to hold off consuming its prey. Sometimes The Chief, cruising the editorial floor of the Journal, seemed to be a man-eater patrolling a tropical lagoon for fresh meat. Roosevelt could fill his always hungry stomach for some time. As far as W.R. was concerned, Gaby was small fry. She'd be gobbled up by the great man in no time if she didn't perform the way he wished. Now, she was trapped between Teddy

Roosevelt, the snorting, pawing bull, and the silent undersea menace of the predatory Hearst.

"Isn't there something I could tell Mr. Hearst to hold him off for awhile, Governor? Just a morsel to feed the big fish?"

"Yes, of course, Miss Irish. I understand your position. Tell Willy you've shown me all the material and I deny it categorically. Say I will launch a full-scale investigation into this matters Add that I will engage the services of this nation's greatest criminologist to ferret out the perpetrator of this fraud."

"If he wishes to print what you have now, there is nothing I can do to stop him. I suggest, however, that a precipitous publication of this material might very well wind up in court. A judgment *against* the New York Journal might be even more than the Comstock Lode can handle."

The great silver and gold mine holdings were vulnerable to attack through the courts by anyone, much less a figure as powerful as the Governor of the state of New York. A wealthy man in his own right, he could command the services of the nation's best attorneys, some as ravenous as Hearst himself in the shark business.

"The Chief's not the kind of man you can easily appease, sir. I'll tell him what you've said. But I need something, anything besides that. He lives on stories. I've got to have some kind of story."

"The story simply is not available now, Miss Irish. But I promise you that when it is, I'll give you exclusive rights to it, a real feather for your bonnet, Miss Reporter."

"Frankly, Miss Irish, I'm not concerned about the veracity of these allegations themselves. They won't stand the light of day. But a smear in the press might be enough to cause the Party to ask for the Vice-Presidential candidate to withdraw for the good of the ticket."

"I won't do that, so we will scotch this right now." He slammed his right fist into his left palm to emphasize his resolve.

One last stab in hope of salvaging something from the interview, "Perhaps, Governor, you could tell me something personal about that famous charge? I can prepare it for the Sunday Supplement. It's *only* two years since the event. Lots of things that happened that day haven't been printed yet." T.R. might give her something to throw into the pit they called an editorial room, instead of her own diminutive body which she feared was forfeit without a big story. Roosevelt responded, "There is one story which has never been made public. I didn't even refer to it in my book, THE ROUGH RIDERS. This is at the request of the man involved. It's about how one of my so-called cowboys saved my life while under fire from Spanish guns. I guess it would be of interest to your employer, but come to think of it, it has another value," the Governor said.

Gaby answered, "I understand, of course it can verify that you were there. If I can hear that story and get a statement from the man who saved you, well that would go a long way to neutralize these allegations Colonel. The cowboy had to be there with you two years ago in combat, please tell me the story."

CHAPTER TWELVE

As Roosevelt began the story he removed his pocket watch, opened it and placed it on the desk before him. He was a man who valued time. T.R's message was clear. He was delivering something extremely valuable, not only the story, but his time.

"It's about how Sherman Bell saved my life," he said.

"The same Mr. Bell, who is on your staff now?" She had noticed the tall raw-boned man with cowboy boots and large handlebar moustache. Who wouldn't notice him, especially when he wore his large "ten gallon" white Stetson.

"The very same, and I'm very fortunate to have him along with me now. He was one of the original Rough Riders and really just developed our presentation campaigning. We have a few of my men in full uniform. A bugler sounds assembly and then we all march in to give the talks. I've been thinking of a color guard too. I think that would give us a bit more panache. There is nothing like Old Glory to rouse a crowd," he smiled at the one time bogus bugler boy.

"I guess flag waving is part of politics, Mr. Roosevelt," Gaby said. It seemed to her that she was engaged in a theatrical discussion rather than a political one. But then, she was becoming convinced that politics was theater after all. Brass bands, torch light parades, patriotic bunting, uniformed color guards and especially rabble rousing emotionally laden speeches. Roosevelt was a master at such things as he had proven in his gubernatorial campaign of 1898. Now, he was going to feed her some tasty tidbit to in turn feed to her boss and keep everyone happy.

"Initially, Bell asked me to not publish that as a story. He's essentially a shy man of action who feels that saving my life was part of his duty and not to be especially noted. But more than two years have gone by and now that he's a civilian again and," the governor laughed, "employed by me, I feel I can tell the tale."

"I feel I ought to do this to help destroy the bogus story and to give you personally some reassurance that indeed, it is bogus. The picture of me which you showed me is undoubtedly one that was taken in Cuba in front of my tent at the front. We were pinned down there awaiting the order to move forward on the Spanish."

"A number of journalists were buzzing about like flies on a cube of sugar. Several took photographs. This part of the picture could well be from one of those *chaps*. The Negro woman is completely unknown to me. How this picture came to be as it is, is a mystery to me. I've never had anything to do with shady women, even at Harvard. There were many opportunities over the years, but I've always tried to lead an exemplary life in that regard. I'm proud to say I've always been true to Mrs. Roosevelt. It's a matter of personal honor to me."

"But let me tell you the story."

"I was leading the charge on my pony, Wyoming. Sergeant Sherman Bell, once a sheriff in Cripple Creek, Colorado, had told me a favorite Indian fighting technique was to pick out the leader and try to shoot him out of the saddle first to disorganize any attacks. He warned me not to mount up, but rather lead the group on foot. You'll be the Spaniard's main target, Colonel, on top of that pony waving your saber,' he said. But I'm afraid some people are right when they describe me as being somewhat stubborn. I thought it was essential to lead the regiment personally and in plain view of everyone, even if it gave the enemy a better shot at me."

The boy governor paused, sipped from his glass of lemonade, wiped his brow with his blue polka dot bandana and went on.

"A sharp shooter stationed beyond the massive molasses kettle atop the hill spotted me and narrowly missed with a shot I could hear whiz by my head. I moved back and forth urging the men up the hill and wasn't an easy target. But another shot did hit the blade just below the grip of my saber. The force of the bullet actually knocked me off my mount and later I determined that the ricochet must have wounded Wyoming on her flank."

"I was on the ground and a bit dazed from the fall. It was then that Sherman Bell, who had been keeping his eye on me throughout the engagement, came along and literally picked me up bodily. He's a strong chap. 'Are you okay Colonel?' he asked. When he was satisfied that I wasn't hit, he pointed to the metal vat atop Kettle Hill. That son of a bitch behind the kettle is gunnin' for you, sir. He knows who you are and he's gonna keep goin' until he holes you,' he said."

"This is the same Bell who's on your team now, Governor, the left handed gunfighter?" Gaby asked. "Very astute, Miss Irish. You noticed he carries his revolver on his left side. But he's only been a left hander since Cuba and that's part of the story."

"What happened Governor?" she asked.

"Sherman saved my life that morning, no doubt about it. Bell placed himself between me and the sniper on Kettle Hill." The lemonade glasses were empty and without missing a beat in his narrative, T.R. refilled his own and the reporter's glass as he spoke.

"The sniper was sheltered behind a mound of earth next to the kettle; he was probably the one who shot the saber out of my hand. Sherman decided he had to get the man. As he protected me with his body between myself and the sniper, he said, if you'll pardon the expression, 'There's the bastard now, I see him.' He aimed the Buntline holding it with both hands in the direction of a pile of earth a few feet from the big kettle. The man fired six shots in a row, bang bang, bang bang, bang bang, at the speed of a Gatling Gun. One of the shots ran the iron kettle behind the mound, but some of the other five must have met their mark. There wasn't any further firing from that quarter."

Gaby was writing furiously in her notebook, as T.R. told his tale, and barely had time to catch up when the former Rough Rider paused for another sip.

"As I was saying, Bell silenced the sniper but was bleeding from the right upper arm. I picked up my saber, pulled out my own revolver, not a Buntline Special, like Bell's, and began up the hill again. I told the sergeant to get back to the medical station and have someone look at the wound which appeared nasty to me. Not surprisingly however, he kept on up the hill. He reloaded his weapon and was at the crest when we raised Old Glory." T.R. removed a framed picture from his desk top and showed it to the reporter.

"Here we are, Bill, Kane, some of the others and Roosevelt immediately after we won. I'm there and you can see a discoloration on the sergeant's upper right arm. I guess I was at San Juan Hill alright," Roosevelt said with some annoyance.

"Yes sir, I can see you. Did Bell have his arm attended to?" Gaby asked.

"Not until the next day after the enemy capitulated. By then, it had become infected and he was in real trouble, almost lost the arm. He still has what the medical men call osteomyelitis. There is no real treatment for it, an infection of the bone. It oozes from time to time, always pus, excuse me I'm terribly sorry."

Gaby became nauseated at the description of the infectious process and held her hand to her mouth and retched just a bit.

"I'm terribly sorry, how indelicate of me. Please forgive me," the governor said.

"Oh no! I have no right to be so finicky when you are describing the problems of a man who risked his life for you and was a genuine American hero," she said.

"A hero he is, indeed ma'am. But he refused to let me write a citation for a medal. Insisted I not do so. Now, however, when I tell him we need to tell the tale to protect the ticket and scotch the vicious story your employer wants to print, I'm sure he'll agree to let it become public."

"Can we get some photographs, I mean new ones, I'd like to have the one you just showed me and I'd like to have some right here. Windy's outside with his tripod and camera, Colonel." Gaby slipped back into his military title. It seemed appropriate to her at the moment.

"Of course! I'm sure Bell will pose for your man. You can see now why he uses his left hand for his weapon."

"And that's why he's working for you now, can't go back to being a lawman," Gaby asked.

"In a manner of speaking, but he's close to forty and probably too old for that kind of trade anyway," Roosevelt told her.

"So he's sort of a bodyguard?"

"I call him my personal assistant. Masterson is the real bodyguard. He's done this sort of thing for several years since he left the west. He worked for old Jay Gould of the New York Central for years after some lunatic threatened to shoot the old man on sight because the railroad stole his land or some such thing."

"Bell's reliable and loyal and can handle his weapon with his left hand. But Bat is a professional. He's quick and incredibly accurate. The man's a dead shot. It's a natural gift I guess." Roosevelt examined his pocket watch, finished his glass of lemonade and commanded, rather than suggested, "Let's get on with the picture taking young lady."

CHAPTER THIRTEEN

Gaby worried about the Chief, she always thought of him capitalized, like God. He'd be unhappy without the complete story He sent her to get. Hopefully, she could placate the man with something for his new Sunday Supplement. W.R. had instituted a device to print colored pictures and illustrate the stories. He believed that adding an extra section would increase Sunday circulation. Besides, he could charge more than the usual penny. He even added colored comic strips.

The story about Teddy Roosevelt charging up San Juan Hill with illustrations in full color might appeal to the young publisher. Gaby envisioned an artist's rendering of the colonel flying through the air as the bullet struck his saber. His horse could be plunging to the ground with blood pouring from its shoulder; Roosevelt could be seen in midair, his gleaming steel saber flying in one direction, the horse pistol in another, and his polka dot blue kerchief floating in the breeze. The Chief would love it.

As Windy put his paraphernalia on Mr. Klein's rig, he gathered up saliva and sent a huge wad of tobacco colored sputum five feet across the gravel to the grass beyond. The man was an addict to Beech-Nut chewing , tobacco. Wads of sputum and tobacco flew everywhere Windy was to be found. He obviously had been most uncomfortable at Sagamore Hill where no spittoons were to be found.

Winterbottom had obviously relished the interview in the trophy room as he could wander outdoors and festoon the grounds with Beech-Nut residue. The old man then commented on the picture taking. "The governor is sure a good subject, Gab. I've taken pictures of all of them, but there's something about that man that appeals to me. Some people just look good in front of a camera. Others come out flat and dull like Major McKinley."

"That Roosevelt, he's something else. When I take a picture of him I feel something's happening. He's in action as I take the picture. Maybe it's his eyes, or the way he holds his body. Bill Cody's like that, too. There's something about the way those people stand and hold themselves that's perfect for the art of photography."

"You know young lady, it is an art. I can do anything with this camera. I can make things look like they're far away when they're right up close, or make them look like they're right on top when they're in the next county. This is a fine instrument to be played like a fiddle. It can sing and dance. I can make it do almost anything."

At the edge of her consciousness, as the ancient mariner rambled on, an idea popped into her mind. She'd learned at the Journal to grab ahold of such ideas and look at them.

"Do you truly mean you can do anything with that camera, Windy? Can you make things appear real that aren't there?"

"What do you mean that aren't there? Do you mean can I make things look different than they are? Sure. I can't duplicate the kind of look Teddy has on his face, but I can change it around. I can make people look different. I can put Teddy Roosevelt's head on Grover Cleveland's body; or McKinley's face on Teddy's neck. I could even take Bryan's head and have him talk from the body of a jackass."

"Well, I guess you can do that in cartoon kind of things, Windy, but can you do it so it looks real? Could you do it so I wouldn't know the difference? I mean, I would know if you had Bryan's face on a donkey's body. But could you do something that looked like an original picture?" she asked.

The old photographer rubbed his ear and stuck his little finger in it as if seeking some bug that had crawled inside. It was a time-consuming device to allow him to think about his answer. "I think I know what you're getting at. I'll tell you something I pulled when I was working for Joe Pulitzer on the *World*. There was this Tammany guy Joe really hated. Joe would support a good man whether he was Republican or a Democrat. He had his preferences, but he'd back the best man. The thing that bothered him the most were real crooks. There was this guy; I think his name was Mulvaney or Mulveany, something like that. Anyway, Joe knew Mulcahey was a crook. The man was a pig. So I got this idea. I cropped the picture of the politician along with one I'd taken at the pig pens in Secausus, when they opened the stockyards there."

"What I did was, I had a file picture of this guy standing at some meeting and fixed it so he looked like he was lying down. Then I superimposed a shot of the pigs in the stockyards wallowing in the mud. When I got through it looked like Muireaney was lying down with the pigs and getting slopped over by them. Joe loved it. He captioned it: 'When you lie down with pigs....'."

"Well, Muldoon didn't like it, not one little bit. He came roaring down to the World. The feller wanted blood. He threatened to sue the paper, Pulitzer and everybody on the premises."

"I never saw Joe look better. He stood up to this guy, and said, Mulhouse, if you can prove that you're not a pig and you can show me in print that you haven't taken money from at least twelve different bartenders to keep their saloons open on Sundays - don't forget, I have their names - if you can show me that you haven't taken money from three or four construction companies I know in this town, to get contracts to build the roads on the west side, I'll take back that picture. I'll print a full retraction. I'll apologize, and I'll not put picture in with those pigs. But until that day comes, that picture stands. You come back here when you have the proof. If you don't, never walk through this door again."

"Well, ma'am, that was Joe Pulitzer at his best. If Hearst didn't pay me twice as much, I'd still be working for the man. He let the piece stand. You can do anything with a picture if you want to."

Gaby pursued her thought. "You mean, you can take two separate pictures and put them together and make them look like one; like two people standing next to each other or even embracing one another?"

"Sure you can. It isn't hard. I could do it now, take one of the pictures I just shot of T.R. and his friend, Kane, and make it look like Roosevelt was buddy-buddy with William Jennings Bryan. I could have Teddy's arm around Bryan and vice versa. When we get back to the paper, I'll show you how. Today's pictures should come out real well. We could make them even more interesting." He propelled an oyster sized wad of saliva to the side of the road.

Gaby considered how to discuss the story with The Chief. It would be a terrible mistake to jump off with a piece that could prove a hoax. Worse, if it were blackmail and The Journal became a tool of the plot. With the information from Windy, perhaps Hearst would hold off until the story was more solid. In the meantime, she had a great Sunday Supplement special. It was important to get the Rough Rider material done in time for dinner with Chuck Majors at the Waldorf. Chuck was interested in the developing story. The price of telling him, along with the assurance that it wouldn't go any further, was a dinner out. Being out on the town was addictive. The more you did it, the more you wanted.

Chuck's expense account enabled them to dine with the rich and famous. Mark Twain was in town, lecturing. He could be abroad tonight. Maybe the Vanderbilts, the Schuylers, or the Goulds would be there this evening.

It was a wonderful prospect, a great life. It was exciting to be alive and in New York at the center of everything in time for the beginning of a magnificent new century.

CHAPTER FOURTEEN

Woodbury Kane and Albert Shaw, both out of Harvard through the Rough Riders looked worried. "I don't suppose you boys think this is true about me and some Negro floozy making love in our tent? Woody, you were there; did I have time to waste with a tramp? Even if it were so, how in hell could I get away with it in the tent? You and Al were in and out constantly."

"If I wanted to, I couldn't have hidden a woman under my camp bed. That is, if she were dumb enough to want to lie there with the bugs and vermin in that God forsaken jungle. I don't know if this is Hearst's work or if he's being used by someone else. He's dumb enough for that."

Kane and Shaw spoke simultaneously. The more forceful Woody prevailed. "Ted, it's none of my damned business if you had a woman in your tent or not, black or white, I couldn't care less. I know you were there on the hill. I was with you. We fought the damn Spaniards together, and won. Anybody who says that isn't true calls me a liar too. I'll fight them to the death, you know that.

"But hell, it looks terrible. I imagine Hearst has a sheaf of other forged papers saying the same damned thing. We have to deny something that isn't true and disprove what we can't put our hands on. It's a criminal disgrace."

"Criminal! That's it! Let's call in the police!" interjected Sudberg, volatile under the best of circumstances.

"A man is innocent until he's proven guilty in this country. That's the American way. Somebody who brings up charges like this is a dirty traitor. Let's get a judge to issue a warrant for the arrest of William

Randolph Hearst, that's what I say! Then we'll see where he got these pictures and the phony documents too. This is blackmail, pure and simple.

"Where's Masterson? He was a sheriff or a marshal for years. Maybe he can find out what's really going on. This sounds like a case of extortion." Rudy "Slim" Sudberg erupted.

"Bat's gone off to the city. He's going to meet Mark Twain tonight for dinner, learn something about the writing trade, I guess," hypothesized Al Shaw. "However, Masterson was a constable and a fast gun. What we need is an investigator of some kind, a consulting detective."

"I've got an idea," Sudberg shouted.

"I'll write a news story that'll make Billy Boy Hearst look like Simon Legree. When I'm through with him, he'll be the most hated man in the United States since George III. How dare he blacken the name of America's greatest hero!"

Sudsberg's erect 6'4", and 280 lb. frame seemed to block the light from an entire French window. Gesticulating, his arms swung wildly as if he were orating on the campaign trail. How he got the name Slim was lost in the obscure depths of the New Brunswick saloons where he spent most of his time while at Rutgers.

After the big man began to lose some steam, Shaw quietly added, "We can't request a warrant for Hearst's arrest. Although I suspect he deserves it for a number of things. And, we can't generate stories denying something that hasn't come to light as yet."

"We've got to scotch this tale before it sees the light of day. We must present such obvious and overwhelming refutation that publishing it, could cost the young man his newspaper and his daddy's gold mine as well. What's needed I repeat is an expert detective. If Sherlock Holmes weren't fictional, I'd suggest calling him in."

Roosevelt slapped his hand on the desk and said, "Of course, Sherlock Holmes, that's brilliant, Albert. The deductive mind of a detective genius, that's what we need. Holmes may be fictional, but Alex Falconer is as real as you and me!"

"Alex Falconer, Governor?' Slim look surprised. "Our poker pal? His stories sound like table talk. Like the one about the mad balloonist in Milwaukee threatening to blow up the city hospital if he weren't paid all that money? That's real? And how about the murder of the three ship captains in the harbor a few years ago, true, Governor?'

"Of course, they're true. Falconer is the genuine thing, a Harvard man. He played baseball for the Crimson, and used the name Al Bird when he pitched for the Giants a few summers back."

"He had a curve ball that looked as if it rolled off the top of a table and a fast ball like a Fourth of July rocket. He was unhittable. After he decided to study medicine, he played only home games. When the Giants went on the road, Falconer stayed in town to keep up with classes. Management dropped him, said they couldn't count on a half time man. A shame, I think it cost them a pennant."

"But a brilliant mind like his wasn't satisfied with merely fooling people with curve balls. Of course, he's our man. He's the expert we need from the twentieth century generation of Americans I've been talking about in my speeches. Alex is committed to the scientific detection of crime. A fine mind. Woody, you remember, we talked in Albany last year about the state police bill, a central forensic laboratory, and the use of fingerprints."

"Of course, I do, Ted. You're right. He can do the job and he's one of us, discreet. We don't know where this may lead yet," Kane agreed.

"Get a hold of him, Rudy .He has a telephone. Run into Oyster Bay and call. Get him here as quickly as possible. Say it's a matter of great urgency to me personally." Such a message was tantamount to a summons from Olympus.

"In the meantime, Governor, we should consider the origins of this material." Al Shaw persisted, "A man is known by his enemies, and you've made quite a few. My first choice would be the Democrats. Bryan thinks he has a chance to win this time. The Cross of Gold speech didn't do it in 96, so he's found something else to shove up his sleeve."

"Bryan! Not him. The man's too thick. The only plot he understands is in a graveyard. Old Senator Foraker once said, the boy orator of the Platte is aptly named. The Platte River is six inches deep and six miles wide at the mouth. That's Bryan, shallow, muddy and thick!' No, not him nor any of his associates. He's not the kind of fellow to concoct or condone back room schemes - dumb, but honest."

"Tammany, now that's a choice. I've made enough enemies at the Hall to spawn a dozen false accusations," mused the governor, as he fingered his pince-nez glasses and unconsciously rubbed them on his vest.

Kane remarked, "Some of our own people hate you, Mark Hanna, Tom Platt and the corporations. Trust busting talks don't endear you to those operators. They can't imagine how terrible it would be if you became president. After McKinley, you're the obvious choice four years from now."

"Add the saloon keepers and slum lords. They remember the police commission days when you closed them down. Don't forget them."

Roosevelt smiled, peered through his glasses and assumed the strutting, bantam rooster appearance he displayed in so many political campaigns. "Well, boys, it looks like I have more enemies than Carter has pills. Corporations, politicians, slum lords, saloon keepers, Democrats, Tammany, you name it, I've got em."

"If a man is known by his enemies, I'm world famous. All of the foreign powers fear the new Yankee colossus. I've never made a secret of favoring American hegemony in the Pacific. Our destiny is to control the Pacific basin and all the lands it washes upon, our natural domain which some would deny us." He was beginning one of his stock stump speeches.

"The Spanish War proved we have the might and the will to control our own future. Others, feeling cheated, will fight, especially the German Empire. I've said publicly that the twentieth century will see the ultimate conflict between our two nations. We'll compete for the markets of the primitive countries in Africa, South America and Asia. If I were a member of the German General Staff, the first person I'd want off center stage in American politics is Theodore Roosevelt. If I thought Roosevelt were to be vice president and later run for president, I'd get rid of him in any way I could."

"You talked about that in your speech at the state convention in Saratoga in April," Kane observed.

"That was the one where you talked about the fruits of the Spanish War. You called Cuba, Puerto Rico and the Philippines three tropical plums just ripe for the picking, very well put," he recalled.

"You've actually been listening to my speeches, Woodbury. I'm dee-lighted." Every time T.R. used the word delighted, he emphasized the first syllable and smiled the huge now famous toothy grin which was a political cartoonist's idea of heaven.

"As you boys well know, I've publicly criticized the motives of those who oppose our annexation of the Philippines. If it weren't for Hobart's tie breaking vote in the Senate, those islands would have been cut free to serve as booty for any group of warlords financed and armed enough to seize them. One vote, Hobart's, made the difference. And now he's dead. Perhaps a detective ought to look into that as well." As he polished his pince-nez, Roosevelt's pale blue eyes gazed off into the mists of yet another mysterious circumstance.

"Yeah, he got some kind of ptomaine poisoning right after that, colonel, didn't he?" interjected the still exercised Sudberg.

"Ptomaine or something worse. He never returned to Washington again. Died a year later of what they said was a heart attack. Alex Falconer should've been called in on that one, the vice president hummph..," the ever suspicious Kane added.

Roosevelt closed the discussion.

"So, there are many choices. Talk won't help. Falconer is the man to get to the bottom of this. Sudberg would you be kind enough to go to town and make that call right now? We have a lot to discuss, and I'm not sure how long Willie Hearst will keep quiet."

CHAPTER FIFTEEN

Arriving at the Journal offices late in the afternoon bought Gaby some time. The Chief was gone, and the paper had been put to bed. With early afternoon editions already on the streets, there wouldn't be much activity until the wee hours of the morning when Hearst returned to ramrod his outfit through another day.

She could lay plans for dealing with her demanding boss. Charles could help. His size and self-assurance was comforting. She'd always felt small and weak, a woman in a man's world.

And, he was always on her side. Even if his motivation was physical, she could handle that. His pawing hands, roving eyes, even the way he licked his lips when they were alone together, suggested Charles Majors envisioned more than a platonic relationship. Yet, there was an animal attraction about him.

Gaby had struggled in this masculine society as far back as high school. She'd been the brightest girl in her class, at Peekskill High. Most of the girls in grade school had gone on to find shop jobs or stayed at home, sewing until they married. Not for her, she was going to make it and make it all the way up to the top. She'd always known that.

Gaby wrote stories for the local paper about events at the high school, the first female to ever draw this assignment. Possibly it was because she smiled so demurely at the editor and publisher, Mr. Blackenck.

Washington I. Blackenck was almost the entire staff of the Peekskill Evening Gazette. Every small town in the country had its own afternoon newspaper. Profits came from the local merchants and businessmen who advertised in the paper. Having a weekly column written by one of the students at the high school was a good idea. It attracted the interest of the parents. The kid was to put in as many classmates names as possible. That would ensure their families bought a paper.

Mr. Blackenck was not devoid of sexual interest. Even though he was quite old, probably in his late thirties when Gaby met him, he was very interested in her diminutive but well formed body. By the tenth grade, she'd reached her full height of 5'1" and had matured physically to full womanhood. Not lost on Blackenck, he displayed the same kind of gaze and lip-licking behavior later perceived in Charles.

Gaby didn't ruin her opportunity. When the kindly old publisher asked her to come to the offices one Monday evening to go over her copy, *she wasn't* surprised he was alone. She never told her mother about that, certainly not father. They thought the nice man was helping their daughter in her dreams of glory. Later, when he suggested she might be able to obtain a scholarship to a women's college, they welcomed his assistance and encouraged her to spend time with this literate and urbane fellow.

Washington Irving Blackenck was urbane enough, thought Gaby. He tried to invade her undergarments early on. She realized that non-accession to his interests would end her career with a high school column.

It wasn't so bad. She kind of liked it. Blackenck was thoughtful and kind and, in his own way, civilized. He understood that his student never had sexual activity before. Wash was slow and gentle with her. He developed a true affection. He even used the new rubber condoms to protect her from pregnancy, and himself from her father and headstrong older brother, Michael. And, he really did try to help with Gaby's writing, giving her small assignments here and there. She did some social reporting, and went to the various picnics and social teas held with great regularity in the small mid-Hudson city.

She never saw herself as a "scarlet woman." After all, Blackenck was a widower. She wasn't breaking any of the major commandments, well, not completely. Later, he helped to get her into Radcliffe. He even assisted with the essay requested by the Admissions Committee and did so with style and grace. When she was accepted, he told the family the Peekskill Evening Gazette had established a scholarship fund for successful writers on its staff, and donated five hundred dollars towards his protégé's education.

At that rate, she figured it to be ten dollars for each time she and her employer had "known one another," a lot of money. Upon arrival in Massachusetts, Miss Irish didn't feel the country bumpkin she might have without Washington I. Blackenck's help; both social and financially.

In Boston her horizons expanded mightily. The city offered a new vista to the girl from upstate New York. There were museums, libraries, great houses, historic places and, of course, the men at Harvard.

The Harvard men, in their narrow way, demeaned most Radcliffe women. But, if a girl was interested in intellectual achievement and the kind of liberal thinking expected of a modern intellectual, Radcliffe was the only game in town. There was Smith, but that was out of town and didn't count much. Smith girls were less attractive anyway, and forget about Wellesley altogether. Most of the local Boston girls sat around with needlepoint waiting for some young man to ask for their hand in marriage. They rarely knew the difference between Grover Cleveland and a small city in Ohio with a similar name.

It was at Radcliffe, working on the college paper that she had her next love affair. That was with Billy Lucas, the editor of _The Harvard Crimson._ Billy was a literary man, as well as a southern gentleman. The son of a state legislator from Georgia, he'd been sent to the bastion of Republicanism to learn the ways of the wily Yankees. This would enable him to return home and assume his rightful place among the ruling classes of the South.

Billy was a courtly, albeit plain looking, young fellow steeped in the ways of antebellum Georgia. He intended, as he told Gaby over and over again, to "bring the South back where it belongs."

But Billy had returned to Atlanta to work his way up through the political network of the South. A ring was never proffered to the Yankee girl. Gaby, not from a wealthy family and devoid of important contacts, would have to succeed solely on talent. If Chuck Majors could help, so be it.

Gaby called Chuck and told him about the interview with Roosevelt. He suggested they discuss things in depth while having an early evening dinner at the Waldorf. She had to get back to the paper well before The Chief. Even in mid-summer, The Waldorf was the focal point of Manhattan night life. Beside the elegant food, an orchestra was available for ballroom dancing, a diversion which the city's elite had recently taken up with great interest.

There was enough time to get home, put on something suitable for evening wear (most of her Journal salary was spent on clothing), and then mix business with pleasure. She loved to be in Major's company. All of the other women looked at her with envy comparing him to their own partners. Chuck stood out in any crowd. Not only handsome, he dressed impeccably. His wardrobe, mostly from London, was elegant and au courant.

Gaby drank in the elegance of the waiter who glided, not walked to their table dressed in gray silk pants, black vest and white tie. The diners at the next table, Mr. and Mrs. John Whitney, (she knew them from her social column) nodded pleasantly at her and her imposing escort. They didn't seem to notice the posh setting, took it in stride as their right and expectation. For the girl from Peekskill, it was heaven.

The maitre d' seemed to know Charles well. "Good evening, Mr. Majors and madame," he smiled deferentially at her. "What is your pleasure this evening?"

Charles didn't bother to consult the menu, "We'll start with iced melon, then a cold vichyssoise, I think perhaps a small portion of Dover Sole and then your excellent Roast Prime Rib, medium rare with all the garnishes. What do you think, Gaby?" He nodded towards her and told the maitre d', "Jean Paul, this is Miss Irish. She is Mr. Hearst's star reporter and soon will be world famous." His voice boomed and clearly the Whitneys heard the prediction.

Gaby blushed and said, "That's far too much for me. Perhaps a small filet mignon, medium and petit pois au Franchais and yes," looking at the menu, "I'd like to try your Pomme Soufflé."

"Excellent madame, I'm sure you will enjoy them. I will personally see that they are as light and delicate as a feather in the summer breeze." He clicked his heels and beamed at the lady.

"And the wine, sir? We have an excellent French Cabernet this evening."

Charles nodded his approval; Jean Paul snapped his fingers and hot bread baked into small loaves, a crock of white and one of yellow butter materialized on their table.

The table was one of the choicest ones in the room, located right next to the dance floor where they could see all of the dancers and others sitting at the margin of the highly polished oak floor. Others could see them as well in mutual evaluation of the prominence and social stature of each party. Gaby loved it.

She also loved the meal. The little slices of potatoes were puffed up into minuscule edible balloons, warm but not hot and as the head waiter had promised were as light as feathers, not chicken but hummingbird feathers at that. "This steak is as tender as veal Charles, and look at the tiny peas braised in lettuce, how elegant," she exclaimed.

"Wonderful," he said as he sucked in his prime rib, slicing and consuming it with one motion. It seemed to Gaby that he barely tasted the wonderful food as he relentlessly plowed through it.

"I think champagne is appropriate for this special evening, don't you, Gaby?" Charles' face was flushed with either delight or the exertion of eating as he raised his hand in the air and waved a white-gloved finger in the direction of the sommelier. He had already drunk most of the Cabernet Sauvignon.

The man with the chain around his neck hastened over and obsequiously inquired, "Monsieur Major's desires?"

"We'll have the Dom Perignon '89, if you agree?" The waiter concurred in the selection, and scurried off to the wine cellar to fill the order. Dom Perignon was only now beginning to become popular in America. Charles, with exquisite continental taste, was quite familiar with the niceties of haute cuisine.

"So he denied the whole thing, is that right? He says there's no such person as Renfield?"

"No, Charles. Listen more carefully. You're so busy with that rib roast that you've missed the core of the thing. He does remember Renfield."

Charles sluiced down a chunk of meat with the remaining red wine, and nodded his head in assent.

"He says that Renfield was always an odd ball and hanger-on. He recruited him personally, remembered him from his days in the Dakota Territory. What he said was that Renfield had always had some kind of obsession with him, trying to dress and look like him and, of course, had the same initials. Well, the point is he said that Renfield was sick, or at least feverish a couple of days before the charge on San Juan Hill".

"I see, sick. You mean he couldn't join the group?" Charles was chewing on a popover smeared with thick, yellow butter.

"Roosevelt doesn't remember whether he participated in the charge or not. A day earlier, he asked the regimental surgeon to look at Renfield. He said the man was strange and babbling. He mentioned something about taking his place, and Roosevelt sent him off to the doctor. He thinks he remembers him later when they had reached the crest of the hill, but isn't sure."

"If this chap's led us on a wild goose chase, I'd like to get to know him." Charles menacingly clutched his meat knife in his right hand, as if it were a steel pike with which he would impale the duplicitous Renfield.

"Well, Roosevelt is going to check all of that out. I expect he'll track down the surgeon and verify that part of the tale. He has the names of the other men who signed the affidavit, and someone will interview each of them. Renfield is probably his first target, though." She daintily dipped a small piece of filet mignon into the light mixture of mustard, mayonnaise and Worcestershire sauce, which rested in a small tub next to her plate, and chewed it slowly as she made her point.

The bottle of Dom Perignon arrived, and Chuck quickly dispatched fully three quarters while still seeming thirsty. He excused himself, presumably to visit the lavatory and relieve himself of the initial portion of wine. Gaby gazed about the room as unobtrusively as possible to drink in an atmosphere reeking of wealth, power and what she characterized as class.

Charles hadn't seemed disappointed in her inability to verify the story nor to print the allegations he had given her. She was glad of that.

He was very interested in what she had to tell him about Roosevelt and his cronies at Sagamore Hill. The colorful roster of friends and especially his counterpart, Slim Sudberg, fascinated him. He wanted to learn more about Woody Kane and Roosevelt's other intimates like Sherman Bell and Albert Shaw.

The man was almost as insatiable in his hunger for information as for food. But he did things with such elegance, at home in this atmosphere of society, wealth and urbanity. She began to wonder if it might not be a good idea to give in to his constant sexual advances. He'd never be satisfied until he bedded her down. Perhaps giving him a taste of the rewards which her body offered might be another step along the path to the pinnacle she sought.

Tonight, she was at the Waldorf, her feet tapping under the table to the rhythm of the Strauss waltz the orchestra played. Men, resplendent in jet black dinner jackets and ebony satin-striped trousers, whirled about the room holding women in silk dresses, decorated with diamonds and ropes of gold. Gaby longed to be on the dance floor with the others. Where was Charles? He'd been gone for almost twenty minutes. No matter she could drink in this glamorous scene all night. It was something she'd only dreamed about two years ago. She'd come a long way from Peekskill.

CHAPTER SIXTEEN

Masterson, who was not a large man himself, albeit barrel chested and well-muscled, was surprised that the giant of American literature was no bigger than himself. Mark Twain, aside from his leonine mane of white hair, was of normal proportions and not especially striking in appearance. The hair alone was indeed remarkable. Otherwise, Mr. Twain, née Samuel Clemens, was an ordinary small town boy from Missouri, just grown up a bit.

"I can tell from your speech that you come from somewhere along the Mississippi River basin," he told the erstwhile lawman.

"I'm a Reuben from the farm country in Illinois, for a fact," said Bat.

"Good! There's an honest midwest twang to your voice and your bearing as well, if I may say so." Twain puffed on his omnipresent cigar. He perused the famous lawman from the top of his omnipresent derby to the heels of his western boots as if he were evaluating his character for a role in a new book.

"Thank you sir," Masterson advised the older man, at least twenty years his senior. "Anything you may say is fine with me, sir. I'm a great admirer of your writing. The best I've read, foreign or domestic."

Twain smiled as he chomped on his stogie. "You also have good American taste, Mr. Masterson. What is it I can do for you? Are you interested in getting someone to chronicle your adventures in the wild west? I know most of the decent scribblers around these parts. I can probably steer you to a good man to recount your days taming Dodge City or Tombstone or the Dakota Territory where you met the hero of San Juan Hill." He was chomping on the cigar more than smoking it at this point.

The two men had just finished consuming a pair of Gary Stone's largest porterhouse steaks, medium rare and smothered with fried onions and mushrooms.

"No, sir, I don't want a ghost writer to help me perfect my stories. Far from it, I want to be a writer myself. I'm a self- educated man, I didn't go to college like the Colonel and his inner circle, but I'm not bad with pencil and paper either." He removed a thick sheaf of pages from the inside pocket of his suit jacket and handed them to the great author.

"I thought you might have a look at what I've done and can do. I'm no hack writer. I want to be an author like you, sir. I know you didn't go to college either and spent a lot of time on the Mississippi as a river boat man..."

"The finest years of my life," Twain interjected. It appeared he'd met his match in audacity and possibly a rival in loquaciousness as well.

"Right, and you've been out west in the mining camps and the Barbary Coast. You've tasted the raw side of the beef as well as the cooked and learned from it, as I have heard. So, I want to follow... ."

"In my footsteps?" Clearly, Twain realized he'd have to squeeze his words in with a large shoe horn. "I've got to give it to you for boldness. Very few men would have enough sand in their craw to ask me to review their work on the first meeting, although most want me to do so, I'll warrant." Twain spoke a little more loudly than usual, his stage or orating voice. To be sure he could have at least verbally overcome the burly ex-marshal.

"I want to write about other things, other than what you find in dime novels you know. I love the city, New York, the people, their frenzy, their multitude-like herds of buffalo before the railroads killed them off. There's a kinship between the masses of people jamming lower Broadway and the great herds of bison racing across the prairie. I want to write about this town the way you wrote about the river. I still think that 'Life on the Mississippi' is your finest work." The ex-marshal tipped his derby hat in deference to the great writer.

"So do I, Mr. Masterson. So do I. The years on the river were as close to heaven as I'll ever get. The sights, the sounds, the very smell of the Mississippi remain in my memory as bright and fresh as Mr. Stone's steaks which we've just devoured. But, I didn't begin to write about them until I learned my craft working as a journalist for newspapers across the country. In all those little towns you mentioned in the midwest and in the west, and even in San Francisco. Doing a writing job every day is the best way to sharpen your skills. If I were you, I'd start looking for a writing job right now," the great man opined.

"Why not?" Masterson agreed. "Do you have any suggestions as to where I can begin? A name, a friend, someone I can drop your name on for effect?"

Twain chuckled; "I appreciate your directness, sir. Yes, I think dropping my name before one of the moguls running newspapers in this city might do you some good, yes indeed. It would help, however, to have a piece to show them. Why not write a news story, a sort of sample, this very night? If it's as good as your conversation, I'm sure I can twist the arm of one of the gentlemen of the press to offer you employment." He ground his already dead cigar in the large ashtray the restaurant provided and immediately put a new one in his mouth to take its place.

Twain bit the end off the cigar, spit the severed piece into a conveniently located spittoon under the table and said, "How about doing something about the fight at the Garden tonight? Two gladiators locked in mortal combat, the roar of the crowd; it's a good way to begin. The best writers, in my opinion, in this town anyway, are the men working the sports page. It'd fit right in. A man of action, in his own element so to speak."

"Let's go to the *fights*, Mr. Twain." Masterson got up from his chair, ostentatiously leaving a five dollar bill to cover the meals and a very generous   tip.

"I'm agreeable. Did you ever hear of the George Washington, the first great passenger vessel on the Mississippi?" he rhetorically queried.

As Masterson shrugged his shoulders in a negative response, the storyteller went on. "She was the largest vessel ever seen on the father of the waters up to that time. So big in fact that she had twenty-three passenger cabins, one for every state in the Union then. The owners decided to give the accommodations names instead of numbers and, therefore, each cabin had a state's name attached to it. The New York room, the Missouri room, and so on. The porter would ask a passenger, Which state room is you in, suh?" he observed as the duo crossed Madison Square to the Garden of the same name.

CHAPTER SEVENTEEN

Some hours after the venerable writer and his western protégé entered at the ground floor, an elderly, rather wizened man sat alone in a private dining room high above the street level of the Madison Square Garden building. In this building, soon to become even more famous for the murder of the building's architect, Mr. Stanford White, a silver maned ancient dwelled upon the death of thousands of those whom he considered his countrymen almost forty years earlier. He also considered the necessity of killing several more people in the present.

A tail coated waiter wheeled in a large pewter serving tray. He lifted its cover to reveal a deep dish filled with a beige colored creamy porridge.

"Shall I wait for the other gentleman, sir, or serve you now?" he inquired of his pale pink and grey skinned guest.

"Jes put it on mah plate young feller. The other gentleman will be here presently, but he may wish somethin' else, thank you."

The waiter bowed slightly after ladling a soup plate full of hominy grits and melted butter before the old man.

A few moments later, the door opened again and the large individual known to the late Robbie "the Robber" Smoot as Mr. D. entered.

"And a very good evenin' to you Peppah, mah boy." The man, lowering his soup spoon full of grits, seemed affectionate in greeting Pepper.

"I'm sorry I was late Uncle Jack, but after I spoke to you on the telephone, I had to get in touch with Maguffin as quickly as possible. He's out there in the wilds of Staten Island and someone had to fetch him down from his house to a telephone at the local gin mill."

"As long as he doesn't frequent the gin mill too often himself. We need sober and serious men foah this enterprise," the elder replied.

"He was able to recall the name of the regimental surgeon, a Robert Clifton, and better yet that the good doctor came from, and planned to return to Trenton, New Jersey. It's along the main line of the Pennsylvania Railroad."

"I told him to go straightaway to Trenton, telephone the local hospital and ask where he could find Dr. Clifton. Maguffin will telegraph me if he cannot locate the man by morning and we'll have to use our resources in the War Department to discreetly locate him," Mr. D. concluded.

"But, when he does find him, can he do the job alone?" inquired Uncle Jack.

"Sir, he's at least forty pounds heavier than I am and two inches taller. None of which represents an ounce of fat, but all muscle and bone. Renfield tells me the man transferred into the Rough Riders from an Indian killing army outfit in the Dakotas. He said Maguffin had a scalp collection bigger than any chief of the Sioux Nation. Our chap is a killer alright."

"And, he can keep his mouth shut?" the old man pressed the question, by now allowing his grit mush to go from lukewarm to room temperature.

"Sergeant Maguffin was cashiered from the Army because he refused to tell the name of the man under his command who butchered a half dozen Philippine villagers with a buck knife and a 45 caliber Army pistol. He insisted he didn't know who it was when he obviously did. That ended a twenty year career as well as his pension with it. The killer wasn't even a friend. He can keep quiet," he reassured his kinsman.

"Alright mah boy. You are doin' well. But we must keep owah eyes on the main object of this campaign. McKinley must go. That is owah goal. When he dies, his successah will set policy."

"The plans are to control all of Central Americah from the Mexican bordah town to Columbia, mebbey furthah. I don't trust that damn Yankee cowboy as president. Git rid 'a him. If ya have to, kill him. No moah pussy footin' around."

"I understand, Uncle Jack, but we don't know for sure. It could be that Roosevelt shares our views. His mother's family was the Bulloch's. Maybe he's just taking the party line and change it if he's president," the big man said.

"Mebbey he will and mebbey he won't. I for one, don't wanna take a chance. Owah man will do what we want. We can have Central America, even Cuba, Puerto Rico, any part of the Antilles we can grab and hold. Roosevelt is a mystery. He might have to stick to the party line, like the late Mr. Hobart."

"If we have to, we kill Roosevelt too, Peppah." He tasted the cold porridge and spit it out. "Ring that bell and git the waiter back. The grits've gone cold," he commanded,

"Yes sir. But Roosevelt's a lot tougher to kill than Hobart or even McKinley will be. He's got a squad of gunmen around him. Masterson and Sheriff Bell, Kane, and Shaw are all quick and accurate with side arms. And they're always armed while campaigning," Pepper informed him.

"I know! I know! You've said it a dozen times. But strong men have to take strong measures. If we can't shoot the son of a bitch, maybe a bomb, or poison like Hobart," said the old murderer.

"I'll cross that bridge when we come to it Uncle. First the blackmail!"

The waiter returned and the two ordered new refreshments.

"Don't evah forget that this is a sacred enterprise," the ancient advised reverently. "We are entrusted to carry out a plan to retrieve the honah of the South." This last word was said as if every letter were capitalized.

"Your late fathah, my sainted sistah's husband, died for the cause at Vicksburg-murdered by the butcher Grant, who Satan has long since called to his own. I was gut shot at Stone Mountain by a henchman of the criminal arsonist, William Tecumseh Sherman." He spit on the floor after mentioning the scourge of Georgia.

Pepper waited patiently, almost reverently as his uncle repeated the chronicle of family tragedy brought about by the War Between the States.

"I have to eat mush and soggy toast because of the Yankee invadahs. They occupied the Confederacy like a Roman legion, rapin' and pillagin' the flowah of Southern womanhood." His alabaster skin beaded with sweat as he drew near the end of his oration.

"When we create the New Confederacy below the bordah, the South will rise again and you and I are fortunate enough to be in the foah front of that endeavah."

"Yes sir, Uncle Jack, and we will prevail, I promise you."

In the arena several stories below, Masterson was writing his description of the boxing match.

CHAPTER EIGHTEEN

SPECIAL TO THE NEW YORK TELEGRAPH

Burcham vs. Schaeffer

Heavyweight Match at Madison Square Garden

by William B. Masterson

Smoke from five thousand cigars filled the great arena at Madison Square Garden last night, so thick it was like a fog bank at sea. Through the haze sailed a modern day Flying Dutchman, heavyweight Charley "Fritz" Schaeffer who was bent on ramming his fistic opponent, lanky 185 lb. Timmy "Rebel" Burcham.

The solidly built 5' 11" Schaeffer, who weighed in at 190 lbs., attacked the "The Rebel" with a series of rapid fire left jabs and a very effective right hand which momentarily stunned his opponent. "Fritz" repeated the strategy through the first three rounds. Burcham, at first seemingly shocked at the Dutchman's nimbleness, could barely fend off the jabs and was cut badly over the right eye. Blood seemed to partially blind him to the quick left hand which fired like a Gatling gun from Schaeffer's side. However, Schaeffer landed no definitive blow at first.

By the beginning of the fourth round, the Dutchman was partially spent and looked arm weary. It was then that the determined Burcham counterattacked. Summoning up previously hidden reserves, the heavyweight mauler from Hampton Roads, Virginia, unmasked a wicked right upper cut which noticeably stunned his opponent. A second right hand to the chin dropped Schaeffer to the canvas just before the bell ended the round.

By round six, in this seesaw match, Schaeffer found his left jab again and the next two stanzas treated the Garden fans to a series of punches and counter punches rarely matched in the famed arena for ferocity and persistence.

As the crowd cheered first one and then the other fighter, the pugilistic opponents displayed a grit worthy of the sport. At the beginning of round eight, both men seemed virtually exhausted by their efforts. Each boxer appeared to be awaiting his respective chance for a knockout blow. The arena itself seemed to be saturated with the haze of cigar smoke, practically obscuring the view of those spectators in the rear seats. The pungent smell, from ringside, was unmistakable, the aroma of sweat mixed with blood.

At one and a half minutes into the eighth round, Burcham landed a mighty and unexpected roundhouse right, a punch he hadn't showed in the entire match until that moment. Schaeffer's eyes glazed over and the Dutchman fell like a hundred and ninety pound stone. "The Rebel" danced back to a neutral corner raising both gloved hands above his head in a display of triumph. Blood still seeped from his now swollen right eyebrow.

"Fritz" didn't move, not a muscle, and ringsiders feared for his life until the fallen man's eyelids began to flicker as the referee, former heavyweight champion Dan "The Mountain" Bear counted down to ten.

Cross out "The Dutchman" from contention. Last night, he was sunk by this latter day Merrimac from Virginia. The South has indeed risen again. This writer expects the public will hear a lot more from this product of the old Confederacy.

CHAPTER NINETEEN

The late train from Newark to Trenton arrived a few minutes behind schedule. It was after two in the morning when Earl Maguffin emerged from the coach and consulted a street map to find the home of Dr. and Mrs. Robert R. Clifton.

It was important for Maguffin to both arrive at the Clifton's house in the wee hours of the morning and to get there alone. He couldn't afford to have a cab driver recall his appearance nor his destination. He didn't want even a streetcar driver remembering someone like him leaving an empty vehicle at 2:00 or 3:00 a.m. near the house of Dr. and Mrs. Clifton.

Maguffin had thought the thing through carefully. If he arrived in Trenton at two, he could walk to almost any location in town by 3:00 or 4:00 a.m., an ideal time to commit murder and mayhem. Almost everyone would be deep asleep. Noises which might emerge from a house would be muffled and passed off by any possible listener as the wailings of a lovesick cat in midsummer passion.

Earl also knew he couldn't afford to be seen by others. Once seen, he was remembered. The man was not blessed with a pleasant demeanor. His dark thick eyebrows conveyed a menacing appearance. Prominent cheekbones, thick lips, and a pronounced glare added to the threatening look. He couldn't help glaring. Earl's dark eyes seemed to want to stay open most of the time, nor did his eyelids blink as did others. He never noticed this. But people did, and he was recognized wherever he went.

How wonderful it was to get the message from Mr. D. to travel immediately to Trenton to meet Dr. Clifton again. Clifton had been the regimental surgeon with the Rough Riders in Cuba. Maguffin had nothing against the man. But work was work. Mr. D. paid well and was his current employer. There was a job to do on the good doctor and Mrs. Clifton. So that's what had to be done.

It was a pleasant way to spend an evening, walking towards the house of an officer, a doctor, probably another bleeding heart, to settle accounts with one more of them. They were the ones who laughed at him, who scorned him, who hated him, who avoided him. He hated them all and he'd settle with two more tonight.

It was 3:30 a.m., the right time to begin. He circled the house twice to get a feeling for the building and how to enter. Two stories with bedrooms on the second floor, it would suit his purpose very well. Mr. D. wanted it to look like an accident.

Maguffin never could understand the squeamish nature of some clients who wanted things to look accidental. But a job was a job. Falling down the stairs would be enough, he thought. An old man like Dr. Clifton and an old lady like his wife, could easily die in a fall. Maybe the doc would die that way and his wife'd have a heart attack when she saw him dead at the bottom of the stairs. That should do it.

Carefully pushing up the kitchen window, already ajar to let in a cooling breeze on the midsummer night, Earl made his way into the kitchen. Fortunately, there was no dog, not even a cat in the house. The Clifton's probably weren't animal lovers. Too bad for them. He took off his shoes because he didn't want to awaken the householder and his wife quite yet. The less trouble, the better; although he did like to see the look on people's faces before they died. He couldn't afford to do that in this situation. A job was a job.

The master bedroom was only a few steps from the top of the stairs. That door was open, too, to allow the air to come in. What unsuspicious fools these people were. Didn't they know enough to lock their doors to guard themselves against intruders and robbers? Cities are full of them. It's a disgrace.

It would be best to quiet the old man first. He could be trouble. He'd been in the army, during the Indian wars and at San Juan Hill too; best to silence him right away. As Maguffin came into the room, the two were sleeping in one large bed. That made it easier. He'd wrapped his .45 Colt revolver in cloth so that it wouldn't leave obvious scratch marks. One blow would be more than sufficient to crush the old man's head.

The blow was swift and sure. It sounded like a watermelon dropping onto the floor, a sort of plop. There were some bloody remnants on the cloth, of course, and a little spurt, which he didn't notice, hit the bedspread and the pillow. The doctor was done for.

The plopping noise seemed to disturb Mrs. Clifton. She opened her eyes just as Maguffin came toward her with the pillow to smother her. He enjoyed the look in her eyes, but he couldn't afford to allow her to scream. No, that would be too dangerous, even though it might be fun. Just a little peep emitted from her mouth before he stuffed it with the end of the pillow and began pressing down. He at least had the pleasure of watching her eyes open wide, as wide as any could, and almost pop out, as she struggled for breath and gazed at him in terror. Her fingers reached for him and scratched at him, but he had on his heavy evening clothing. She barely managed to get a few tiny threads of cloth in her fingernails. That's all the damage she did before he finished her off.

He probably pressed a little too hard on her neck at the same time as he stuffed the pillow in her mouth. Something crunched a little bit. But she was dead in less than two minutes. It was faster than most of the Filipinos he'd killed, not as quick, of course, as breaking someone's neck or crushing their skull. But she was dead. She stopped moving.

Her eyes stayed open. He'd have to close them. It wouldn't look good if they were wide open. Well, maybe not. Maybe he should leave them open. After all, he reasoned, she's just seen her husband fall to the bottom of the stairs and crushed his head at their foot, and she'd be wide-eyed in terror. Yes, leave it that way. He could put his shoes back on now. There was no one to hear him anymore.

He moved the two bodies, one under each arm, towards their new resting places. Earl threw the old man's body down the steps. That would lend a more natural appearance to the final position of the remains. He then deposited Mrs. Clifton more daintily at the top of the stairs. It would look as if she'd heard her husband tumble down, come to the head of the stairs to see his limp and inert form and then dropped of a failed heart on the spot. A neat job, he thought. It was done. Exiting the same window he had entered, Maguffin partly closed it so that it would appear it was open just a crack as had been intended, to cool the house.

He considered setting the house on fire to cover up any evidence. But that could create more questions than it was worth. Besides, it would attract attention. Earl didn't want to be noticed as he walked back to the railroad station. No one had seen him on the way in, and no one would see him returning. It was dark, and darkness was his friend. He could get back to the station by dawn and return to Newark.

When he got home, he sent this telegram to Mr. D.: "Thank you so much for recommending me to the good doctor. I have seen him and I feel much better. I'm sure you will as well. Your friend, Earl T. Maguffin." He knew that Mr. D. would enjoy this little touch of humor and, at the same time, understand the meaning of the message. A job is a job.

CHAPTER TWENTY

Sudberg met Falconer at the station. "The governor was disappointed we couldn't reach you in time to get here last evening. You missed a terrific barbecue. The boss roasted a steer the way they did when he was a rancher, a whole side of beef over an open fire, delicious." He tried to stifle a rather large belch by holding his hand over his mouth as the sound of escaping gasses issued around his closed fist.

"They had a keg too?" It didn't require a feat of great detection to divine that Slim's protruding belly was just as likely due to his taste for beer as for red meat. The abdomen, in fact, flopped over his belt as he sat driving the buggy.

"I do eat and drink a little too much. Of course, I'm under a lot of strain in this job. Being a press relations man for a man like T.R. isn't easy. He's always up to something, never stops running around. Sometimes he says things I have to explain to the press. I'm on the go day and night. I had to get ahold of you, then explain why we couldn't get you till today. Maybe I take refuge in eating and drinking, you know, drown my sorrows in roast beef and beer."

"I understand. It's difficult to keep up with great men. It must have been hard for the people who worked with Napoleon or Bismarck to keep their camps in order. It's a big job, but you're big enough to handle it. Tell me why the governor called me and why the haste?"

Sudberg filled him in on recent events.

Each piece of information Alex received spurred more questions. As the journey proceeded, and the scope of the problem unfolded, the usual train ride drowsiness disappeared as a major problem unfolded.

Every cell in his brain seemed stimulated. Falconer couldn't wait to talk to Roosevelt.

"Governor, it looks like you have a puzzle that needs solving. There are a number of questions only you can answer. You know my methods. I need every available piece of information. Each fact is linked to another. My job is to sift through them all and see how the chain is forged."

"First, tell me about the picture. I understand it shows you amorously embracing a Negro lady. Is it genuine or not?"

Roosevelt raised his eyebrows and bristled, like an animal facing a predator, in both rage and fear. "Genuine? Of course not. First of all, even though I have been a stalwart for the colored race, do you think I'd be foolish enough to allow a picture to be taken with some dark skinned lady of the evening, and have her inscribe it to me?"

"Nonsense, utter nonsense. I may seem impetuous, but I'm no fool. The picture is genuine, at least half of it is. And so is the inscription. The problem is that it's been doctored up, changed in some way."

"I don't have a copy of it with me. The reporter, Hearst's messenger, took it back with her. It shows me with a lady and is signed by somebody named Winnie. Winnie is an English gentleman."

"His full name is Winston Spencer Churchill, a British writer. You know, a kindred soul. I've done my share of books and magazine articles myself. He was in Cuba as an observer. Because of his sympathies to our cause, and his political position, we didn't make his visit public, nothing nefarious about it. Renfield, the fellow who signed the affidavit, was a photographer. He shot us outside of the tent. We weren't embracing, just shaking hands and grasping each other's shoulder. The fellow must have changed the picture by some trick, removed Winston's image and replaced it with the woman's."

Falconer queried, "Obviously Churchill inscribed the photograph sometime after Renfield took it. Isn't that so, Governor?"

"Certainly, the photograph was in a frame here in my study. Winston signed it while on a visit here last year. It was among a number of others on the wall. Obviously, it's gone now."

"Someone must have doctored the image. Anyone proficient with a camera can do that." A thought formed in Falconer's mind, related to last evening. Someone who wanted to destroy something of great value, a paper, a document, a picture, a negative! "The original picture was genuine. It means that someone had seen it before. Someone, not Renfield, who knew what the inscription said, and formulated a plan to use it against you."

"Yes, put that way, it's quite logical. Someone must have been in this room, seen the inscribed picture and decided to use it in another context. Someone who realized that Winnie could be either a man's or woman's name."

"A great many people must come to Sagamore Hill, Governor, reporters, politicians, business people, and foreign dignitaries. Let's calculate the last time you saw the picture and who was here in the interim."

"You're right but I can't begin to count the number of people in and out of this study in the past month alone. Ever since the convention, at least several hundred. The last time I actually saw the picture? I recall pointing it out to someone three weeks ago, a British visitor who said Winston's in South Africa now, reporting on the Boer War. Since then, two hundred others have come through this door who might have seen the photograph and read the inscription."

"Are there any other missing documents, artifacts, or the like? Think carefully about this, it's quite important. Anything of value that's missing, gold frames, something like that?"

"Of value? Yes, I see what you mean. If a thief were here, it might be hard to pass up something of value." He scanned the cluttered room. "The gold coin; here." Roosevelt displayed an indented velvet presentation case in which a coin was intended to rest.

"Here, this is or was a souvenir of the Columbian Exposition of 1892 in Chicago. It was given to visiting dignitaries, politicians, and the like. It's solid gold. Christopher Columbus was on the face. Hard for a thief to pass up, it's probably in the pocket of the same criminal responsible for stealing the picture."

"You're right, impossible to pass up." Falconer eschewed mentioning the coin in his study and began moving about the room, studying every aspect of it from carpet to ceiling. He carefully manipulated the windows; and removing a pencil from his pocket, flipped up the lock from the inside. It moved easily. He opened the window and stepped outside. He then asked, "Mr. Roosevelt, would you please close the window and turn the lock back in a closed position? Thank you."

T.R., unaccustomed to taking orders from anyone, looked surprised. But, with his usual dispatch, leaped from his chair, went over to the window, closed it briskly, and pushed the lock shut. A moment later,

Falconer, jiggling the frames, manipulated a small opening between the two closed portions of the outwardly opening windows. He then inserted his pencil into the aperture, flipped the lock open, this time from the outside, and reentered the room.

"It's obvious how the burglar entered. A professional would lose no time in testing each opening until he found the one that gave him the easiest and quietest entry. He was lucky here because this door gave him easy access for a quick, clean job. The thief got greedy with the coin, obviously that wasn't the job he was sent to do."

"This was no ordinary burglar robbing a wealthy man's house. This man knew what he was looking for and where it was. The gold coin was his personal bonus. Whoever hired him knew nothing of it. That may be of great help to us later. We have a criminal betraying his employer in a small way, the way most petty crooks do. If we're lucky, it can help us to track him down."

Falconer went on, "You said something about papers, documents, sworn statements. Tell me about that."

Roosevelt reported what he'd been told by Gaby Irish. "The documents attested to Renfield's statement, that I was in the tent and didn't lead the charge at all. Nothing could be further from the truth. Not only did I lead the charge, as all of my men will swear, but Renfield was actually sick."

"I told the reporter the man did resemble me somewhat, and liked to prance about calling himself 'Little T.R.', or 'Teddy Too'. I kept my eye on him more than the other troopers. I noticed he looked sallow and yellow around the edges. We were all concerned about Yellow Jack then. I asked him to see the regimental surgeon a day before combat began."

"The surgeon must have a record of it, at least a recollection. The files, of course, are likely lost deep in the bowels of the War Department. Dr. Clifton recently retired. He wrote and offered to work for my campaign in Trenton, New Jersey. He'll remember Renfield's illness. He's worth talking to, to confirm my story."

"It isn't important that I confirm your story, Governor, I'm convinced. The public must believe it."

"You're right, Alex, we've got to stop this lie before it sees the light of day. Once a yarn is aired in the newspaper, no matter how ridiculous, it becomes incumbent upon the accused to prove it false. That mustn't happen."

"I agree. That's why I want ironclad refutation to show Hearst. It must be crystal clear that if the charges are printed, he'll be sued for libel. I'll gather every bit of information concerning this matter and disprove this nonsense. I also intend to get to the bottom of who's behind it and why. There's much more here than a newspaper story. Someone wants to destroy your career. And for reasons I don't understand, yet."

"I'd like you to ask your friends in the War Department for the whereabouts of Renfield and the soldiers who support him. I want to talk to each one and develop my own feeling as to why they signed the false statement."

"They can lead me to who's behind it. I want the address of the regimental surgeon. I'll get a sworn declaration from him concerning the truth of the matter. If we present that to Hearst, we'll stop him from printing the story despite his phony picture."

"Of course, Alex, bully! I have good contacts in the War Department. We'll get the names and addresses of the soldiers, including Renfield. Shaw can find the doctor's letter. Clifton lives in Trenton somewhere. I'll get on those things right away. Is there anything else I can do right now?"

"I'd like to go over this room with a fine-toothed comb. I want to look in every corner to see if there's something else that might give me a clue as to what happened here and who did it."

"I'd like your appointments secretary to show me the names of the people who've visited Sagamore Hill in the past couple of months. Whoever directed this petty thief to steal the picture on your wall must be familiar with this room and your house. One of your own staff, a servant, or a frequent visitor comes to mind."

"It could be someone with a trained eye here only once." Falconer was already prowling about the room like some great cat, sniffing every nook and corner, touching but not moving objects and, raising his whiskers to pick up whatever vibrations might remain from the unwanted visitor.

Roosevelt agreed to alert his staff to cooperate in every way with the detective. He added, "Of course, you'll stay to supper."

"Edith lays on appetizing summer feasts out here. It's a much better place to entertain than the governor's mansion in Albany. We'll have a fine time this evening. Some of the boys from out West are still with me. Sherman Bell plays the guitar, and sings too. Masterson will be back from town as well. He has a nice tenor voice, surprisingly nice. We'll all join in and have a lot of fun. Please stay."

"I'll be happy to stay, Governor. My work here will take all day. It'd be best to get a good night's sleep. Sleeping on things helps me to organize facts more effectively."

"Bully, bully." T.R. was truly pleased, like a boy whose little friend was allowed to sleep over. "I'll tell Edith you'll stay. We'll have a room prepared for you. The barbecue is at seven. See you then," and the great man strode off, intent on other thoughts and other pursuits.

Falconer stared at a small spot on the floor beneath the missing picture. Despite the brushing and cleaning of the carpet by the household staff, there was a tiny brown stain on the carpet. He took a tiny scissor and small envelope from his shirt pocket and snipped around the carpet, removing only the tufts of material colored with what he thought was blood. He placed them in the envelope for later perusal. The material would be put in solution, individual cells floated off and examined microscopically; another part of the robber's trail.

He now knew where the gold coin in the tramp's pocket came from. The connection with Harley's suffocation fell into place now. The detective physician unconsciously hummed "There'll Be a Hot Time in the Old Town Tonight" as he snipped. Those who observed him from a distance might have said Falconer was on the hunt. Like the bird of prey from which his family took its name, he was homing in on a target from a great distance. With the falcon's incredible sense of vision and perspective, he knew exactly where he was going and enjoyed the pursuit immensely.

CHAPTER TWENTY ONE

The governor, away so much in Albany, stayed close to the family during the summer. All six children were there, including teenage Alice. The first Mrs. Roosevelt had died one day after giving birth to their only child.

Eating was an important family activity. The meal was typical for the Oyster Bay ménage.

A row of chickens turned slowly over an open fire. Mrs. Klein laid on gobs of orange-yellow barbecue sauce to glaze the birds as they rotated on the spit. Several game hens freshly shot in the marshes of Long Island sizzled on the coals of the barbecue pit, wrapped in corn husks.

"It's Indian style, Alex. I learned it out West. It gives the bird a special flavor and keeps the juices in. I hope you'll like it. It's one of my favorites along with the fresh corn the husks came from."

Most members of the entourage were present, including the family and Slim Sudberg. Woodbury Kane, the Rough Rider captain, conversed with Al Shaw, another member of Roosevelt's shadow cabinet.

Shaw, slight in appearance, dressed in a business suit even on this warm summer evening, didn't appear to be a man who'd stormed a hill that day in Cuba. But, he was there and now part of Roosevelt's brain trust.

Sherman Bell had just returned from Westchester where he'd been glad handing the politicians in that key New York county. He had the gaunt, big-boned appearance of a horse wrangler complete with boots and ten-gallon hat. Bell brought Bat Masterson over to Falconer.

"Doc, Bat here wants to be a newspaper writer and a lawman too. I've been giving him some hints on how to do peacekeeping without gettin' himself shot full of holes. He's pretty good with a gun but, as I've been tellin' him, that's not the whole story keepin' the peace. Us professionals know it's more complicated than that. You're gonna set things right in the detective line for the colonel, right?" Bell's sarcastic grin suggested less than blind faith in Falconer's scientific approach.

"Oh, sure, Sherm. Alex has been telling us about his detection work while cleaning us out of poker hands all summer. If he's as good a detective as he is a card shark, we both better listen up real good," Masterson attested.

"Thank you, Mr. Masterson. As to guns, I don't think modern society is civilized enough to go without them. I carry a pistol with me when I'm working on a case. You might say it gives me a kind of insurance. Perhaps someday we can go out and have a shoot. I'm sure you can show me how to improve my marksmanship."

"Well, I sure would be happy to do that, Doc. From what I hear from the colonel, you don't need much instruction in most things. He says you're pretty good at everything you do."

"Well, I'm flattered you've heard so many nice things about me. I'm really not that good with the gun. The only time I've ever had to use it, I wasn't very successful. It was a case I got into in Wisconsin. A balloonist tried to drop a bomb on a Milwaukee hospital. During the chase, I fired at him with a pistol, missing each and every shot. I seem to be better on the range than I am with live targets."

"Let me tell you one thing, Doctor. I practice a lot with my gun. It's real important to feel comfortable with it. But I never pulled it on a person unless I had to. I was told by an old cowboy years ago, never pull your gun less you can't help it. Avoid it if there's any other way out. But once the iron's in your hand, use it and shoot to kill, and keep shootin' til it's empty. That's a hard thing to say. But it's the only way to stay alive if you're gonna get to go up against another man with a gun," the ex-town tamer explained.

By now, the meal had begun in earnest. Servants moved about with platters of fowl. A serving table groaned with vegetables of all kinds from nearby farms. Falconer had a game hen, two roasted Long Island potatoes and an ear of corn.

He sat down next to Sudberg. The man was drinking from a very large stein of lager beer, and holding a joint of chicken in his other hand.

"Food's good wherever Teddy Roosevelt is, Dr. Falconer. You can see that. It's one of the extra added attractions in working for T.R. In my case, maybe not the best thing. I've gained twenty pounds in the year since I got this job. If he gets to be vice president, it'll cost me my figure altogether." Rudy patted his bulging abdomen and ungraciously belched.

"I saw you talking with Sherman Bell and Masterson. They call the governor a cowboy, but Bell's the real cowboy around here. Give him half an excuse and he'll say something like; 'Let's have an old fashioned hoe down.' He'll strum that big guitar and sing songs. Masterson'll join us too. It'll begin as soon as dessert's finished, you'll see. Speaking of dessert, they've got hot peach pie. I'll get you some," Sudberg added, as he stuffed in the last morsels of meat, talking with his mouth full.

"I've had enough peaches today. I had some this morning, thanks anyway."

"Well, I'm going to go get some for myself, and peach ice cream. How about some of that? No? I'll be back in a few minutes. We can watch the hoe down from here," said Sudberg, wiping his greasy face with his left shirtsleeve.

The Roosevelt children had gathered around the campfire after the feast. It was traditional on summer evenings at Sagamore Hill for the Governor to sit with his offspring before the campfire and tell stories. He favored ghost stories, always well received. But this evening, because of the presence of Masterson and Bell and the frontier flavor of the party, the kids pressed their father to tell them stories of his days out west.

Governor Roosevelt, the erstwhile Dakota Territory rancher, had written extensively about it in several magazines. Many of his stories had to do with people he'd met like cowboys and wranglers, rustlers and horse thieves, and all the characters in between.

To the children, their father was the hero of all the stories. "Tell us about the time you captured the rustlers, Daddy, that's your best story. Tell us about that one, I love that one," Archie, who was six, insisted. Ted- twelve, Ethel- nine and the diminutive Alice, the young lady of sixteen, said, "Dad, the one about the rustlers is your best story. Tell us about that again."

The Governor's famous grin showed his ample teeth and caused the wrinkles in the corners of his eyes to bunch together. It was obvious that he loved his family and children even more than the fame and power he'd acquired over the years. T.R. often told friends that family life and the raising of children was the single most important thing anyone could do.

"Well, if it won't bore some of our guests, I'll try to remember that particular yarn. It was back in the winter of '86, in March to be precise. I'd been out in the Dakotas for about a year raising Texas longhorns who could live off the land."

Roosevelt spoke with intensity; his short, clipped words emphasized by hand motions, punching up and down with clenched fist to make points.

The children's mouths hung open in awe as they gazed at the great man who was their father and hero. Roosevelt smiled from time to time at each as he described events which occurred before they (with the exception of Alice) were born.

"It was the coldest winter that anyone could remember in those parts. The river had frozen solid; it was only beginning to break up by March. Huge floes of ice were coming down the river so thickly that the jam increased rather than diminished as the floe laid in. It was still bitterly cold day and night. A central current of speeding water kept the gorge in the middle of the river moving. We had a boat that we had brought with us. It was really only worth about thirty dollars at the time, but it was essential to us for transportation and we tied it up to a tree near the river."

"Early in the morning of March 24, however, I went out into the piazza and found the boat gone. It had been cut loose with a knife. Nearby, at the edge of the water; somebody had dropped a red woolen mitten there."

"I was so angry that I wanted to saddle up my horse Manitou and go down and pursue the devils. Mr. Sewall who was working with me at the time, a backwoodsman from Maine who knew about these things, pointed out that that wouldn't be of much value because the river was walled off on both sides with ice. He told me I'd never get within a mile of the men in the boat. All they had to do was keep floating downstream. The current was so strong that they couldn't possibly have gone upstream.

"There was only one thing to do. We had to build a makeshift scow and follow them. The thieves probably felt that we'd never be able to come after them. We had the only serviceable boat on the Little Missouri at the time. They were probably leisurely sailing down the river thinking they had made their getaway. I was the chairman of the Stockman's Association and a Deputy Sheriff of Billings County at the same time. I felt that I was bound to pursue these lawbreakers and bring them to justice. I knew who they were. They were three hard characters who lived in a shack or a hut some twenty miles above us. We had suspected them for sometime as horse thieves, and they probably decided to get out of town or out of the area by stealing our boat and making their getaway down river. They never suspected that we'd be able to pursue them at that time and they didn't want to wait till spring when justice would be dealt out to them for their horse thievery. The leader was a man named Redhead Finnegan, a long haired gunman of vicious reputation. He had two associates, a half-breed named Bernsted, and a half-wit named Pfaffenbach. They were all desperate characters or they never would have made a break in that kind of weather. I knew that if they were chased they would shoot for their lives."

The Governor, wearing the same bright checked vest which a New York Tribune reporter had described as being 'so loud you could hear it from thirty yards away,' took a healthy drink of Mrs. Klein's homemade Birch beer and proceeded with his tale.

"It took us six days to put the boat together and we had a seaworthy scow with which to pursue the criminals. We thought they'd be going down the river in a leisurely fashion stopping often and sleeping late, thinking that they had gotten away with the only boat on the Little Missouri. We had every confidence that we would catch up with them. The river current was strong and with Mr. Sewall steering and my other ranch hand, Dow, from Maine watching the bow we took off after them. The river was moving rapidly but there were ice walls looming up on either side in crazy glittering stacks. Every now and then overhanging pieces would break off and slide into the stream with a loud, sudden splash, like the plunge of some great water beast."

He looked around at his audience to make sure they were attending every word and continued. "It took us three days with little sleep and little stopping to catch up with them, but on the morning of April 1, coming around the bend we spotted our other boat. It was moored against the bank. From among the bushes some little way back, the smoke of a campfire curled up through the frosty air. Our overcoats were off in a second, and after exchanging a few muttered words, the boat was hastily and silently shoved toward the bank. As soon as it touched the shore ice, I leaped and ran up behind a clump of bushes, so as to cover the landing of the others, who had to make the boat fast. For a moment we felt a thrill of keen excitement and our veins tingled as we crept cautiously toward the fire."

"We took them absolutely by surprise. The only one in the camp was the German (Pfaffenbach), whose weapons were on the ground, and who, of course, gave up at once, his companions being off hunting. We made him safe, delegating one of our number to look after him particularly and see that he made no noise, and then sat down and waited for the others. The camp was under the lee of a cut bank, behind which we crouched, and, after waiting an hour or over, the men we were after came in. We heard them a long way off and made ready, watching them for some minutes as they walked towards us, their rifles on their shoulders and the sunlight glittering on their steel barrels. When they were within twenty yards or so we straightened up from behind the bank, covering them with our cocked rifles, while I shouted to them to hold up their hands the half-breed obeyed at once, his knees trembling as if they had been made of whale bone. Finnegan hesitated for a second, his eyes ferally wolfish; then, as I walked up within a few paces, covering the center of his chest so as to avoid overshooting, and repeating the command, he saw that he had no show, and with an oath, let his rifle drop and held his hands up beside his head."

By this time, not only were the children hypnotized by their father's storytelling, but every adult within earshot had stopped all other activity and sat in rapt attention.

He concluded, "We brought Finnegan and his two companions back. It took ten days in the ice and snow, but we brought them back, and justice was served."

"After we returned to our spread, I never again heard of Finnegan nor his pals. I suspect they were dangling from the end of a rope not long after we returned to our ranch. Justice out west is swift and sure."

The children leaped gleefully, clapping their hands together. "Tell us another one, Dad, tell us another one. Like the time you faced down the redskins who were charging at you with rifles," shouted Ted, caught up in the excitement of the tale.

"Not that one," said Kermit, "I want the time you killed the cougar." On and on it went, the children clamoring for more tales, and Roosevelt smiling and chuckling as they leaped around him in their ardor to hear more adventures.

"No, children, it's time to stop my tales and allow someone else to have center stage."

During the story telling, the servants had cleared the dinner plates and several sweating containers of ice cream had appeared, along with hot fruit pies, steam rising from their surface.

True to Sudberg's prediction, a few minutes after the story telling ended, Bell invited everyone to join in the western music. He announced he was going to sing an authentic Texas song (even though he came from Colorado) called "The Red River Valley." Falconer, not *familiar with* range music, was fascinated by the sad music and the lonely, plaintiff lyrics of the cowboy whose lover was going away.

Bell followed this with "The Streets of Laredo," another melancholy western tune. This time Masterson sang along with him. Alex resolved to read more about the frontier and its people. Nothing worth knowing should escape attention.

Roosevelt strode over, having sent his children off to bed.

"Falconer, Rudy, what about a game of poker? The boys want to get some of their money back, from you two. This time we'll get Sherman to join us. What do you say, men?" Roosevelt was beaming his toothy smile, glowing with energy and anticipated pleasure.

"I'm sorry to disappoint you, Governor, but I haven't had enough sleep yet. Too many ideas are spinning around in my head. One of my methods of crime detection is to sleep on ideas. A resting brain has more ability to concentrate than it does when awake."

"Sorry you can't join us, but I understand. We'll recoup our losses later. I respect your theories, Alex. With your deductive mind and acute observations, it's better you don't play poker with us right now. I can't afford another losing night, besides we probably all should turn in early. Kane has set up a full day of campaigning in the Northern New Jersey counties tomorrow. He plans to make it a rehearsal of sorts for the national tour in September." He grinned again and clapped the larger man on the shoulder, and Sudberg in his wake, turned to other plans.

Alex, filled with good food and fascinating thoughts, had sleep come easily. He hadn't had much during the past twenty-four hours. With the sleep came another dream. As soon as he awoke, Falconer wrote it down on notepaper. Dreams were crucial in understanding problems. The notes read:

"I saw a man who looked like Roosevelt, moustache, rather protuberant teeth, pince-nez glasses, in a military uniform racing up a hill. He was grabbed from behind by a much larger man in a green and black coat. The big fellow grabbed T.R. and began smothering him. I saw him and realized that this was the one who had killed the photographer. I knew the next victim was going to be the future President of the United States. I had to save him."

"The large man was now chasing Teddy up the steps of the Capitol Building in Washington. It was Inauguration Day. There was a crowd, and a speaker's platform."

"I was certain the big man intended to kill the President. I didn't have a gun. I looked for it, but my pocket was empty. All I could find was a large gold coin, the one bigger than a silver dollar stolen from T.R.'s study. I had no other weapon. Knowing the killer was ready to strike, I threw the coin at the head of the assassin with all of my strength. It impaled itself in his forehead, like David throwing the stone at Goliath. The man fell with the coin impaled above his eyes. The last image in the dream was the gold gleaming at me as the man fell backwards. I had foiled the plot."

Having recorded the dream, Falconer went back to sleep, "I'll figure that one out tomorrow. I'm on to something."

CHAPTER TWENTY TWO

Falconer had arranged to meet Miss Irish for lunch at Sherry's. He had to get the source of her information. She'd be reluctant to reveal it, but it was essential to the investigation. He'd use his charm to discover what he wanted. The physician—detective retained the Victorian view of women as being occasionally clever, but never a match for a man's intellect. There were exceptions, but he'd never met any woman, aside from his late wife, who met the rigid criteria of intellectual prowess he expected of those with whom he became associated.

Alex made it a point to get to Louis Sherry's fifteen minutes early. It was flattering to a woman to know that the man awaited her. It also gave him an opportunity to look her over as she entered the room, and plan his strategy. The first thing which struck him was her beauty. Her auburn hair was piled atop her head, crowned by a small sailor hat. Au courant with the styles of the day, she wore a white crinoline gown appropriate for the luncheon hour. She hardly presented the picture of a toiler in the presses. No ink stains appeared on her hands nor did thick spectacles block her chestnut eyes. She strode erect, self-confident, a woman who knew where she was going, what she was doing, and how to get what she wanted. This would be a pleasant challenge, socially as well as intellectually.

As the captain brought her to the table, Falconer rose to his full six foot two height, smiled and bent over to the diminutive lady, almost a foot shorter than he even with her high-heeled, buttoned-down boots.

"Miss Irish, it's a pleasure to meet you," said Alexander L. Falconer. "Governor Roosevelt has told me a great deal about you. I'm delighted to have the opportunity to get acquainted."

The reporters and editors at the <u>Journal</u> had given the tall professor a good review. The jaded journalists never mentioned his good looks.

"Well, I'm happy to meet you, too, sir. My colleagues have told me a good deal about you. I was pleased to get your call and I'll try to be of whatever assistance I can." She sat down demurely and accepted the menu proffered by the overly obsequious waiter with the questionable French accent.

"I love Sherry's, not just the desserts. The whole menu is charming and unique, don't you think, Dr. Falconer?" She smiled and very slightly batted her eyelashes at the large man.

Gaby's demure flirtatiousness was not lost on Alex. Even though he'd not been spending much time with women of late, Alex Falconer recognized perfection in its every form. Her flirtatiousness was neither too overt, nor too subtle to hit the target. Her demeanor said she was interested in him, wanted to know more about him, and was receptive to the notion of having a more meaningful relationship. This, all in a glance, a smile and a few words, coupled with the slight movements of her long and curling eyelashes.

"I agree," responded the physician. "Sherry's is one of my favorite places. I really enjoy the sweets. Although they don't help to keep you trim. Mr. Sherry's ice cream and special flavors are the best in New York. Even though he's made his reputation on desserts, his menu is tops too. My boys love Sherry's more than any other place in town. They hound me to take them here on their birthdays and mine and any other occasion they can imagine. Maybe I indulge them too much. But then as a single parent, I have to play the role of both mother and father."

Falconer had neatly informed Gaby that he was not married, had a family, and was interested in the finer things of life. He also pointed out that his sons needed a mother, but they were getting along very well without one, thank you, at the moment. She recognized and responded in kind.

"I didn't realize you were a widower. I assume that's true. You're not divorced, are you?" She went on, as Falconer simply shook his head in reply. "Did your wife die in the TB epidemic?"

"No, something worse than the TB bacillus took Marjorie." He looked down at the menu, staring at it while going through a painful recollection of the past.

"She was the victim of a maniac. You probably don't recall this, you're much too young. There were a series of rapes and murders on the upper west side five years ago. The press at first weren't aware of the rape aspect of the crimes. They were reported as random killings."

"The police didn't connect the crimes, let alone the motive. They made no effort to understand the killer. The tragedy is, it could have been prevented. The lunatic could have been stopped if only someone had applied reason, deduction, understanding and even a small amount of thinking to deal with this crime. Marjorie, it happened, was his sixth and last victim."

Falconer looked up from the menu at a pensive and obviously sympathetic Gaby. "But this is no subject for luncheon conversation. Besides we have other matters to discuss."

"Nonsense, Dr. Falconer, I can see how important it is to you." Her tone encouraged him to go on.

"We met in Cambridge. Roosevelt told me about your interview for the college paper. You do remind me of Marjorie. She was slight and, if I may say so, very attractive, just as you are." Tears welled in the corners of his eyes. He was starting to give in to the years of dammed up emotion.

"Excuse me, I try not to be emotional when working, but it was Marjorie's death which demonstrated to the governor how scientific approaches in crime detection can be more valuable than chasing after people with night sticks. I was able to see a pattern in the crimes, (too late for Marjorie), which had escaped the police."

He was into it now, and was going to tell her the story. This young girl seemed interested and could absorb the material better than anyone he had known in years. Why? It was one of those intuitive leaps he made when everything came together. This was, indeed, the kind of person he could talk to, who could understand what he was saying.

Gaby confirmed this. "That might be the reason you have pursued the legal aspects of medicine, a personal motive to account for your success over the past several years in detecting crimes."

He nodded, "I agree. No one had paid attention to criminal patterns. You know, they do follow a kind of pattern, a modus operandi', the same thing each time. As I reviewed the victims, I saw that every single one, including Marjorie, was a red head. They were all attractive and young. Married women; each was killed when her husband was away, at work or out of town on some kind of business activity. The killer had to be someone who had thought it through, observed his victim and knew when to make his move."

"Further, each crime occurred in a small geographic area on the upper west side, within ten blocks of one another. I drew a map of the sites. While the police had a vague notion that the criminal was common to all, they'd never spent time putting it together. They hadn't thought of a psychological motive for the killings, like a need for revenge, or a hidden sexual drive relating to married, red headed women."

"I reasoned, since he'd spent so much time and energy observing his victims, the killer probably didn't have a job in the neighborhood, the police theory, if they had one. He was someone who lived there, and didn't have to work, for one reason or another. Therefore he could spend his time stalking his victims."

"I decided to set a trap. I found an attractive red headed woman of the proper age, and installed her in a house in the area. Fortunately, I am of independent means, having inherited a reasonable sum. We made it appear as if a colleague of mine were her husband. We installed her in the house and had her go about the neighborhood, to the grocer, the butcher, the baker, and so on."

"Since the killer took time to stalk his prey, I'd reciprocate to track him down. It became my obsession, as you can imagine. It was important that the woman be beautiful, young and have flaming red hair. I had no fear that the maniac would do anything on the streets. Each and every crime was committed in the home and while the spouse was absent."

Falconer gripped the napkin in his hand as if it were the throat of his wife's murderer.

"With the other doctor acting as husband, I hid in the house and never left. I didn't want to risk the likelihood that the killer had seen me while tracking my wife. Therefore, I remained inside the house until the day I caught him. By now, you know I did." His smile was forced and almost demonic.

"The counterfeit spouse made his schedule quite obvious. He *was* gone every week day from 8:00 in the morning until 6:00 in the evening. He went out every Tuesday and Thursday for some unannounced errand and returned at midnight. We felt that if we kept up this charade long enough, the lunatic would spot her, be attracted as a moth to a flame, and we'd have him in the same trap he was setting for her. It took many weeks, but I wouldn't give in."

Gaby, caught up in the tale, found herself holding her bread knife as if it were a weapon to defend herself against Falconer's villain.

"To make a long story short, it did bear fruit. The monster couldn't resist a beautiful victim with a husband absent two evenings a week, every week, like clockwork. In the third month, during a Tuesday evening when my friend was away at a poker game (where he went regularly on Tuesday and Thursday), the fellow followed him to his regular gaming spot. Assured that the doctor was, in fact, on the other side of town; the villain returned to the house. I, of course, was inside as always, especially alert during the evenings. Each of the murders occurred after dark."

"His method was to come at night, assault his victim in her sleep by knocking her unconscious and then truss her body in a spread-eagle fashion to the four corners of the bed. Thus, with his victim tied and dazed, he'd cover her mouth with sticking plaster to keep her silent, and then in this helpless and gagged condition, rape her repeatedly. I had determined this from my own postmortem examinations. After that, the fiend killed each woman, presumably so she wouldn't identify him."

"My deduction was that he was red headed himself. On the occasion of my wife's a death, I painstakingly went over the murder scene and found red hairs on the floor which were not hers. The police, of course, hadn't done a careful examination in the previous crimes, so I couldn't be absolutely certain of this fact. But it seemed likely to be one piece of the puzzle. I suspected his mother had been red headed too and the crimes related to a distorted sexual drive as well as rage against her."

Gaby shivered as the grisly story went on. She was a reporter and tough. But not that hard yet.

"On the evening in question, I, as usual, was hidden in the alcove of the bedroom, in an area with a drawn curtain so that I'd be unobserved by anyone entering the room. I expected the killer to come in, cosh the victim and then complete his murderous ritual. I planned to leap out of the alcove as the assault began, and stop him in his tracks. As you know, I'm something of an athlete, baseball and crew at Harvard and I exercise daily. I knew I could subdue him when the time came. In the event, it wasn't so easy."

"It was after nine and very dark outside, the time I'd choose if I were the killer. I was on my guard when Evelyn, the counterfeit wife, went to the bathroom down the hall."

"I never considered following her. I'd miscalculated the man's modus operandi. He was in the hall and slugged her there. It was only after I heard the door opening and saw the fellow dragging her into the room that I realized he'd already knocked her senseless."

"It was then that I lost perspective. I actually became melodramatic. As I saw him dragging her through the open doorway, I leaped from the alcove, shouting, You're through, you fiend. This is the last helpless woman you'll murder."

"Of course, that only gave him warning. I was still several feet away. He roped her, turned and produced the largest knife I'd ever seen."

"As I saw the blade gleam in the gaslight of the bedroom, I knew I had to use every ounce of athletic ability in my power. I was rushing at him and tried to twist my body to one side. He held the blade in front of him to impale me as I flew at him. I managed to turn slightly to the left, and the blade skewered my coat, my skin, and sliced a rather large chunk under my left armpit above the rib cage. I hardly felt the blade. By then, every ounce of energy and every scintilla of concentration in my being was focused on throttling the man."

"It was as if he were once again attacking my wife and I still had time to stop him before she died. I turned with my right hand to grab his shoulder. It threw him off balance, and he fell to the floor. He still held the knife, and was going to use it when I grabbed his wrist with my wounded left arm. At the same moment, I pushed my good arm under his chin and ground it in with all of my strength. The knife dropped from his hand. I began beating him over and over again in the face, the neck, the head, the chest. I kept on for two or three minutes. We later determined I'd crushed his larynx with the first forearm thrust to the neck. I'd killed him instantly. The later blows were unnecessary and only examples of my pent-up rage."

"The maniac had surprised me with the weapon. If I weren't in top shape, Evelyn and I would have become his seventh and eighth victims. I still keep in condition with daily exercise. I take a brisk walk every morning for at least an hour at dawn, rain or shine, and then work at eye to hand coordination at home for another hour."

"I should have anticipated the knife. He had to complete the final act of his macabre scenario. You see, he cut the throat of each of his bound and gagged victims. As they looked on helplessly, he gashed them from ear to ear." His voice cracked, and his speech stumbled as he completed the sentence. Alex stared at the table setting; gleaming crystal, china and silver. Gaby reached over and placed her small hand lightly atop his huge, clenched fist, still throttling the napkin.

"You must have loved her so," she said, tears filling her eyes. If only she could share a love so intense, and with such a man.

"It took several months for the wounds of my rib cage and arm to heal. Actually I still have some scars there which aren't pretty. It taught me a lesson as far as dealing with criminals is concerned. I carry a Smith & Wesson .45 caliber revolver with me at all times." He smiled in a sardonic way and chuckled.

"You never know when the other fellow's going to have a six-inch knife to thrust at you. If he does, a Smith & Wesson does the job, especially if you're two or three feet away from the blade. The bullet doesn't take long to cover the distance." The detective stopped his description, looked at his lovely luncheon companion and said, "But this isn't much in the way of table conversation, is it? Please forgive me. You're such a ready listener. Something I haven't had for a long time."

"Oh, please don't apologize, Dr. Falconer. I'm fascinated by what you've had to say, and I'm honored to have you share your feelings with me. Please go on."

"No, I've imposed upon you enough. Let's order luncheon and then talk about the business at hand. The problem that faces us, while not as emotional as my sad tale, may be vitally important to our country. What do you say to one of Mr. Sherry's crabmeat cocktails, some fresh bing cherry ice cream, and a little champagne to wash it down?" He beamed, as if a great weight had been lifted from him.

"I'd be delighted to let you make all of the selections, doctor. Obviously, your taste in food is as impeccable as your reputation for detecting crime." Her demure and slight flirtatious smile indicated to both that a meaningful friendship could be forming.

As the meal went on, Falconer made it clear it was essential to know the source of Gaby's information. He insisted this was a matter not only of national importance, but which might rebound to the detriment of her employer.

"I have every reason to believe that the individual who stole the original picture of Roosevelt, and that's what it was, a stolen picture doctored by a criminal photographer, has gone even further. I suspect him of murdering the photographer who altered the picture. I'm sure he'll stop at nothing to destroy the governor's career."

"Why go to such lengths? Killing, forging, and so on. I mean, politicians don't have clean hands, we all know that. But murder?" She seemed interested in the answer as well as the answerer.

"I'm not certain as to his motive yet. It may be political, economic, God knows what. But I do know we're dealing with a killer as dangerous and as distorted as the one I told you about before lunch."

"Aside from that, if the documents are forged, there's another problem. Mr. Roosevelt could, if your boss prints this material, destroy the entire Hearst empire after a successful libel suit. It would affect your employment, but Mr. Hearst would be the greater loser."

His logic was irrefutable. Hearst with no newspaper would mean Gaby without a job. No paper would hire her if she were responsible for bringing in the story that laid Hearst low.

"I understand. I'll speak to my source this afternoon, ask him where the material came from, what he knows about it, and let you know. I'm sure I can convince him. He's caught in the middle too."

"You won't regret it, Gaby." He thought he'd risk the first name now. "Whatever you do now won't be so much for Mr. Roosevelt as for the whole country."

His hand reached out and grasped her upper arm in a firm, enveloping manner. Instead of further physical contact, he went on to describe his feelings about his current client.

"Roosevelt is capable of becoming one of the great American presidents. He's in line for the election of 1904. He can be the leader who'll make us an international power, the colossus of the twentieth century."

"Someone, or a group, wants to stop him by any means they can. I have reason to believe they murdered the photographer who altered the picture. This morning I learned the army surgeon on duty at San Juan Hill who actually treated Renfield, was dead. The bodies of the doctor and his wife were found this morning. A report came in by wire after I inquired concerning an interview to get his statement. I intend to go to Trenton on this afternoon's train to examine the bodies. I suspect they're the latest victims in this plot, and of one criminal."

"You think one man is orchestrating this whole thing? The phony picture, the affidavits, and the killings?"

"Absolutely. We might be only seeing the beginning of a series of crimes which will go on until we track him down and stop him."

Falconer's fork pressed deeply into Mr. Sherry's linen, almost puncturing the tablecloth in the unconscious acting out of his anger. They had finished their meal and were sipping their Moët champagne as Alex intoned these ominous predictions.

With moistened eyes, he remarked, "You can't imagine how much you put me in mind of Marjorie."

"I know you couldn't offer a greater compliment," she said softly. Even Louis Sherry's select bing cherries could not sweeten the bitter reminiscence they now shared. The crimson dessert softened and melted in its silver bowl and went untouched by either diner.

Realizing the moment was too soon and the conversation too intense to continue, Gaby closed with, "I'll go to the Journal right now and call my source. I'm sure I can arrange for you to meet tomorrow."

Alex's farewell wasn't quite business like. "Adieu, I'll look forward to seeing you again in the very near future," he said with intensity. He swept her body, from head to toe, in a gaze which signaled his intention for a much closer relationship.

"And I, too, Dr. Falconer. I can't say how much I've been impressed by our meeting." The message was received and reciprocated.

Alex stood for a moment watching her cab move away, uncharacteristically forgetting, just for a moment, that he had things to take care of. He hailed another hack, and began the journey to Trenton to pursue the deadly business at hand.

CHAPTER TWENTY THREE

"What a grand and glorious time to be an American, my fellow citizens. Our nation stands at the brink of a new era. The twentieth century looms big before us with the fate of many nations at stake. If we stand idly by, if we seek merely swollen, slothful ease and ignoble peace, if we shrink from the hard contests where men win at hazard of their lives and at the risk of all they hold dear; then the bolder and stronger peoples will pass us by." His clenched fist raised in the air.

The crowd erupted into cheers. Calls of "You tell 'em, Teddy!" and "Up with the Star" flew through the air along with streams of red, white, and blue crepe paper and handfuls of confetti.

"Jersey is with you Colonel!" shrieked a plump burgher from Newark.

The candidate held his hands outstretched in the air to indicate he had further comments.

"Our opponents say give back Guam, the Philippines, Cuba, and Puerto Rico. Cut them loose, let them find their own destinies. I say there is no stopping the American colossus. Don't let the scalawags and filibusters have lands to exploit to further their own greed. What greater achievement is there than to add more stars to our glorious flag, in the Western hemisphere and across the broad Pacific! Up with the Star!"

More huzzah, shrieks, Indian war hoops and howls and cries of "Columbia the Gem of the Ocean," "The Rough Rider forever," were drowned out by the traveling brass band striking up the stirring sounds of "Rally Round the Flag."

"The Union forever,

Hurrah boys, hurrah.

Down with the traitor

And up with the Star."

With this, T.R. in his cowboy style broad-brimmed black hat and his honor guard of Rough Riders, in full uniform, marched off the platform and headed toward the Vice-Presidential candidate's campaign train.

The triumphal march was interrupted a hundred times by Roosevelt stopping to pump the hands of the dozen well wishers on each occasion. Several of them shouted, "After the Major, the Colonel for president!" McKinley had been a Major in the Union Army.

The cold bottle of milk which the Governor had swallowed in two long drinks, had colored his reddish brown moustache a pearly white. Removing his polka dotted blue Rough Rider bandana from his rear trouser pocket, Roosevelt brushed his mouth and observed. "I love campaigning. It's the ultimate expression of American democracy. The people, in their wisdom, decide who will become their leaders, not some archaic rites of descent. What's our next stop?" he asked Kane.

"Passaic for a ten minute stop at the platform, then Patterson and Hackensack for whistle stops and finally down along the Erie Lackawanna track to Jersey City for a torchlight parade and rally. We'll take the ferry home from there at eleven, spend the night at the Astor and then take the New York Central line up the Hudson Valley for a sweep and back to Albany." The former First Volunteer Cavalry Captain was now ramrodding the mini tour of nearby eastern towns and cities, helping Sudberg polish his leader's ten and twenty minute speeches, arranging for proper brass band martial music, setting up star spangled buntings for platforms, placards for rallies, and three color McKinley- Roosevelt buttons for the assembled multitudes. All in preparation for the big railroad tour of the midwest where the GOP bigwigs expected their biggest battleground with Bryan.

"They love the parts about expansion to the Pacific and Caribbean," Masterson noted. He was chronicling the candidate's rhetoric for his future career, as well as acting as chief body guard. A snub nosed .38 caliber revolver bulged from the breast of his already tight suit jacket.

"Some people think I go too far in the direction of the New American Empire. They say I'm power mad," mused the still incumbent governor.

"Mark Twain thinks you're crazy." Masterson liked to drop a conversational bomb from time to time, if for no other reason than to get a word in edgewise when his charismatic leader was holding forth.

"Crazy? That unreconstructed Missouri Democrat is a good one to talk. Crazy indeed! On what does Professor Clemens base this diagnosis, pray tell, Mr. Masterson?"

"Well, Colonel, I'm not his apologist. I don't share his ideas, you understand. But he says your need for action and power are going to get you killed. Some mad democrat, some out of work political hack, an old fashioned confederate, a saloon owner you put out of business, who knows? He says you talk so much and write so much, you're too God damned righteous, those are his words. Roosevelt's too righteous' to quote him precisely, and he's made enemies on every side.' He told me to get into the writing business as quick as I could because going around in the campaign watching you, I'll likely stop a bullet myself; maybe even get blown up by a bomb."

"Dammit man, I'm not going to change a word of my convictions nor will I ever alter anything which I consider to be just and fair. Once I have set my course, I stick to it. If that's righteous or mad, then I plead guilty on both counts."

"Like the charge up Kettle Hill leading a skirmish line of dismounted cavalry? Sitting on your horse, into enemy fire, the biggest target anywhere in sight?" former U.S. Marshal said.

"Precisely. It was my duty to lead those men, set an example for courage in the face of the enemy. I would no more change my views on political strife than shirk my responsibilities in mortal combat. Right is Right!" said Roosevelt.

"No assassin's bullet will strike the righteous, Colonel?" Bat asked.

"I'd never be foolish enough to say anything like that. Captain 'Buckey' O'Neill, the former mayor of Prescott, Arizona said that to one of his sergeants. He said, 'the Spanish bullet isn't made that will kill me.' It wasn't a moment later before a Mauser shot went zing into his mouth and burst out the back of his head. The biggest, handsomest, laziest officer in the regiment was dead by the time he hit the ground. If fate rules that I be struck down while exercising my responsibilities in this campaign just as I did in Cuba, so be it. I will not swerve! Neither you nor the fanciful master of fiction, Mr. Mark Twain, not withstanding."

That was his final word on the subject as the train rolled northward. He left the rear platform at the next whistle stop to tell the citizens of New Jersey why President Mckinley of Ohio should be re-elected, and he Theodore Roosevelt of New York, Dakota and points west, should become the new Vice-President of the United States.

CHAPTER TWENTY FOUR

More than five thousand excited citizens of the great state of New Jersey had gathered at the Hudson County Fair Grounds to meet and greet the military hero of the Spanish War. The sun had just set and the grandstand at the harness track was lit by more than a hundred paraffin and kerosene soaked torches held aloft by party faithful scattered throughout the stands and on the infield of the track.

A speaker's platform, festooned with patriotic bunting, stood in the center of the track infield facing the grandstand. Eight very large torches lit the platform casting an orange glow upon the faces of the local dignitaries awaiting the advent of the speaker. T.R.., as was his invariable custom, arrived a few minutes late. "Not enough to annoy the audience, mind you; just ten or fifteen minutes to get them excited, not angry," he advised Woody Kane earlier.

With the quarter hour having been fully expended as predicted, the Governor of New York State made his dramatic entrance. Roosevelt was flanked by Color Sergeant Albert Wright in his blue shirted Rough Rider uniform complete with golden chevrons, and campaign ribbons. The sergeant carried Old Glory and bugler Emil Cassi held his trumpet at port arms. Sergeants Buck, Taylor and Sherman Bell fell in behind, along with the omnipresent Woody Kane and Al Shaw, both attired in officer's dress khaki, spangled with several medals on their chests.

T.R. was dressed in a black business suit, with his broad-brimmed Stetson as the only symbol of his western identification. Indeed, his bright pink shirt and yellow cravat might lead the uninformed to describe the man as a dude. If they did so to his face, it was at their own peril. He had demonstrated that many times in the past.

Heralded by bugler Cassi's trumpet blast, the full brass band, which the Hudson County Republication organization had hired, began a medley of Sousa marches as the candidate and his entourage marched in military formation from the grandstand to the speaker's platform at a relatively slow pace, to enable the excitement to build.

Removing his Stetson, drinking a glass of water, the war hero allowed the last strains of Semper Fidelis to fade, and slowly scanned the multitude eagerly awaiting his opening remarks. He reached inside his suit coat, removed a sheath of papers presumably containing his remarks for the evening, and waited a little longer.

Finally, the great man began to speak in his slow, high pitched carefully enunciated style.

"Good evening fellow citizens. My name is Theodore Roosevelt and I am here to urge you to vote for Mr. McKinley and me and the whole Republican ticket on election day in November."

Before his first sentence was completed, a storm of cheers, the peeling of cowbells, loud whistles and war hoops filled the air. A shout informed the man on the podium, "We are with you Teddy boy." Others screamed, "On to Washington," "Cuba today, Toronto tomorrow," and "Hurray for Teddy, the trust buster."

He held both arms aloft as if signaling a horseman to rein in his mount. After five full minutes he said, "Whoa, my friends, let me speak, a train load of Democrats couldn't do a better job in keeping Roosevelt quiet." The expected laughter arose from the multitude. He went on without once referring to the typed notes in his hand. Rather, he used them rolled up as a baton to orchestrate the responses of the crowd.

"This time, we're not only going to re-elect McKinley and bring me in to back him up, we're also going to sweep in a full slate of Republican legislators in Congress to carry out the President's policies. And the year after this, the good people of New Jersey will sweep out the deadwood. And by that I mean the Democrats from their corrupt perches on municipal, county, and state government!" The sheath of paper, now held in two hands, was being used to symbolically sweep the air in front of Mr. Roosevelt.

"You tell em cowboy!" shrieked a corpulent citizen while energetically waving a small blue pennant which read: McKinley-Roosevelt.

"He can really turn them on!" Kane told Masterson. "They're in a frenzy!"

"Yeah, Captain, but a wild crowd makes me a little scared. It's hard to tell the real lunatics from just excited Republicans," said Bat.

"I'm scanning the crowd and there are a few characters I wouldn't invite to Aunt Betsy's for afternoon tea, I'll tell you that," Masterson added.

"I'm keeping an eye on them too, and I've instructed Bell to slip around behind the speaker's stand to watch Ted's rear," Kane said.

"Good idea, in another ten minutes, he'll be plunging into the crowd like a diver into the water heedless of the consequences. The man thinks he's invulnerable. He likes to shake every hand in the county. He'd do it too. I'm afraid one of them will come up with a knife or a pistol."

Kane blew out his breath forcefully in exasperation, "You really think so?" he asked.

"Most lawmen are more afraid of knives than pistols," said Masterson. "They're quiet, easy to conceal and can be just as deadly in close quarters as a gun. Hell, you can stab somebody, deep and hard, drop the weapon and fade into the crowd without ever being detected." He shuddered at the thought of a blood soaked end to today's glorious campaigning.

"They all look like good, solid Republicans here tonight," Kane said as he continued to peer into the five thousand or more faces.

"It only takes one, Mr. Kane, only one," Masterson warned.

With that, their leader concluded his speech, the band struck up The Battle Hymn of the Republic and Teddy literally leaped from the platform, away from his uniformed troopers and was engulfed in the adoring masses. He clapped backs, grabbed shoulders, pumped hands, grinned his enormous toothy smile and seemed to gain sustenance from the humanity crowded around him.

Kane, Shaw, and Masterson plunged after their charge and reached him after a few annoyed citizens complained, "What's your hurry, soldier boy? Don't push! This is my only chance to shake a future president's hand".. . .and so on.

"We've got to catch the 11:00 p.m. ferry, Theodore!" Kane only used his friend's full first name when annoyed, like a parent chastising an exuberant boy playing too late with his friends.

"Then we'll get the one at twelve, Woodbury," T.R. shouted and pumped more outstretched hands. "These are my people. They love me and I love them. I love the raw energy here, Mr. Kane, don't stop me now."

They boarded the midnight ferry to Manhattan with only minutes to spare.

As the boat slipped into the Hudson, Masterson, Kane, and the candidate stood on the upper deck viewing the city to the east.

"Crowds like the one in Jersey City scare me, Colonel," said the old gunfighter.

"They're good Republicans, Bat. A bit loud, but a bully bunch, believe you me," T.R. insisted with his usual enthusiasm. "He could be right, Ted," observed Kane. "You never know when there's a joker in the lot. Some troublemaker, crazed Democrat, who knows?"

Masterson, gazing across the harbor and tugging his Derby down tight on his head against the cool evening breeze, observed, "Puts me in mind of the crowd in Sacramento about ten years back when I was doing security for the Central Pacific Railroad. They'd just built a new terminal there in the State Capitol and set up a big grand opening party to celebrate. Attracted people like flies to a honey pot. Free food and worse, for that town, free beer." Bat once again patted his Derby to make sure it was still on his head.

"An unruly crowd, eh, Masterson?" asked Woody Kane.

"Unruly? The only rule they knew was where is more beer. Every saddle tramp, Candy dancer, and loafer in Northern California showed up."

"The Governor was going to unveil a brass plaque on a cornerstone of a new building and that attracted the political crazies too," Masterson noted.

"What kind of political crazies?" the boy Governor inquired; ever attuned to anything political, crazy or not.

"The ones who wanted to secede from the Union and go back to the old California Republic. Others who wanted to make the Bear state, the bare state (he spelled it for them). They wanted everyone all naked. And then the usual loonies, you know, woman suffragette agitators, W.C.T.U., holier than thou grandmothers..."

"There's something to be said for the Women's Christian Temperance Union, Bat," T.R. observed.

"Sure, but not in a crowd of rowdy, liquored up hooligans, no sir."

"What happened?" asked Kane.

"Where?" Bat replied.

"At the grand opening at the railroad station of course."

"Oh, that. Nothing terrible. I did have to shoot one real bad actor."

"Shoot and kill him, Masterson?" asked Kane.

"I don't shoot at somebody unless I aim to kill him. I'm not leaving a wounded adversary around to get me later, not me," Masterson said.

"You killed someone in the crowd?" T.R. asked almost incredulously.

"Had to, a real mean, sour faced character named Needlenose Mickey Milton," he answered.

"Needlenose Mickey Milton, what an odd name," Kane noted.

"Oh, I don't think so. I knew a whole family back in Illinois named Milton. Right, honest God fearing people they were," he said with a straight face.

"The Needlenose I meant, of course," Kane said with a little exasperation.

"Oh that. They called him Needlenose because he had a nose that was long and as thin as a darning needle. It even had a little hook on the end of it. And little beady eyes, and a head the shape of an egg with the narrow part on top."

"And it was the man you shot and killed?" Kane asked.

"Didn't mean to, he drove me to it. I tried to maintain my composure, but the varmint pushed me. You see, he knew who I was. The railroad people had advertised that I was taking to oversee security for them all along the line, and they had my picture in the Sacramento Bee, on the first page big as life," Masterson recalled smiling a bit and patting his stomach.

"So he challenged you to a gunfight?" Roosevelt assumed.

"No, that was the hell of it. The needlenose, beady eyed, egg headed son of a prairie dog tried to get me into a fistfight. He said something like, 'You think you're a big man because you can shoot a gun. What can you do without none?' He said again, 'I ain't afraid of you Miss Masterson.' You know, like he said it on purpose, Miss."

"What did you do, Masterson?" Kane asked.

"I put my right hand on my Colt, a move which I figure menaces most jaspers looking for trouble. But this troublemaker stands there with a thousand people all around him and raises his hands up in the air. He says,

'I ain't got no gun Miss Masterson, will you fight me like a man without no gun or are ya too yeller for that kind of action?' he says, the little pinheaded, cross- eyed, varmint ridden pig." Masterson was sputtering with rage as he recanted the tale and once again tapped his Derby down on his head as if it might have gotten loose in the wind.

"Did you hit the creature?" asked the former leader of the Rough Riders, always ready for a fight and always anxious to prove his manhood.

"Hell no! I'm a gunfighter, not a street brawler. I pulled my revolver and I fired a shot slightly to the left of his leg. That's usually enough to scare off the meanest of troublemakers. I'm standing there with my gun pulled bare out firing a shot. The bullet actually ricocheted and nicked Needlenose's cap, just barely." Masterson gazed at the oncoming shadows of the buildings of the great city.

"Then what?" asked T.R. as the ferry approached it's slip in Manhattan.

"Then the fool, with his hands still up in the air, reached behind the neck band of his shirt and pulled out a six inch knife. The rat must have planned to use it all along I figured later. He threw it right at me, one motion. I saw him reach and his arm go forward all at once. The damn knife hit me in the chest, right over my heart." Masterson tapped his left breast pocket, "Right here."

"Obviously, it didn't kill you. What happened man?" asked the incredulous Kane, already aware of Masterson's reputation as a teller of tall tales.

"The black Derby topped ex-lawman, reached into his left breast pocket and removed a metal flask. "I was saved by the demon rum, Mr.

Kane. Saved by strong spirits you might say." He unscrewed the flask, held the container in the air and asked, "Would either of you gentlemen care for a sip?"

As both nodded no, he added, "It's genuine Kentucky sour mash, one hundred proof, very good stuff. No? Well here's to you." He took a small sip, screwed the cap back on and commented, "It sure takes the chill off a cool river crossing."

"The knife blade hit the flask? Is that what happened?" asked Woody Kane.

"It hit right here." Masterson pointed to an indentation just below the neck of the metal container.

"And Needlenose?" asked the Governor.

"Needlenose?" he briefly lifted the Derby giving the onlookers a fleeting glimpse of the sparse strands of black hair across the top of his head.

"The knife thrower, of course," Kane said with now obvious exasperation.

"I shot him, of course," Masterson answered.

"When the knife hit?"

"Before; when his arm came forward, I fired, the knife hit me and Needlenose was dropped, all at once." Another pat on the top of the hat ensued.

"So you killed him with one shot?" Kane asked. *"As* dead as a door nail. I hit the bastard right on top of his ugly needlenose, just between the eyes. He was dead before he hit the ground. Sure you don't want a little nip?"

CHAPTER TWENTY FIVE

"I'm very happy to meet you, Dr. Falconer. I've read your articles in the Journal. The one concerned with identifying human blood and especially the last January issue where you talked about the new role of the pathologist in crime detection. They're fascinating. I'd love to attend your lectures at Columbia, if I get away from Trenton for a couple of weeks." The tall, bespectacled physician played with his fountain pen as they spoke.

"Thank you, Dr. Waterbor . I am flattered by your interest, but I wonder how it was that your call came as quickly as it did. After all, the bodies were only discovered early this morning." The August sun was about to set as they spoke.

"It's a curious combination of circumstances, doctor. The Cliftons were found early this morning when the milkman came to collect his monthly bill. Mrs. Clifton always met him at the door. She was an early riser. When she wasn't there, he became concerned. It was totally out of character. The Cliftons, you know, are local celebrities. What with Dr. Clifton being a war hero, the regimental surgeon for the Rough Riders et al. He was the Grand Marshal in last month's Fourth of July parade. Anyway, Mr. Petit, the milkman, went down the road to Mrs. Weiss' house. Jennie Weiss is Abby Clifton's sister you see. He told the sister that Abby didn't answer, said he pulled the doorbell over and over and pounded on the door as well. Mrs. Weiss then went right over there. She has a key, went in and found what you see." Waterbor pointed his fountain pen at the corpse at the foot of the stairs.

He then raised it upward to show his visitor Mrs. Clifton's corpse. "It's rare that I get to an actual murder scene you know. I guess that's what you think it is or you wouldn't have called me in. It's rare, I say, that the bodies haven't been disturbed," Falconer commented.

"It's not every day that the town hero is found dead along with his wife who happens to be the Police Chief's sister-in-law," Waterbor explained.

"Jennie Weiss called her husband straightaway and he called me at the Mercer County Coroner's Office. That, plus the telegram he got from Governor Roosevelt's office about locating the doctor. Well, this clearly was a very special case in every respect. The police chief's sister-in-law, our local celebrity, a fellow physician, you know. I decided to call you and told Weiss."

"He got a hold of Roosevelt's office in New York by telephone and somebody there said he'd have you here in no time, that you were working on the case anyway. Can you imagine my surprise. Thank God you're here now. Something must be up."

"I assume," Alex said, "that the telegram asked the sheriff to locate Dr. Clifton. There is, or was, some information he could've supplied better than any other source."

"Right, and now that knowledge is gone?" the coroner asked.

"Not entirely, but it will take a long and tedious search of army records to find it if we can."

"Something that Clifton knew about what?"

"I'm not at liberty to say at the moment," said Alex. "The case is still under investigation."

"Well, if you wanted to know anything about Yellow Fever, Clifton was the one. He gave talks about it at the County Hospital, the Medical Society meetings, even wrote an article for the New Jersey Medical Journal last year. He had a thousand stories about 'Yellow Jack'," Waterbor commented as Falconer bent over and carefully, painstakingly examined his late colleague's body.

"Did he ever talk about Yellow Fever causing dementia or delirium?" Alex asked as he peered first into the corpse's left ear and then the right using a reflecting head mirror and the fading rays of the setting sun through the open front door.

"Did he ever? A hundred times. I remember one colorful story at the Society meetings last month. It was about a private who, in his delirium, thought he was Teddy Roosevelt himself. He said the guy even dressed like the Colonel, had a little moustache and prominent teeth. He even missed the famous charge up on San Juan Hill, but told everybody that he was there and so on."

Falconer was examining the victim's head and nodding his own at the same time.

"What did you make of this skull injury, Waterbor?"

"Aha! I knew you'd see it. The crushing injury to the skull could never have come from a fall down the stairs. The deep indentation, the lacerations and bleeding of the scalp only in the center are certain evidence that a heavy blunt instrument caused the wound. Bouncing and bumping his head down a flight of stairs would have never resulted in the central depression we see. That is, unless a pointy huge flat iron were at the foot of the stairs, he flew directly down on it; not tumbled as the perpetrator wanted us to believe," the Mercer County coroner concluded.

"Exactly, all of the bumps and bruises were certainly postmortem. He must have been dead for a few minutes when thrown down the stairs. I imagine our killer would have been a big man to lift Clifton up and toss him like a sack of clothes down like this," Alex deduced.

"Or there were two killers?"

"Possibly, let's keep looking at the evidence."

"And, upstairs I think you'll find that Mrs. Clifton did not die of heart failure. Her medical history, Chief Weiss, and her sister confirm this, is totally absent of any coronary problems. Her skin has a bluish, cyanotic discoloration indicative of someone who has smothered or choked to death," announced Waterbor.

After Falconer had concluded the second examination, he said, "I think both smothering and choking in this case. Note the small abrasions on the perioral skin around her mouth and inside on the mucous membranes. Someone shoved something in her mouth, a careful examination of the bedroom may reveal a towel or pillow or blanket with remnants of saliva on it. Also, you'll see the slight discoloration in her neck, just here." He pointed to the area of the Adam's apple. "I suspect autopsy will reveal a crushed larynx. So, if I'm right, the killer choked her with one hand on the neck and smothered the woman with a wad of cloth over her mouth and nose at the same time," the pathologist-detective concluded.

"I'd best take your courses at the College of Physicians and Surgeons as soon as possible; remarkable indeed!"

"Thank you. Also, inspect the bedroom. I think that's where the crimes were done and I suspect some blood may be found there. Look on the sheets, the floor, the rug, I'm sure you'll find something. Clifton's head injury did result in some bleeding. The killer seems a bit sloppy and may have missed the blood in the dark."

As the train rattled down the Main line of the Pennsylvania Railroad from Trenton to Manhattan, the day hadn't yet begun as the grainy feeling under Alex's eyelids told him his constitution couldn't tolerate much more all night detective work.

He was puzzled by the slovenliness of this latest pair in what was becoming a chain of homicides. This crime was nowhere near as neatly done as the one in Manhattan, nor even the murder of Smoot, which was supposed to look like a train accident. As far as the arson case in Manhattan, the photographer's death had been missed entirely as a homicide by the police. Only an astute observation by a former student revealed it. His own observations indicated that the killer was meticulous in his attempts at creating a pseudo-accident. This wasn't the case in New Jersey. Something didn't ring true.

He returned home on the milk run train arriving in time for his morning constitutional. Sleep hadn't been possible on the trip. With his brain running at full speed, Alex reviewed the facts.

He compared the Trenton findings to the Nassau County murder. The death of Robbie, the robber, was a cleverly constructed ploy. The body was indeed soaked with alcohol. There was ample evidence that it had been crushed by the train. If it weren't for the fact that Falconer meticulously examined the body, it would have gone unnoticed that the petty thief was killed by a smallish blunt instrument thrust with great force into his skull. It was, just as the photography studio crime, a cleverly concocted scheme. Only careful examination of the body and clothing of the victim had connected the crimes. The discovery of the Columbian Exposition souvenir coin had forged the link between the murders.

Clifton was killed to keep him quiet about the imposter with Yellow Fever. His wife was there and had to die too. The three crimes fit together. But something was disturbing about it all. Why had the killings in New York and in Long Island been so cleverly done and the one in New Jersey botched? Was there another killer?

Falconer thought this through still again as he strode briskly down Riverside Drive approaching the newly completed Grant's Tomb. It still seemed new although it had been in place for more than three years.

Two men loitered at the entrance to the tomb. It was unusual to see anyone at the monument on a weekday morning. The shabbily dressed fellows in front of the tomb aroused his suspicions. What were they up to? Both stepped in front of him and blocked his way on the sidewalk, obviously looking for trouble. His hand, inside his sweater pocket, finger on the Smith and Wesson. He thought, "When they see this they'll start running the other way."

He heard a whirring sound from behind him and realized too late, someone had snuck up to attack him from the rear. He tried to duck his head to one side. Alex later decided this saved his life. As he moved his head slightly to the right, the heavy lead pipe skidded across his skull just above the left ear, and smashed into the shoulder on its way down.

It was a solid blow, enough to make even a great athlete stagger. He was a great athlete, both at college and later in professional baseball. The blow forced him to his knees but he didn't lose consciousness. Remembering the two fellows in front, Falconer squeezed the trigger of the .45 and fired the weapon through the pocket in the general direction of the other two assailants. The report roared in the early morning silence, and the bullet, because of its low trajectory, caromed off the sidewalk and found its way in the general direction of the assailants.

Recalling what Sherman Bell had said about firing the gun repeatedly, Alex continued to fire one bullet after another toward the assailants, obviously wounding one of them. He heard a shriek and then a guttural scream, "He hit me, he hit me!" The other shouted, "He's got a gun, get out of the way. Let's get out of here. I didn't sign on for this!"

The fellow with the lead pipe, apparently fearing the weapon would be turned on him, had run off in another direction. Alex found himself seated on the sidewalk in front of Grant's Tomb, blood trickling from his left ear, a very hot Smith and Wesson in his pocket, with several holes in his good sweater.

Partially assured that the assailants had fled, he ostentatiously removed the revolver from his pocket, and looked about, holding the gun in his hand. He got up and made his way slowly and painfully home.

Flossie Malone, the housekeeper he'd hired several years ago to take care of him and the two boys, was there with his usual hot breakfast.

"What in the world has happened to you, professor? You've been at it again with some loafers, I can see it. And you're covered with blood. Your hair is covered with blood; it's all over your clothes. You smell like your sweater's been on fire. Look at that great hole in it! My God, what has gone on here."

Mrs. Malone's broad Irish brogue revealed she was only a few years away from "the auld country." Concerned and reliable, she was more of a mother to his two sons than he could provide alone. She took it upon herself to be his mother as well. "Now let's get you cleaned up. Are you all right? It looks like a rat's been chewing at your ear."

"Yes, Mrs. Malone, a human rat. A pack of them attacked me outside of Grant's Tomb. My head feels like it's been sliced open, but there's no apparent damage, I'm sure of that. Please get me some clean towels and a basin of hot water; I think I can take care of this without having to call one of my colleagues."

"You'll need some stickin' plaster too. Oh, my, my, professor, you do get yourself in all kinds of scrapes. You've got to be more careful. Who's goin' to take care of these beautiful little boys if somethin' happens to you? I'll have to do it all alone, a poor widow woman like me. These walks early in the mornin' can't lead to any good. There's all kinds of bums and louts hangin' about the streets these day. Stayin' up all night goin' to morgues, and such. You had a telephone call a few minutes ago just before you got back here. It was from the governor himself. He wants you to call back immediately. But first take care of your head."

"Were there any other messages while I was out?"

"You got a call last night from a young lady, who calls herself Miss Irish, don't sound Irish to me. I was to tell you she had talked to her friend and he was interested and willin' to meet you and the governor too. She said she'd get in touch with you this mornin'."

"Here, let me have a look at that. Don't be touchin' it. Doctors don't know everythin'! After I clean it up, you're goin' to sit down and have some hot oatmeal. Somethin' to stick to your ribs. A warm meal'll do you a lot of good. You haven't been eatin' well. Look at the rings under your eyes."

"Mrs. Malone, I appreciate what you're saying, but. . . .Ooo, ow, that stings. That really hurts."

"It sure does. Looks like one of them loafers hit you with a two-by-four. Well, I've got the bleedin' stopped. I'm goin' to put this plaster on it. That'll do the job. You're lucky your ear's still on. You're a handsome fellow, but if you keep gettin' into trouble, you're goin' to be all scarred up like an old war horse.

"Here, I've written down the numbers of the governor, and Miss Irish, and then some other fellow from the medical school, somethin' to do with blood tests, or that, on carpets, I don't remember. He said somethin' about carpet blood bein' human blood, whatever that means."

"Thank you, thank you, Mrs. Malone. You're priceless, better than a private secretary. This whole house hinges on you."

"I'll do the job without the sweet talk, thank you very much. The boys'll be comin' in any minute lookin' for their breakfast, and I'm tryin' to clean up so they won't think their father's been in a barroom brawl. There, that'll do." She finished her ministrations, tying up his wounds as well as any Florence Nightingale.

Falconer, with time to collect his thoughts, ate his hot oatmeal and put some facts together. The assailants were sent by his adversary, whoever that might be. The man who had killed or caused the killing of the doctor and his wife, the petty thief, and the photographer. The same fellow who set up the scheme against Roosevelt.

He must have decided Falconer was in his way, but why? "Some thread strings these crimes together. Something's escaping me. The killing of Dr. and Mrs. Clifton and the attack on me indicate the opposition has information about my plans," he said to no one in particular. Speaking his thoughts out loud seemed to crystallize them better.

"It looks more and more like an inside job. How did the killer know the original photograph of Roosevelt and Churchill was there in the first place? How did he know about my plan to visit Dr. Clifton about Renfield's state of health? How did he even know I'm on his trail? Someone's feeding him information."

"I'll have to sleep on this, and I haven't been getting enough lately." He thought, "I'll go to Sagamore Hill and meet Gaby's source. I have to put as many of the pieces of this puzzle together as possible. I know I can suck the killer into my own trap. There must be a way I can set it up just the way I did with Marjorie's murderer. Still, something's missing."

The kids arrived and said he looked like one of the characters from the picture of "The Spirit of 76," the one with the bandage around his head.

"I am sort of fighting for my country, boys. Someday I'll tell you the story. Right now, let's eat breakfast and get about our business. You fellows have tennis lessons this morning, and I have to go out and play my own games."

"But your games are a lot more fun, dad. Didja get into a shoot-out with the bad guys?" asked Lexie, cramming a spoonful of cereal into his mouth.

"What makes you say that, son?" Where did this kid come up with such an accurate perception, he wondered.

"Your Harvard sweater's lyin' on the hall chair all holed up like Nick Carter's coat when he faced down the Black Domino Killer. Besides it smells like gun powder from my .22 rifle." The juvenile detective actually licked his chops savoring not the breakfast food, but his deductive triumph.

"The apple doesn't fall far from the tree," a proud father thought.

CHAPTER TWENTY SIX

The persistent aching in both the back and front of his head and especially over his left ear, which also had a very high pitch ring to it, told Alex that he had suffered from a concussion of significant proportions. He had to get to bed and to rest. But the role of single parent dictated that he must spend some time with the boys. Besides, if the thugs who waylaid him this morning knew his daily walking habits, then they also knew about the two small boys and possibly even their tennis lesson.

"Instead of tennis this morning, how would you young men like to help your dad in the lab?"

"Gee Dad, can we do some detective work, did you bring some clues from Trenton?" asked Gideon.

"I did and I'll need your help in investigating them, both of you. Come on along."

The three went to Alex's study which, in addition to being crammed with medical journals in German, French, and Italian, also included several American and British periodicals. A huge stack of texts stood in one corner with pieces of notepaper sticking out from most of the volumes to mark germane passages. On a flat table near the window, sat a black tubed Bausch and Laumb microscope, a Bunsen burner, a rack of glass test tubes, several glass stoppered bottles labeled in capital letters with such names as: CHARCOAL, SULPHURIC ACID, CALCIUM CARBONATE, and so on. A large retort attached to a coiled glass tube issuing from its top was half filled with a purple fluid.

Alex pointed to a small covered beaker at the bottom of which rested several fibers. "Those are the fibers from the carpeting in Governor

Roosevelt's home. They're soaking in a normal saline solution. Do you boys know what that is?"

Lexie said, "That's salt water, dad. You told us about it a couple of weeks ago when we went to Rye Beach. You said salt water is the same as we have in our bodies, normal saline," he proudly reported.

"Yes, sir, one hundred percent correct. I'm glad you remember."

"I did too," said Gid.

"Of course you did, son. The idea here is to see if there are any human blood cells still intact and on the fibers. Most will have been destroyed by the air drying them out and causing the cells to disintegrate. If my guess is right however, some of the red blood corpuscles will have stuck together in little rolls, doctors call them roulettes, and a few will still be intact if we can float them free in the saline. Do you understand boys?"

"Sure, dad, then you can see them in the microscope" Lexie responded.

As Alex nodded Gideon again said, "I knew that too!"

"In this case, it's not especially important because I'm certain the blood is there and it's not paint or dye or an animal's blood. My colleague from the College of Physicians and Surgeons left a message about that this morning anyhow. I saw a small nick on the hand of the man found run over by the locomotive and I knew that he had to be the one who stole something from the governor's house," Alex told his open mouthed boys.

"Then why do it at all, dad?" Lexie wondered.

"To perfect the technique, learn what can go wrong, see if blood lying on the carpet for so many days is recoverable at all. It's not just for one case that you do a scientific study, men. It's for all the future cases."

Both of his sons smiled when he referred to them as men. They really were part of the team now.

"Over here." Alex pointed to his set of glass slides laid on a wooden board to the microscope. "I've prepared slides of scrapings from under the fingernails of the first two murder victims and I'm going to add some samples that I have in my pocket taken from the victims in Trenton last night."

"Wow!" said Lexie.

As Alex prepared the slides of the two latest fingernail residues, he placed them under the microscope and advised his sons, "If you look through the scope, you'll see that there are fibers from some kind of woolen material on number 2, the photographer found in a downtown fire. And on number 3, Mrs. Clifton which I just got from Trenton last night, there are some strands of a cotton material. Numbers 1 from Mr. Smoot and 4 from Dr. Clifton are unremarkable." He scanned the four slides one at a time in rapid succession.

"What does unremarkable mean, daddy?" asked Gideon.

"It's unremarkable, you dummy," taunted Lexie.

"Unremarkable means there is nothing special to talk about in it. What is remarkable is that the older brother should never belittle his younger brother for not knowing something." He looked at his older son and namesake pointedly. "The older chap should try to help and enlighten someone less experienced in life. Don't you agree, Alexander?" The last, full first name thing was a sure sign of disapproval.

"I'm sorry, Gid. Well, sometimes dad uses words even I don't know and he tells me what they mean. So, I'm sorry I called you a dummy. You're not."

"Good," smiled their father. "You see," as first one and then the other child peered through the lens, illuminated by a mirror reflecting the brilliant midday sun through the nearby open window, "The woolen sample consists of black and green coarse fiber. It's most likely from a heavy suit jacket or even a topcoat. The other material is from a light brown or khaki cotton cloth, most likely a shirt or blouse."

"What does that mean, dad?" asked his namesake.

"It's most likely that the victims clawed out as one of their last conscious acts and scraped the coat or shirt of their killer or killers. If we encounter similar garments on a suspect later on, we can compare the fibers under our scope to see if they match," he explained.

"And then we'll know!" shrieked Gideon.

"Not exactly know, son. But, we will have a clue. It's like a mosaic pattern where hundreds of tiles of different colors and designs are put together and fit into one picture. They become a picture from so many different little pieces. You understand that?" The two boys nodded their heads solemnly yes. "These slides can be part of that portrait. You do see that?" he again asked.

Both boys nodded once again in the affirmative.

"What I'd like you men to do now, however, is to examine the photographs of some documents I received in the morning mail from the Evening Journal. I asked for the people at the Journal to send them so that I can examine the typewriting instrument they were made with. These documents all appear to have been prepared on the same machine. I've only just glanced at them, I'd like you to help.

"I'd like you, both of you, to take these magnifying glasses and look at every letter from A to Z on the pages of the documents. I want to know if any single letter is abnormal, distorted, has missing pieces, blurred type, or any other clue that will help us to identify a typewriting machine if and when we find it. This work, if you do it well, can also tell me if all of the affidavits are from the same typewriter. That will help. Are you gentlemen up to it?" he asked.

The two boys snatched the magnifying glasses from their dad's work table as Lexie said, "I'll take the first four pictures, you take the other two, Gid, I'm older."

Three Falconers were on the job now. With these odds, Alex knew that no malefactor could long remain undetected.

CHAPTER TWENTY SEVEN

Despite the early and oppressive heat and humidity of mid-August Manhattan, it was quite cool aboard the ferry boat heading across New York harbor from South Ferry to St. George in Staten Island.

"Peppah, Ah'm afraid we will have to go inside the cabin, mah boy. It's too cool out here for these tahrd bones." The pale old man made slow progress with his tiny steps across the wooden planks on the passenger level of the double decked steam vessel which sailed across the upper harbor of America's busiest port.

"I'll help you, Uncle Jack," offered the large man, while grasping his uncle's elbow.

"I kin do it mahself young man. I kin do things a damned sight better than yoah incompetent hirelings. That's for shuah. Am ah right in deducin' that they, all three of the fools, bungled a simple thing like cavin' in Falconer's head?" He sourly gazed at the glassy waters of the harbor and the white foamy wake which the <u>Governor Clinton</u> made in its half hour passage from one island borough to the other.

"Yes, sir, I'm afraid so. It seems they knocked him on the head, but either it's too thick to cave in, or the man who swung the lead pipe wasn't strong enough. They called me from a tavern an hour ago. One man was wounded by Falconer's fire..."

"His fire? He's armed? You and your people didn't know that I expect. The man walks around New York City with a pistol, a revolver, I expect."

"Yessir, he does. It was a six shooter, they told me. He got one of our men in the upper body…"

Jack interrupted yet again. "One of yoah men, not oah men. They are surely not mah recruits. They can't take a man when the odds are three to one, disgraceful."

The pair had entered the main cabin of the cross harbor boat. The top deck, devoted to passengers, was practically empty on the trip to the rural island, away from Manhattan. The vessel had already deposited several hundred turn of the century commuters. Wall Street and the entire financial and commercial districts of the largest city in the United States were a short walk from the ferry terminus on the city side.

Three separate plank ways on the sea level deck allowed room for horses, wagons and even the occasional motorized vehicle to make the short voyage.

"One man was uninjured, another fellow was seriously wounded and the third twisted his ankle as he fled Falconer's bullets." Pepper reported.

"Fled the bullets? Did the dunce think he could out run them? What happened, did he turn his dainty little foot?" Uncle Jack was fuming with rage. Small dribbles of saliva emerged from his mouth and some flew through the air in the general direction of his beleaguered nephew.

"Falconer was in Trenton all last night both with the coroner and, I am told with the county sheriff. I'm afraid he's become as dangerous as Roosevelt, or more so."

The Governor Clinton plowed majestically through the busy harbor as the almost apoplectic uncle sputtered, "As dangerous! More so. He might uncover the whole scheme. I don't have to tell you, Peppah, theah are people in very high places countin' on us. People of money, and position, and powah." Jack sunk back onto the wooden backrest of the ferry seat and dabbed his mouth with a large silk handkerchief. "You are goin' to have to do somethin' verrah specific, and now. Get rid of Falconer, Roosevelt, and the whole caboodle of Yankee trash, and now!"

"I've arranged to meet Maguffin, the man who silenced Dr. Clifton at the ferry terminal."

Uncle Jack's upraised bony, alabaster hand stopped Pepper in mid sentence. "I will not speak to or even be seen by that hired assassin, no suh. How dare you."

It was Pepper's turn to halt his uncle's thought. "No sir, no not you. You're not involved. He knows nothing of you, nothing of any of our principals. You simply stay on this boat and return to New York. I'll meet him, tell him what must be done and come back on the next ferry."

The aging Confederate calmed a bit and advised, "It must be a clean and thorah job. Roosevelt, Falconer, and the whole nest of cowboys and gunslingahs. A cannon shell might do the job." He smiled as the notion of cannonading Sagamore Hill flew across the screen of his mind.

"Something like that, Uncle; and soon. I'm going to discuss it with Maguffin. He's said to have wiped out several Filipino villages in the insurrection last year, until he was cashiered. He knows his work." It was Pepper's turn to grin as he considered the fantasy of a professional killer turned loose on the ancient enemies of his kind.

A whistle announced the arrival of the boat at its southern terminus, and the few passengers aboard began to gather at the ferry slip end of the vessel. Some were within earshot of the two conspirators.

"It will be a grand party. We're going to throw it tonight. I know you'll love it." Pepper rose to leave.

As the Clinton made its return voyage to the tip of Manhattan Island, it passed for the thousandth time, the great statue in the harbor. A half dozen school aged children ran to the portside rail to gaze at the new colossus.

"Does the light stay lit all the time?" asked one.

"No numbskull, only at night," replied a friend.

"It must burn a lot of lamp oil," another observed.

"It's electric, you silly!" replied the omniscient ten year old. The remaining youngest laughed.

Uncle Jack noticed neither the children nor Miss Liberty. His thoughts and dreams were half a century old and a thousand miles away.

CHAPTER TWENTY EIGHT

It was easy to find an empty double seat on the early afternoon trains going out to Long Island. Most passengers came in to the city earlier and didn't return till some hours later. Alex dozed as the cars rattled through Queens and into Nassau County.

Despite the noise, he got some rest and had snatches of dreams. They were about the assault against him earlier in the day. His head still ached from the blow. During the third dream, he saw the two assailants lounging against the monument once again, but not the one who hit him from behind. At the very end of the image, he noted the third fellow wearing a bright blue bandana around his neck, tied in cowboy fashion. Its vividness and its white polka dots struck him.

It fit! The Rough Riders, their insignia, or someone trying to make it look that way.

One of the assailants may have had a direct connection with the Rough Riders. The blue polka dot bandanas were unique to that unit.

Rudy Sudberg met Alex at the station. Slim, as usual, was unable to stop talking throughout the ride. He told him that Gaby Irish, Winterbottom, and a man named Majors had already arrived by an earlier train.

Slim described Majors as "a large fellow, athletic like yourself; Doc, bigger around the shoulders. He's well spoken too, and very interested in Miss Irish. He kept reaching for her hand and touching it. She wasn't that receptive, though. She played coy with him. You know, she'd take his hand and move it away, then smile and divert his attention. I think he's a Yale man. He had a blue ring that looked like Yale, and that tight-mouthed, clipped New England accent you hear with those fellows. It's almost foreign, the way those people talk. You know, not a real New York accent like you or the governor or myself. I mean, even though you and the governor went to Harvard, you sound like real people."

Falconer, half listening to Sudberg, was thinking about the polka dot bandana. Something Slim said struck a chord, and he responded, "You say she was putting him off, moving his hand away from her like she didn't want his attentions, is that right?"

"Yeah, it was as if they had been friendly, and now she didn't want to be close anymore. At least, it came across that way."

"That's very interesting. What was that you said about the blue ring, a Yale man?"

"That's right, Doc, a Yale ring. You know, the pale blue color on the stone, and the funny accent like I said."

"Well, here we are. The governor's expecting you. You know how he hates to be kept waiting."

Gaby and Chuck Majors were already seated in the study sipping Edith Roosevelt's lemonade. Winterbottom was on the grounds with his camera presumably shooting background pictures. The governor paced back and forth discussing his view of the world. "Haiti was another issue. It was clear that the Imperial German High Command wanted to have a piece of Haiti, or all of it, and my job as Assistant Secretary of the Navy was to make sure the Caribbean remains an American lake. I'm sure you understand ah, Falconer, we've been waiting for you. I'm afraid I've been lecturing these good people on my views of world affairs. You recall the Haiti business. The Germans sent a warship to take over before the

Spanish War. But let's get down to the business at hand. Miss Irish insisted we await your arrival before proceeding."

Alex had forgotten for the moment about his wounded appearance. Both Roosevelt and Gaby Irish appeared shocked at the bandage and his wound.

"My God, Falconer, what happened to you? You look like one of my Cuban casualties. I've seen men with smaller wounds in hospitals," Roosevelt shouted, and drifted, as he did when excited, into a high-pitched voice.

Gaby, her mouth agape, came over to Falconer and said, "Have you been hurt, Alex? What happened? Oh, my God. It's terrible to see you like this." She appeared frightened. The blood had drained out of her cheeks.

"I'm getting closer to the trail of the gang who cooked up this fraud, and they know it. Three thugs attacked me this morning on Riverside Drive. Fortunately, I was armed, and chased them off. But not before one of them hit me from behind. It feels almost as bad as it is to look at.

"We've got business to transact here, and no time to waste. Whoever is responsible for this won't stop now till they get what they want."

Falconer got right down to brass tacks. "Where did you get the material you gave to Gaby Irish, Mr. Majors?"

"It came in the mail, to Democratic party headquarters addressed to the press representative, that's me. There was no identifying information except a note printed in block letters saying: "WE THOUGHT YOU'D LIKE TO SEE THIS."

"That's all, is that right?"

"Yes, Dr. Falconer," responded Majors. "There was nothing else on the paper, no marks, no signatures, nothing written, nothing to identify it. Just a plain piece of yellow paper you'd get from any child's note book. As soon as I looked at the material, I realized it was dynamite, potentially very destructive to the governor and to the Republican Party. I'm sure that's why it was sent to our headquarters."

"I felt it deserved further investigation. That's why I took it to Miss Irish. Miss Irish and I have a personal relationship," and with this he beamed a proprietary smile at Gaby.

Seeming uncomfortable with his description of their relationship, Gaby gazed down at the floor and, in a most subtle way, moved her head in a vague negative manner. Falconer, at least, thought this was for his edification. Majors went on.

"I wanted to help her. I thought if she checked to see if the story was factual, it would promote her career and keep our party out of it. It should never have appeared to be politically inspired. You can understand that."

"I can, Mr. Majors, and I appreciate your forthrightness. Tell me, did you have any idea where the package came from? I mean, you say it came in the mail, was there a postmark on the envelope?"

"I'm not sure. There was nothing special about it. It came in a large folder, the kind that might be sent by a photographic studio. There was the picture enclosed and the documents. It was wrapped in plain, brown paper. Come to think of it, maybe there was a New York postmark on it. I can't say for sure. I threw it in the trash. That was a few days ago. I'm sure it's been swept up and carried away by now."

Majors seemed to be genuinely searching his recollection to help out. It was belated, thought Falconer, but the man was trying. He was good looking too, Alex noted. No wonder Gaby seemed interested in the fellow, even though he was a Yale man.

"And you say there's nothing else you can remember about it, is that right, Mr. Majors?"

"Nothing at all. It came in the mail. I did as I have said and brought it over to Miss Irish." Majors looked puzzled.

"And nothing since. Is that right?" asked Falconer, staring at Majors, his blond flowing hair and his blue Yale ring.

"No, not a peep, not a note, nothing."

"Do you have any idea why anyone would want to send this particular package to you? Aside from your being in the party, what reason someone would have? Do you think it's politically motivated?"

"You mean, do I think someone in our party might want to destroy Governor Roosevelt's career and ruin the opposition ticket? Sure, he has plenty of enemies at Tammany. I've heard a lot of talk around the Hall about the governor and the problems he's caused them. There's no love lost there for Theodore Roosevelt. I can promise you that." Majors, although serious, wasn't unhappy about that statement. Alex considered that Chuck might be behind it all. No fact or even possibility should be dismissed. Yet this notion could be his own personal thorn. Alex then dismissed this as a product of Major's proprietary air around Gaby Irish.

"Yes, I dare say that's true. I'm sure you'll agree, Governor. You have no friends in Tammany," Falconer responded.

"Nor do I want any. They're the scum of the earth. Tammany is a scar on the body politic of the United States, especially New York. Anything I could do to get rid of them would be a boon to the public, the state and the city." T.R. was on his soap box again.

Politicians seemed intrinsically unable to avoid polemics, even amongst close friends. Alex wondered if the governor talked this way to Edith in the bedroom. "I find it hard to believe that even those louts would involve themselves in something so despicable." The governor's campaign speech was cut off when Mrs. Roosevelt came in and invited everyone to high tea on the veranda.

Chuck had been in shirt sleeves when they met. The detective watched him tap his pipe empty after Edith Roosevelt's announcement, go to the hall clothes tree and place the pipe in his jacket pocket. It was a British woven black and green garment, too heavy to wear in the midday heat even on the shore side of Sagamore Hill.

Tea time at the Roosevelt's was always a scene of pastoral splendor, sipping Darjeeling al fresco in the fresh country air, with the birds singing, the cucumber sandwiches and scones issuing from platters of plenty liberally distributed by the staff, along with heavy fresh country cream and dishes of golden brown honey.

During the repast, Falconer couldn't keep his eyes off Charles Majors' left hand and the blue ring on it. Majors held his fork in that hand while munching a cream and honey laden biscuit. Little wheels began to click in Falconer's mind.

"Mr. Majors, you have an unusual surname. Majors? Majors? Not a common name at all, sir," Alex observed. "I recall that name from my philosophic studies. A John Major it was, I'm sure, a Scotsman. Perhaps one of your ancestors? He wrote Historia Majora Brittaniae, tam Angliae guam Scotiae' if I'm not mistaken...." He nodded omnisciently towards Gaby, the Radcliffe graduate, while rendering the translation.

"Although his book was written in 1521, it still stands strong today. Archibald Constable translated it from the Latin a few years ago, 1891 I believe, a fine objective book. Are you familiar with it, Mr. Majors?" Alex could be insufferable with his pedantry.

"I'm afraid not. I can't claim any relation to the gentleman either. Our family name is Majors with an S at the end. We have no philosophers or historians in our tree, I'm afraid."

"Where are you from, Mr. Majors, if I may ask?"

"We hail from Adams County, Mississippi. Good Democrats, all of us...."

"Adams County, isn't Natchez the county seat?"

"Yes, are you familiar with the town?"

"It's one of my hobbies, attaching cities to the county in which they are located. Often they have Indian names like Natchez. Usually its in reverse: the cities like Columbus, Georgia, in Muskogee County; Fort Sill, Oklahoma, in Comanche County; Springfield, Illinois, Lincoln's home, in Sangamon County, have English names in Indian named counties. So you grew up on the banks of the Mississippi? Didn't some of the early filibusters come from Natchez? I have a vague recollection about that ...."

A vague recollection from Falconer, was akin to only a full page from the Encyclopedia Britannica as compared to a volume. "Filibusters? I'm not sure what you mean. Are you referring to one or two of our senators talking too much in opposition to some Yankee generated bill during Reconstruction?" Majors appeared perplexed.

"No. . . to the adventurers who went South to Mexico, Central America and Cuba. Their idea was to take over these countries by force of arms and plunder their wealth. John Quitman and William Walker were the best known of these rogues."

"Draws a blank with me doctor."

"Curious. May I say that your years at Andover and at New Haven have removed almost all traces of your Southern accent. Just the occasional prolonged vowel remain."

"I suspect that's a compliment, from a Yankee that is. But how did you know I went to Andover?"

"Just an assumption based on your background, collegiate choice, and the fact that four years in New Haven would never have been enough to erase a Mississippi drawl. That is unless your prep school was in New England, northeast Massachusetts, more specifically from the A's in Adams, Majors and Yankee." Falconer's plumage gleamed after this tour de force.

"Simply astounding, Dr. Falconer. I can see that one not only needs to be careful with what one says, but how one says it in your presence."

"I'm afraid Alex can't help but be a showoff, Mr. Majors... I suspect he was born bowing and strutting and displaying whatever attributes he may have had, even then," the Governor observed. It takes one to know one.

Falconer continued his pursuit, "Surnames are something unique to each person, isn't it so, Mr. Majors? For instance, Miss Irish has a name which seems rather simple altogether. It probably has to do with somebody who traveled to Ireland in Cromwell's time and then returning home was given the name of Irish, something like that, pretty simple. Of course, it's also possible that it could be derived from another ethnic root. For instance, the name Iris is a common German name, is it not?"

Majors responded, "I really wouldn't know about that. I don't know much about this whole name business. I'm happy with my name the way it is, and don't spend time thinking about others. It seems to be the kind of intellectual pursuit Republicans enjoy. We Democrats don't have enough time for such games."

"Touché, well struck, let's get on with the business affairs at hand," added Roosevelt. "You've put Falconer in his place. I'd say we've had enough of that for the present. We are now in the business of pursuing criminals and killers. That's the hunt before us, don't you agree, Professor Falconer?" Roosevelt was disposing his forces in the imperious manner to which he was accustomed.

"Certainly, Governor. Mr. Majors and Miss Irish have been very helpful. I greatly appreciate your help, Mr. Majors, coming forward with this information. You can be sure we'll use it to the best advantage. Now, I know that you have to return to the city. There's a 6:30 train. I'm sure Mr. Sudberg will be happy to take you and your party to the station."

Gaby, shocked at Falconer's abrupt dismissal, added, "I do have a deadline for tomorrow's Journal. I thought I'd do a story about the governor and his entourage. My photographer can take some pictures and perhaps Mr. Sudberg could provide information about the Midwest campaign tour on the way back. I could use it, if you agree, Governor, in tomorrow's paper?" Putting on her best face, she looked at Falconer in an injured manner, and arose.

The governor said. "Of course Miss Irish, you may use whatever information Sudberg gives you at your pleasure. We cooperate with the press, even the Democratic press, in every way possible. Please give my best wishes to Mr. Hearst. And tell him we're going to get to the bottom of this matter shortly."

"Can I use, Dr. Falconer, the information that there may have been murders associated with the campaign? It would make an incredible story."

"I'd rather you didn't attach the deaths to anything, right now. They've been announced separately in the press. But at this moment, we won't make any connections precipitously. I'm sure you understand. Even the attack on me, earlier today, has not been reported to the police. We're trying not to alert the other side as to what we know. Press exposure would only help their cause. I'm sure you understand." His expression indicated he was overwhelmed with the pressure of the governor's business and she should comply.

Gaby got the message. Although not pleased with it, she was so distressed by his sanguine appearance, blood seeping through the bandage on his head, that she decided not to press the issue further. Raising her hand so he might grasp it to bid her adieu, she left to summon Winterbottom and get some photos for the story.

CHAPTER TWENTY NINE

After the pictures were taken and the guests had left, T.R. presided at a meeting including Kane, Shaw, Sudberg, and, of course, Falconer.

"Gentlemen, let me fill you in on my inquiries thus far. This turns out to be a far more dangerous business than we imagined at first. We're dealing with more than one man, probably with a well financed organized group. One with many resources."

"Well formed, organized, who the hell are we up against, Alex?" asked the ever cautious Woodbury Kane.

"Let me continue, Woody. I think I have some answers, and a lot of new questions as well."

"The murders of the man, whose body was found on a nearby Long Island railroad track..."

"Cut right in half, as I recall," Kane interjected.

Ignoring the interruption, Falconer went on. "The arson- murder episode in the Manhattan photo studio a few days later, and now the double murder in Trenton two nights ago are all connected."

Roosevelt began polishing his pince-nez exhaling moist breath on first one lens and then the other, while removing imperceptible dust with his blue bandana.

"They have, it seems, access to our plans and even to my own movements. I was attacked by three men early this morning on my regular walk. They were, in effect, lying in wait at Grant's Tomb, where I take my exercise daily. There were three of them and I believe there are at least two more who killed the murder victims. They move about from Long Island, to Manhattan, to New Jersey, or have agents in several places."

"There may well be someone in Washington, D.C., a possible source of information for them."

"You're talking high level people," Albert Shaw observed.

"Indeed I am. I believe the killings were all part of the basic crime. The theft of the governor's picture; to create an incriminating blackmail scheme and then one murder after another to cover up the basic plot. The assault upon me was meant to be the fifth murder. I fear the plotters may be going off the track, overreacting and thereby becoming even more dangerous as they perceive we're on to them. That's why I was targeted. I truly fear the governor may be next," Falconer said.

"I told you, Ted! These handshaking jaunts, mixing with the crowds! The whole regiment couldn't protect you from an assassin in a mob of thousands," Kane warned.

"You've always been afraid of the masses, Woody. It's my duty to meet the people. They can protect me, even without our men," Roosevelt replied.

"They didn't protect Garfield or Lincoln, Colonel," Al Shaw reminded him. "I think Woody's right."

"I'm afraid even Sagamore Hill isn't truly safe gentlemen," Falconer added.

"The picture was stolen from this room, as was this." He produced the gold Commemorative coin and offered it to the governor.

"Smoot stole this when he took the picture. He had it in his pocket when I examined the body. Perhaps you'd like to put it back in its original place."

"Keep the coin as a souvenir of this experience. I want no grisly memento of this episode. I hope to soon put the entire mess behind me. But who is Smoot? Is that the fellow who stole the picture?" T.R. asked.

"I was about to tell you I in fact have used your name with the police department. As I'm sure you know, you still have a good many friends there and they're still loyal. I asked some of them to keep me informed of any unusual inquiries about missing persons, especially adult males over the past couple of weeks. I want to get a line on the body found on the Long Island Railroad. The one I am certain stole your photograph in the first place."

"Fine Alex, anything we can do to get to the bottom of this mess. Certainly you can use my name if you think it will help," T.R. replied.

"Well it has I'm certain. A woman, named Joanne Bednar, came into one of the downtown precinct houses two days ago to report that one Robin Smoot had not returned home and that she suspected foul play. She said he'd been hired by a gentleman, as she put it, to do a job on Long Island. She didn't go further about what the job was except to say that Smoot expected to have enough money from it to last through next winter."

T.R. polished his glasses with his bandana and said, "A bit thin, wouldn't you say? A job on Long Island? It could be any job, a roofing repair, fixing an oven, even repairing one of those new horseless carriages," Roosevelt observed.

"Yes, there are lots of jobs possible but not for a known sneak thief," Alex answered.

"Oh."

"The sergeant who took the report knew Smoot. He was nicknamed 'Robbie the Robber' and had a record dating back to a boy's detention home in New Jersey. A very unsavory character altogether, he told me on the telephone. I didn't have enough time personally to check out Miss Bednar's story, so I asked one of my former students to follow up for me.'

"A trustworthy fellow? This is a very sensitive issue you know," the governor added.

"Stanley Kern was the man who picked up the discrepancies in the Manhattan photography fire I mentioned earlier. He's very bright, perceptive, and follows my methods carefully. I had no hesitancy in trusting him and as it happens, he got a lot of information from the woman."

"Such as?" asked Woody Kane.

"Such as, Smoot described his client physically to the woman. It was, it turns out, a robbery case. Kern is a good interviewer and got her to admit it to him. She didn't want to talk to the police about robbery, but she felt he would be safe. Some swell in Oyster Bay she said. Is that enough corroboration, sir?" Alex looked at the assembled brain trust.

"I don't enjoy being called a swell, but you're right. That was certainly our man. And the description?" Roosevelt asked.

"Not unlike our recent visitor, Mr. Majors. Hasn't he been here before? Didn't I see his name on your secretary's list?" Alex asked.

"Yes, I believe so. And a group of political people who were interested in forming a Democratic McKinley-Roosevelt ticket. But Majors? Do you truly suspect him? And why?"

"I'm not entirely certain as to motive. A Democrat party functionary wouldn't go as far as murder. Blackmail perhaps, but multiple, vicious, pre—meditated murders. I don't think so. Something more. Something very ominous, in my view," Alex added.

"What did this woman tell your friend, Kern?" T.R. asked.

"Specifically, Smoot described a 'fancy Dan' character dressed in what he called expensive English clothes. She even recalled him describing a woolen coat, black and green, very much like the one Majors wore here today."

"I didn't notice," admitted T.R.

"I do that sort of thing for a living, Governor. I note details such as his habit of cutting his food with his right hand and eating with the fork in his left. That suggests spending some time in England or on the continent. Perhaps we'll be pressed to learn more about that as well as other things as we proceed with the investigation."

"In any event, Miss Bednar said Smoot had visions of lots of money and she pointed out that well paying jobs come along attached to big risks. She warned him and he said she was his insurance. That's when he described the man, big, blond, fancy dresser, and an unusual accent, foreign. Sudberg noticed his accent too, he told me it sounded foreign'," Alex reported.

"What was all this business about names, origins? It went over my head," T.R. asked.

"Just an attempt, abortive I fear, to extract something germane about his origins and something which I haven't as yet determined, the motive. What is this murder and mayhem supposed to bring about? I'm not certain." Alex had an unusual, for him, perplexed look.

"The thing about Filibusters?" Roosevelt ventured.

"Aha, I'm glad you picked up on that. A Yale man and Andover too, would certainly know about Filibusters from his state. That was too coy a response to suit me," Alex said.

"Why would Filibusters try to eliminate Theodore Roosevelt from the national ticket?" T.R. wondered aloud.

"The obvious answer is to put in their own man," Alex replied.

"Why worry about their own man as Vice-President? Why not replace the President directly?"

"Maybe that's the next move. It's far easier to replace your man on the bottom of the ticket than on top, isn't it?"

"Of course," Roosevelt answered. "I was extremely reluctant to take the spot myself. But why all of this machination? Eliminate a Vice-President, then a President? Why and why Filibusters?"

"That's what we need to consider, why indeed? Let's wait and see as we go along with our discussions."

"The inquiries to the War Department has born some fruit, as well," the governor announced.

"We've obtained considerable information concerning the men who signed the affidavits. First, Renfield, the chap who fancied himself my double. As far as the War Department is concerned, he's missing entirely. His last address before the army was in Kansas City. Since his discharge in 98, there's been no contact. He may be difficult to round up."

Roosevelt, reading from a paper prepared by Shaw, went on. "The only ones we can locate for certain are Maguffin and Lieder. Sergeant Maguffin was dishonorably discharged from the Army of Occupation in the Philippines. They caught him in open brutality against Filipino citizens. As I remember, he was a rough and tough one, isn't that right, Woody?"

Woodbury Kane nodded and laconically added, "Maguffin was a good soldier, but mean. We'd have had the same kind of trouble with him in Cuba if we'd have stayed there in occupation. I wasn't surprised to learn about him roughing people up. He's big, nasty, cunning, but not terribly smart. Probably got what he deserved in the Philippines."

Roosevelt went on to say that both Maguffin and Lieder had been located at the same address. Lieder, discharged after the 1898 hostilities, had gone back home to Staten Island. Maguffin, after his dishonorable discharge, had informed the authorities that was his destination as well.

Shaw added, "Obviously there's a relationship between Maguffin and Lieder, being in the same town can't be a coincidence. That relationship must be looked into. Especially since they both signed the same damning document."

Roosevelt completed the roll call. "The Private Small, who signed the document, the last one on the list, originally came from Trenton, New Jersey. He, too, left in 98, no current address."

Shaw interrupted again, "Trenton is interesting. Dr. and Mrs. Clifton were killed there. Kane, what do you recall about Small?"

Kane sat back in his chair. Sucking on a pipe, he looked at the ceiling. "Small? Small, as I remember, wasn't. I recall thinking, a man named Small who's large. There isn't much else about him. I'd recognize him if I saw him, but that's about it. Sorry I can't be of more help. I'll think about it."

Falconer pleased with the information offered, "A good day's work, gentlemen. We have, in fact, located two of the four men who signed the documents. We have one address for both, making it easy to track them down. Insofar as Renfield is concerned, Yellow Fever can affect the brain. He may be a tool of the perpetrators or even be held by them in some way."

Alex loved nothing more than pontificating before a receptive audience. He filled his chest unconsciously as do some of the great apes when demonstrating their ascendancy over their peers.

"I wouldn't be surprised to find him in Staten Island, too. My inclination at this point is to get out there, interview Maguffin and Lieder and see where that trail leads us. We're on to something now. Things are narrowing down. Two of the four are in one spot. Renfield may not even be alive. I have a few ideas, however. First, I may want to take advantage of your contacts in Washington again, Governor." Falconer, flushed with excitement, was again in a fever pitch of thinking, as while talking to Majors earlier.

Roosevelt said, "Every resource of the administration will be lent to this investigation. Anything I can do will be done. Just ask it."

As a second line of inquiry, Falconer suggested a wire be sent to Robert Pinkerton in Chicago. "I want to make inquiries of his detective agency to find out everything they have about Mr. Charles Majors. There may be something there in addition to checking further in War Department archives!"

"The Pinkertons?" asked Roosevelt. "I fail to see why they would know anything about Majors. What connection does he have with train robbers?"

"The specific information I want is related to their efforts before and during the Civil War. Even though the United States has no national police apparatus, as you all know, Alan Pinkerton's agency served in that capacity to protect the president and to run an espionage system throughout the South during the War of the Rebellion. In this case, they still have a lot of information in their files about agents, spy rings, and so on. If you asked them to tell us about Majors, giving his description, his background, and the information we now have about him, I expect an interesting response."

Kane asked the obvious question. "The Pinkertons know something about Majors? I mean, just because he is a Yale man doesn't mean he's a spy. Besides, if he were a spy, what purpose would it serve? They can't really think hurting Roosevelt will prevent McKinley's re-election. Even if T.R.'s out, another candidate will take his place on the ticket. Interfering with his career would be of no value to them. It doesn't make any sense at all."

"You might be right," said Falconer. "Except for the most obvious reason. The man who is elected to the vice presidency has immediate accession to the top if the president dies. Or perhaps they anticipate that the vice president under McKinley in 1900 will become president in 1904 and again in 1908. These are crucial years - years in which we will be confirmed as a true major power in the world. The Spanish War has given us a global empire. The Philippines, Guam, Cuba, Puerto Rico, all at one stroke. Many of our fellow citizens, especially Southern Democrats, don't want colonies or anything like them. Some, like the old time Filibusters, would prefer we cut these dominions loose. Possibly, they have plans of their own. A Caribbean or Pacific Confederacy dances before their eyes. That's what I have in mind."

Roosevelt agreed. "Of course, the motive for the blackmail, the reason to discredit me. The intent of it all makes sense. What's at stake is more than a vice presidency or a political career. It's the presidency, the succession! You're right, Alex!"

Falconer added, "Most of my conclusions are speculations at this point. But they stem from a number of facts, and ideas which I've put together. If these things are true, we have no time to waste and an extremely dangerous enemy to overcome. I'll draw up a telegram to Pinkerton and send it tonight. I suggest the other inquiries be made as rapidly as possible. I'd like Lieder's specific address from the War Department. We'll need to check on the availability of transportation in Staten Island and the possibility of armed assistance should trouble arise. I'm afraid it might." Roosevelt smiled,

"Armed assistance, Dr. Falconer? You have right here at Sagamore Hill the nucleus of the best military force the United States has ever seen. The Rough Riders were the most skilled combat outfit this country has ever produced. Myself, Kane, Shaw, and Bell were at the core of it. It goes without saying that Masterson can help. Even our friend,

Sudsberg, can account for himself in a scrape." The colonel's face was flushed with the excitement of potential conflict.

"I'd rather not take this outside of this room. If you're right, we will need experts at soldiering and no better cadre could be found than here. If you're wrong, we could be terribly embarrassed by bringing in the police or even the Pinkertons. We must be careful about how to proceed in this matter, you can see that." When Roosevelt asked you to see, he was giving a command.

"I am the governor of this state, and Staten Island is in it. Therefore, I hereby appoint myself as head of the Special New York Volunteer State Militia, and appoint you, Alex, as one of my adjutants. These other gentlemen are also appointed to the force. If your suspicions prove out and you need armed assistance, you can count on us."

Roosevelt's eyes gleamed with pleasure. He looked like a man about to enter combat, expecting victory. He had the situation well in hand, in command just as on the day he decided to charge San Juan Hill, before the orders came from General Headquarters.

"I couldn't agree more, Governor. This group will be more than sufficient. I doubt if the other side have more than four or five men. If they're the same gang who attacked me and turned tail when I fired my pistol, we won't need more than this group to handle them. Let's go into the details of my plan. The Staten Island locale could turn out to be a hornet's nest." Falconer once more with a chance to pontificate was in his glory.

They spent the rest of the afternoon discussing their alternatives. By then, Masterson and Bell had returned and Sudberg filled the group in on his talk with the photographer. "The old man, you know the old photographer, with bizarre clothing, was outside the house playing with his camera and I was sitting there eating some broiled chicken and some rye bread under a tree. He came over to me and said, 'Can I take your picture young fellow?' I asked him why me and I said, 'I'm not one of the big time politicians around here, and I wasn't with the Rough Riders either. Are you sure you want me?'

"He said, 'I think you're a good photographic subject young man, I can't recall ever seeing a man eat so much, so fast, even after a full day's work on the range, punchin' cows'."

"I asked him if he was a cowboy in the past and then I asked him his name. He said that it was Winterbottom and that he came from the state of Maine and told me that he was a scout for Custer and he had been a sailor on whaling ships around the world and he said to me, 'I never saw a mechanic with a knife and fork as good as you anywhere.' I guess I was flattered and I asked why do you want my picture anyway? He said he wanted to have a picture of me eating the melon that was lying at my feet. Mrs. Klein had given me a watermelon and I was going to cut it in quarters and eat it after I had finished the chicken and bread. He said, If you plan to eat that melon now I'd like to take your picture.' And I told him I did and I started to cut it in quarters. He said, 'Lay onto it son and I'll make you immortal.' And he started to take pictures. I began eating the stuff and I asked him, 'Did you see the picture of the Governor in Cuba with that tart?' And while he was taking the pictures he said to me that he sure did and he said, 'You can do anything with a picture if you know how son.' That's what he said and he said, 'That was a pretty good fake, but the lighting on the black woman was wrong.' He said the sun was at the wrong angle, that is he said he looked at the picture of the Governor that was one angle of the sun, but the woman had a different angle altogether and that was a fake picture. He said, 'I could tell as soon as Gaby showed it to me. I let the Chief know too. It's as queer as a three dollar bill.' That's what he said."

"After that I said, 'So Hearst knows somebody faked the picture? What's he gonna do with it.' I thought you ought to know about this. Winterbottom said that it didn't matter if the picture was a fake or not, that he would have rather had a story about Theodore Roosevelt being involved in his tent and all that stuff, but a story about faking a picture of T.R. was almost as good as the first one."

"I asked him if he was real sure about the picture being bogus and he said to me, 'I know as much about picture takin' as you do about eatin'.'"

"And I asked him why he thought maybe somebody would want to take a picture like that. Why go to all that trouble, and he said, 'Politicians will do anything to get power. They want T.R. out and somebody else in. I don't know who or exactly why, but it has to do with power, you can bet your boots on that'."

"I thought I'd tell you guys about this as soon as they left. Hearst knows that the picture is a fake, he's not going to print it except maybe he'll print it and say it's a fake and then raise the issue as to why. It might be good for us, I don't know, that's why I brought the information in to tell you."

Kane thought about it and said, "Nothing that even implies a smear is good for us, Rudy. We'd rather not have any of it and I think the next move is to tell Hearst we don't want that picture published even under these circumstances and that we'll sue for that too. That might keep him quiet."

It was getting late when Mrs. Roosevelt interrupted.

"Gentlemen, it's almost supper time. I'm sure you'd all like to freshen up before dining. Our boys have been fishing on the Sound, and they've landed a big catch. We'll have home fried potatoes, garden fresh vegetables and Mrs. Klein's special lemon Bavarian cream for dessert, which I'm sure you'll enjoy." Edith Roosevelt, an ideal future first lady, enjoyed her role as hostess. She regarded the men, in their late thirties and early forties, as more boys playing at cowboys and Indians. They had to be reminded by mother it was time to go home and wash up for supper.

All sat on the porch digesting their supper before the evening poker game. Falconer relaxed in a rocking chair next to Roosevelt. Masterson and Bell further down the veranda, fooled with guitars and sang cowboy songs for the Roosevelt boys, at the feet of their western heroes.

"Alex, I'm amazed by your problem solving abilities and how you've worked this out, this far. No one who ever worked for me could have done better," T.R. announced in a voice for the entire assemblage to hear.

"Well, sir, I learned a lot about problem solving in medical school. Solutions require a fresh perspective and no preconceived notions. Conundrums usually have simple answers. In fact, it's all basic stuff if you know enough. The key is information. Observe everything that goes on around you and consider all in its entirety." It was a line from a lecture Falconer gave at Columbia College.

"What I'm trying to say is that you must think of things in three dimensions, just as you would in life. A problem shouldn't be two dimensional like a picture. It should have depth as well as width and length. That's why I like to be at the scene of a crime, to get a feeling for the place. It was important for me to be in your trophy room, crawl on the floor and touch the rug, touch the walls and check the doors. I want to get a feeling for the ambience of the room. That's why I had to personally examine all of the bodies too. I've been immersing myself in this case. Now I believe I have a feeling for it. I think we're on the right trail." His confident demeanor suggested he was certain he was right, not just thoughtful.

"The amazing thing for me is how you take such disparate input and create a new image," the governor observed.

Falconer went on. "The notion of the simplest solution being the most obvious is the key to my thinking. It's similar to a rule I learned in medical college. A professor, teaching us how to make a diagnosis, said to use the Bear Theorem. I asked who was Bear. He said 'it was a forest animal. Why, he said, do bears seek out beehives in the woods, even though they get stung? Why, I asked. Because that's where the honey is. The same thing is true in solving any problem. The most obvious answer is probably the correct one. We shouldn't fear being obvious. When we have enough facts, solutions are obvious. It's quite simple really, isn't it?" Falconer's smile of certitude beamed across the dark porch like a beacon in a stormy night.

Roosevelt was about to reply when a black object came hurtling through the air. It was a bomb, the kind anarchists had been throwing at Russian royalty for twenty years. A terrifying device whose sputtering fuse was about to expire.

Falconer, the bomb flying toward the spot where he and Roosevelt sat, reacted immediately. He snatched T.R.'s walking stick with his right hand and with one sweeping motion, swung at the missile in mid flight. The ex-big leaguer struck the thing with the makeshift ball bat, just as a slugger would hit a hanging curve ball. The heroic swing of the erstwhile New York Giant sent the lethal ball hurtling away from the porch in a line drive. It exploded forty yards away with a tremendous roar and blinding, orange flash.

Everyone on the porch was covered with soot. The concussion knocked the governor off his chair. Falconer, in his standing position, staggered backwards from the force of the explosion. The boys and the guitarists, were dazed. It was a prodigious bomb, clearly meant to destroy the vice presidential candidate, his chief investigator, the Rough Riders, and the family, all in one blow.

A dazed Falconer mumbled, "We can all see they mean business. There's no more time to waste." Pursuit through the darkness at Sagamore Hill by the would-be victims turned out to be fruitless. The assailant was gone but the battle had been joined in earnest. The other side had been given too many opportunities to strike first. It was time for the Rough Riders to hit back.

To: Alan Pinkerton

Vice-President

Pinkerton Detective Agency

Chicago, Illinois

From: Alexander Falconer

c/o The Office of the Governor State of New York

Executive Offices, New York City

INTERESTED IN ALL INFORMATION AVAILABLE ON CHARLES MAJORS CURRENTLY EMPLOYED PUBLICIST DEMOCRATIC NATIONAL COMMITTEE NEW YORK STOP NEED TO KNOW HISTORY EDUCATION OTHER BACKGROUND STOP CHECK FAMILY HISTORY IN NATCHEZ MISSISSIPPI RELATIVES IN REBEL ARMY POSSIBLE CRIMINAL CONVICTIONS IN FAMILY STOP ALL MATERIAL URGENTLY REQUIRED USE ALL MANPOWER NEEDED COST NOTWITHSTANDING STOP SUSPECT HIM TO BE INVOLVED IN POLITICAL FOUL PLAY FALSE REPORTS FORGED DOCUMENTS AND PICTURES STOP SPEED IS OF THE ESSENCE END OF MESSAGE

CHAPTER THIRTY

Gaby's story announcing the vice-presidential candidate's campaign plans got ink on page eight. It wasn't the kind of piece to make her a household name. That one was still unwritten. Her yearning to write it was like a sexual desire which pleaded for fulfillment.

Apropos of sex, she was also perplexed about Alex Falconer's sudden change in attitude. He'd been so warm and giving, so much in contact when they had lunch at Sherry's. But at Sagamore Hill, he was distant and cold. He seemed to push her toward Chuck Majors, almost as if he wanted nothing to do with her. Maybe it was that blow to his head. Perhaps it affected his personality, made him irritable and cranky. Whatever the reason, she was disappointed but determined things would change.

The letter which came in the morning mail told the ambitious journalist that here was her big chance. This story could solidify her career and also reinstate close contact with Falconer. Gaby didn't even call Chuck Majors, even though the letter referred to him specifically. It was more important to get a hold of Alex. She rang him immediately.

"Alex, I'm so glad I caught you in. I've just received a letter having to do with the Roosevelt case. I called you immediately." Her voice betrayed not only excitement about the story but the need to be in touch with him again.

"A letter about the case," he tried to say in a matter-of- fact way, not being totally able to mask his pleasure. "Please read it to me exactly as it's written! It won't interfere with your journalistic rules if it has to do with a murder, I assure you."

"I want to read it to you. It bothers me, but it may be the break we're looking for. You, to straighten things out, and me, to finally get my big story. If you like, I can bring it over. But I thought you should hear it now." Her excitement sang through the telephone wires.

"The letter is as follows: "Dear Miss Irish: I am writing to you because I know a woman can understand me better than a man. I know Mr. Majors was the one who my husband's good for nothing friends sent the papers to in the first place. I know he turned it over to you. Thomas, he's my husband, he's been very confused lately and gotten in with a pack of troublemakers who were with him in the Army."

"These men are bad actors and I know they'll get Tom in deeper. One of them comes home this morning with a gunshot hole in his side. They patched it up with bandages. He was in a lot of pain. They didn't even take him to a doctor. They said they'd take care of it themselves and asked me to change the bandages. I don't know nothing about this kind of thing. It looks ugly. I'm afraid. They've been sitting around all day smoking cigars, drinking whiskey and grumbling about how they are going to get that damned New York swell, Governor Roosevelt, and his Harvard fancy pants chum too. That's exactly what they said."

"I'm really scared. I know that a woman like you can help me to protect my husband. I don't want him hurt no more. He's a sick man. He's mixed up, and someone's gotta help him."

"Please. The loafers plan to be away tomorrow night. I know you'll get this letter in the morning. I don't know when they'll be gone again. If you and Mr. Majors come here, you can get Thomas to leave this place with you while his so called friends are gone. I'll help too. It's only a short ferry trip from downtown where the Journal building is."

"We're at Emerson Hill on Staten Island. Please come alone with Mr. Majors. My husband would be scared of too many strangers."

"If you catch the 9:00 o'clock night ferry and catch the Richmond Road trolley, I'll meet you at the Emerson Hill gate at 10:00. I'll wear a polka dot dress."

"Please be there. You won't be sorry for it. Sincerely, It's signed, 'Mrs. Thomas Renfield'."

"What do you make of it, Alex? Would it be safe for Chuck and I to go there tonight? Don't you think it might be better if you came along, or if we called the police? I'd rather not involve the law. It might scare her off if we arrived there with officers. Maybe if just you came along with us?" The usually self-assured journalist betrayed anxiety, as well as excitement over the phone.

"Tell me everything you can about the letter. Does it look like a woman's handwriting?" Falconer, at a distance, felt the trained eyes of a reporter might help.

"Yes, certainly a woman's hand. It's on pink paper, such as a woman might have for correspondence. There's nothing special about it nor the envelope," Gaby reported.

"The postmark, markings on the envelope, stamps, return address; tell me anything you can about what you see," Alex insisted.

"It's postmarked Stapleton," and she spelled it out. "There's nothing else. Stapleton, New York."

"That will be near Emerson Hill itself," Alex added. "It's the spot where Ralph Waldo Emerson lived toward the end of his life. I know the place. That part is easily verifiable. As for the rest, I'm not sure."

"Discuss my joining you with Majors. If he agrees, we can meet later today and talk over our plans. I'll call you this afternoon at the Journal. Then we'll decide on specifics," Falconer concluded.

Gaby was physically tingling with excitement, from head to toe.

"Alex, it's frightening but, of course, I want to help. I'll call Charles. I'm so glad you think I can help. I do want to work with you. Isn't it a stroke of luck that Mrs. Renfield wrote to me?" she said ingenuously, or so it seemed to Falconer, from the other end of the telephone.

"Yes, it would seem to be a stroke of luck, but remember, we're dealing with dangerous and clever people. Everything may not be what it seems on the surface. Keep that in mind. I'll talk to you later," the criminal expert intoned.

"Danger? Do you think there's danger of someone else being killed? I mean, do you think they'd involve me and Charles as well? Well, Alex, you know far more about these things than I ever hope to." She was actually sexually excited by the titillation of the situation and the opportunity to be working with Falconer. At the same time, she was scared to death.

Falconer rechecked his Smith and Wesson to make sure it was loaded. He took along six extra bullets which he placed in his left-hand coat pocket as "insurance." He then made his way downtown to the offices of the Governor of the state of New York.

Roosevelt and his entourage had moved to the city that morning. T.R. wished to establish a central headquarters to control the events which he believed would follow in rapid succession as they unraveled the blackmail scheme.

As Alex entered the gubernatorial suite, the young chief executive vigorously waved a telegram at him. "Falconer," he said, with even more energy than usual, "the wire from Pinkerton has arrived. It's incredible!"

"Good, Governor, I do want to hear about it."

Falconer's lack of enthusiasm implied he knew the message would confirm his deductions. He had more important things to discuss.

"First let me inform you, sir, that I've had a rather important telephone call from Miss Irish, of the Journal. She's received a letter from someone claiming to be Mrs. Thomas Renfield." He then went on to describe the contents of the letter and what he thought was a further plot against them.

"We've got to plan carefully to deal with this fellow. He's clever and well informed. We've been lucky with the coroner's findings and the coin thus far, but careful planning and thoughtful preparation make their own luck." The physician detective then asked, "What's in the telegram? I assume it's from Pinkerton himself and concerns our man."

"Indeed it does, Falconer. You were right. I had great respect for your abilities before, but his takes the cake!"

"Robert Pinkerton telephoned me to confirm your wire was genuine. He was happy to cooperate and get us this information. Here's the text of the wire. Read it for yourself." He handed the transcript to Falconer.

It read as follows: **MAN YOU DESCRIBE KNOWN TO US STOP FORMERLY POSED AS BRITISH JOURNALIST IN CUBA, MANILA AND CENTRAL AMERICA FATHER WAS NOTORIOUS FILIBUSTER STOP EDUCATED AT YALE AND OXFORD AND KNOWN TO SPECIALIZE IN POLITICAL AGITATION STOP WE BELIEVE HIM TO BE EXTREMELY DANGEROUS AND PROBABLY RESPONSIBLE FOR SEVERAL DEATHS IN CENTRAL AMERICA STOP DETAILS TO FOLLOW BY COURIER END**

"How the devil did you know this fellow was a political agitator? It's beyond me. I had no clue." Roosevelt's speech erupted in an impatient geyser of surprise.

"Well, Colonel, I had several. I take all the clues and examine every bit of information with extreme care. Real detection means looking at any possible alternative and examining details one by one. With enough information, you can solve any problem. The secret is to keep an open mind and consider even small things. For instance, the drop or two of discoloration on the carpet in your study might have been blood or claret or something entirely different. The only way to know was with examination in a laboratory. It proved to be human blood."

"How in the world do you know that?" asked T.R.

"I read the scientific journals. Just as you study and review histories, newspaper articles and the like about political figures for your many books and articles, I review journals from around the world. A serologist named Paul Ulenhuth described his technique in a German periodical this year. I asked a friend at the College of Physicians and

Surgeons to follow the sample from your carpet. It is human!" he trumpeted.

"The problem was where did it come from? The corpse from the railroad accident had a small cut on the left hand. It was the kind of thing that might come from the edge of a picture. Not much, but an essential part of my method. Details first, then letting my intuitive powers take hold."

Roosevelt looked quizzically at the detective physician and said, "Intuition? that's the realm of women. It smacks of magic and voodoo."

"On the contrary, it's actually due to the incredible powers of our mind. Modern science tells us there are more than fifteen billion cells in the human brain. Each capable of connecting with the other in an infinite number of permutations. We only scratch the surface with ordinary thinking. Some people feel that the brain uses only ten percent of its capacity at the very most. A genius uses only twelve or fifteen percent. I believe intuition is the exercise of those extra percentages working unconsciously, beneath the surface of individual awareness. It gives us extra power, brain power, if you will. That's what I call intuition." Falconer looked increasingly pleased, truly delighted with himself. He was reverting to the pedagogue, as when lecturing to his medical students. Only this time, the audience consisted of one man, a potential president of the United States.

Roosevelt spurred him on. "But specifically, how did you determine that this man was a political adventurer, a Filibuster? How did you even know that he was a southerner?" His face was red with exasperation.

"Let me tell you some of the things that entered into my considerations. First of all, as I drove out to Sagamore Hill to meet Gaby and Majors, I was speaking to Sudberg, a bright fellow by the way, who puts things together. He doesn't always understand why he has them together, but he's clever enough. He told me he'd been speaking with Majors when he drove him to your home earlier. He said something about his Yale accent. He described it as almost a foreign accent. Well, we've all had our feelings about Yalies. Those fellows from New Haven do have something about them, an air, something uncomfortably different than men from Cambridge. But we can scarcely call it a foreign accent. Sudberg's ear detected an accent that the others hadn't noted. I, myself, had not met Majors before, but when I did, I had that little clue in the back of my mind." Falconer's hands moved in the air, creating little boxes apparently encompassing each idea with invisible geometric containers.

"Another thing had been rumbling around back there. Things seemed to happen after each contact with Gaby Irish. If you recall, during our interview with her, you told of Dr. Clifton examining Renfield in Cuba. Then, the doctor and his wife were killed. It happened that very night, as a matter of fact. Somehow the killer must have known of your conversation. He probably hadn't initially been told by Renfield about visiting the physician. He had to silence the doctor, and do it immediately."

Falconer's pupils were dilated as if he'd injected a large dose of cocaine into his veins. Unlike his fictitious British colleague, Holmes, the stimulant was natural. It poured forth from his brain in response to the intellectual challenge of the hunt.

"Another thing, the killings weren't all done in the same way. The deaths of the photographer and petty thief who stole the picture were much more clean-cut, closer to real accidents, and required great skill to detect. The murders of Dr. and Mrs. Clifton were less professional, almost sloppy. It occurred to me that those deaths were ordered by someone not in Trenton. Someone who sent another party to do the crime."

"The attack on me was something else. I had, only the previous day, told Miss Irish about my dawn exercise, that is, my walk along Riverside Drive. I told her when and where I walked daily. The very next morning, I was accosted by the three thugs. That was another fact that rattled around somewhere. I didn't want to give credence to the possibility that the reporter herself was in with the criminals. It just didn't ring true with my intuition. But there was some connection."

"Then it became clear. Gaby was in regular contact with Majors. He was the source of her story in the first place. She would lean on him and ask for advice. She was, and is, an aspiring journalist looking for every angle she can find. It would be logical for her to talk with Majors."

He went on almost without taking a breath. "Then, what is the source of the filibuster connection? There must be motivation for every form of human behavior. Why was this plot mounted, these crimes committed? I wasn't happy with explanations about slum lords or rival politicians. It isn't the sort of thing sane men, even greedy ones, in our society do. It's not part of our nature. It hasn't happened before in our history. That word stuck in my mind, 'history'."

Falconer was literally thinking aloud for the benefit of his gubernatorial audience of one.

"I'm something of a history fanatic like yourself, you know. I catalogued American history to consider if there were episodes when ambitious or greedy men had set ruthless schemes in motion. The Aaron Burr business when he was accused of conniving to set up an independent nation in the Louisiana Purchase territories. A vice-president of the United States involved in such madness!"

"I agree, Alex, there have been several absurd plots to set up separate nation states on this continent." Roosevelt, the author of several scholarly historic books himself, mused. "The Republics of Texas and California were formed with some considerable plotting, scheming and bloodshed as well," the governor added.

"I thought of those, too, sir. And the schemes of the Confederates to form their own slave empires in Central America. I'm certain Lincoln's assassination was connected to those people as well." Falconer was tracing boxes in the air again.

"That's when the ideas merged." Two ephemeral boxes were interlocked as he drove home his point.

"The Filibusters like John Quitman, once governor of Mexico City during the American military occupation after the Mexican War, and William Walker who made himself president of Nicaragua just before the Civil War. There were others, one of Quitman's young lieutenants was a man named Light Horse Harry Majors from Mississippi. It all started to come together." His hands now traced concentric circles with the right index finger pointing to a phantom bull's eye in the middle.

Roosevelt nodded in agreement and understanding. "You're right, Alex!" Roosevelt pounded his desk.

"To be even more certain," the punctilious professor continued, "I called a friend at the Washington Star. Majors was a reporter for them assigned to the Senate and to Vice-President Hobart. My contact said Majors took an inordinate interest in the vice-president and literally followed him about, until his so-called heart attack. I wish I had been there to examine him. Did someone or some group expect him to go the other way?"

"Of course! Hobart cast the deciding vote in the Senate against incorporating the Spanish territories into the United States. You think he double crossed these plotters?" Roosevelt wondered.

"His sudden death would suggest that. If those tropical islands were independent, wouldn't that be a tasty dish to set before some would be king?"

"Remarkable," interjected Falconer's newly formed acolyte who was also governor of the nation's most populous state.

"Yes, that and, of course the final clue." Alex went on. "After we had our conversation in your study, Majors took his pipe, went to the hall coat rack and placed it in his jacket pocket. It was a green and black British made woolen suit coat. When I examined the photographer Harley at the morgue, I scraped material from under his fingernails. The Bednar woman spoke of English cut clothing. Microscopic examination revealed green and black woolen threads under the nails of three fingers of his right hand. He had clawed at his assailant as he died and managed to scrape off some bits of material from his killer's clothing. Green and black wool fell into place in my thinking."

"That's when I started to play the name game, that is, the surnames. I had decided by then that I should follow the Bear Theorem."

Roosevelt smiled, a broad toothy grin. "I remember that lecture, professor. That's where the honey is."

"Exactly, after the meal it all made sense. That's when I asked you to contact the Pinkertons. I knew if this man were indeed a new generation of Filibusters in an operation of this magnitude, that agency would probably know of him, and his family. If we described him and what we knew of him, they might give us much more."

"I played the name games to get a reaction from him, but only succeeded in getting a small response. I believe he suspects I'm on to him however. We may have pushed him to the point of desperation. The bomb last night! The letter Gaby Irish received is surely his creation."

Falconer went on as if giving a dissertation on the anatomy of a frog to a bright student, rather than conferring with the chief executive of the nation's richest state.

"I'm not sure what he's got up his sleeve, but it's some kind of trap, I'm certain of that. We must act as if we're falling into his hands. You'll agree that it's always good to have the element of surprise on your side and let the other party think they have everything under control."

Roosevelt listened with astonishment and satisfaction. Astonished at the range of Falconer's mind; satisfied that he had picked exactly the right man for the job. "Crackerjack thinking, Alex! First rate! I agree about surprise, but why not just take the man into custody? As the chief executive officer of this state, I can put him under arrest, or surround that place on Emerson Hill with a hundred police. I can activate the National Guard, if necessary, and take them all in hand. Action is what's called for now."

"I agree, Governor. Action is called for. But we need proof of Major's crimes. We don't have enough hard evidence. We've got to get him to tip his hand and do something overt in front of witnesses. Everything so far is supposition, based on my observations. In a court of law, a clever lawyer could point out to a jury that it's mainly speculation, deduction and circumstantial evidence. We must catch the fellow red-handed." Roosevelt, who studied at Columbia Law School, nodded in agreement as Alex continued.

"I'm sure Gaby Irish isn't directly involved. There's our witness. If she and I go along with Majors to where Renfield allegedly is held, the man will make his move. Then both of us can be witnesses. You are our ace in the hole. If we get into trouble and he tries to do something to us, you'll be there with your men. As our reserve, you'll still have an opportunity to come in and personally place him under arrest at the right moment."

Falconer calculated that Roosevelt's well known ego and political astuteness would opt for a personal arrest of a multiple murderer, two months before a national election.

"I hope to stall him until he becomes confident, and starts to brag and swagger and tell us how clever he is. Then we'll be able to stop him once and for all."

Roosevelt looked pensive, "You're probably right, but I don't like the smell of it. You and Miss Irish could be sacrificial lambs. We'll be outside safe. I'm not cut out to sit around safely while someone else takes risks. Let's consider every possibility, leave no stone unturned. We must be certain of where we are, what we're doing and how to do it. This fellow's a killer. He's demonstrated that. The Pinkertons have confirmed it. I won't give him an opportunity to injure you or the young lady."

"We'll get a map of the area on Emerson Hill where the meeting is to take place. I'll call the city assessor's office. We can check the topography of the area as well. It's a hill, probably one or two houses. We'll lay our plans as to how to have our reserve, as you put it, approach them exactly; where and when to dispose our forces; that's your area of expertise. Then we'll decide on what kind of signals to arrange. We must be certain to arrive before the fellow does any damage."

Warming to the task, T.R. thought aloud as he moved toward the telephone to call the proper bureaucratic office. "I think my force should take an alternate route. I wouldn't be surprised if the man has the ferry watched. You'll take the 9:00 p.m. boat, of course, but if we follow you, he'd know it. We could take an earlier one, but that might be risky, too. I would anticipate that if I were he."

"But he likely isn't familiar with other routes to Staten Island. I can take the Weehawken ferry, travel down to Bayonne, and then cross at the ferry point there. In effect, we'd flank the fellow. We'll arrive at Emerson Hill a short time after you get there, and go up from the gatepost described in the note. After infiltrating the gates and the hill, we'll gradually move up to the house itself. You give us a signal when ready,

and we can pounce on him and lock him up. How does that sound?"
Roosevelt smiled with all of his dental plentitude.

"It sounds as if it were a good thing the Spanish surrendered when
they did. Otherwise, you'd have led the Rough Riders to Madrid itself and
invested the city." Roosevelt turned red as a beet. The man hit the mark.
T.R. would have enjoyed further military adventure even more than
becoming Governor of New York State.

"It's agreed, then. I'll gather my men together. I can count on Bell
and Shaw. Masterson's still in town. Sudberg's right here with my old
regimental captain, Woody Kane. With the exception of Slim, they're all
dead shots. We'll reconstitute the Rough Riders one more time." He
preened his moustache with his forefinger, and actually smacked his lips as
if he could savor the taste of forthcoming battle. He loved it.

CHAPTER THIRTY ONE

As Falconer expected, Majors acted surprised at the notion that Renfield's wife wanted to meet with Gaby Irish and himself. His objections to Falconer coming along were almost too brief.

"Perhaps she'll be scared off if she sees you along with us, old chap. I mean, she did write that she only wanted to meet the two of us, didn't she?"

"You're right Majors. I can wait at the ferry slip," Alex offered.

"On the other hand, Gaby can allay her fears when we arrive. You know; the woman's touch. I suppose it'll be all right. If you think it best, we'll do as you say. You're the expert after all. I'll help as best I can." Falconer was now sure he heard a Mississippi accent hidden amidst the tight jawed Yale sounds.

"I do feel I can contribute more if I'm there, Majors. You know on the spot!" He reassured the schemer.

"I hope those men don't come back before expected. You do have a gun, don't you, Falconer?" Charles seemed genuinely concerned that Alex be armed to protect them all against "those men."

"Oh, yes, I'm armed. I don't anticipate much difficulty however. The woman seems quite frightened. I read the note carefully. It was written in fear and anxiety. Besides, if we can get to Renfield, and uncover the truth of this matter, it'll once and for all put an end to this entire sordid business."

Falconer studied the lights of the harbor as they steamed across from Battery Park toward the ferry terminal on Staten Island. The journey took about thirty minutes by steam ferry.

The summer evening quickly cooled in the chill night air at mid harbor. Gaby shuddered a bit and wrapped her cloak more tightly. Majors wore his black and green wool coat. The blond giant seemed impervious to the cold.

Alex Falconer, lost in his thoughts, wasn't aware of the change in temperature. He fingered the Smith and Wesson revolver in his right hand pocket. In the left were the six extra bullets, he hoped he wouldn't need.

As they approached the terminal in Staten Island, Alex pondered how he'd end the affair. The .45 should be sufficient to do the job. Still, since Majors knew of the weapon, Falconer expected that his opponent's men would jump him before he could bring the gun into play. He counted heavily on Roosevelt. At this moment, T.R. was crossing on the Bayonne ferry from the flank. He'd be there with his men ready to surprise the murderous adventurer and his henchmen.

Gaby, huddled against the chill harbor winds, was obviously excited or was it frightened? Her "big" story was at hand, a career maker. She'd get to interview the man who had blackmailed Teddy Roosevelt.

Tomorrow's scare headlines in the Journal could well read: "REPORTER TRAPS BLACKMAILER" and under that "Several wounded in shoot-out on Staten Island." A scary but promising prospect for the would-be Nellie Bly!

Falconer looked something like the bird from which his ancestor had taken the family name. The sharp brown eyes, the tapered thin nose, even his shiny brown hair reminded one of a falcon soaring through the heavens searching out his prey. Indeed, he was on the hunt right now. He stared at the Lady of Liberty as it faded from sight, both hands thrust in his coat pockets.

Majors had the appearance of a palomino stallion with golden hair and rippling muscles; a sexual object for a young girl if there ever was one.

As far as Alex could tell, Majors showed no sign of frustration despite recent failures. Both the ambush on Riverside Drive and the bomb had failed. The man had to consider the idea that they were on to his involvement in the crimes and were at least suspicious of the bogus letter.

He had something up his sleeve. The frightened wife had to be part of the ambush scene. But Roosevelt and his men would be ready. The colonel could react quickly when necessary, history had proven that.

An enigmatic smile crossed Majors' lips as the ferry nudged its blunt nose into the dock pilings at the terminal. They had arrived on Staten Island, and the final act of the drama was about to be enacted.

The little group quickly alighted from the boat and found the Richmond Road trolley. The line led to the village of St. George, the commercial center of the island. It then wound on south through the small island. Filled with hills and valleys. Staten Island, with the exception of a few hamlets and farms, was mainly occupied by small homes, thick forests and a large number of cemeteries to accommodate the needs of the nation's largest city. It was, in effect, an island of the dead.

The trolley took twenty minutes to reach the Emerson Hill stop outside the hamlet of Concord. In a few moments, the three reached the gateway described in Mrs. Renfield's letter. A small, slight woman stood there peering at them and looking past to see if anyone else was nearby.

"Miss Irish, Mr. Majors? Who is this other man? I asked you to come alone. I'm Elaine Renfield, this is a very bad business. Who did you bring with you? Is he a cop?"

"Please don't get nervous, Mrs. Renfield. I'm Gaby Irish, and this is Mr. Majors, as you asked. We've brought along Dr. Alexander Falconer. He's a great friend of ours and can help. He's a medical doctor. If your husband is very sick, Dr. Falconer can help." A reasonable way to calm the woman, it worked immediately, possibly aided by Charles Majors' ever so subtle nod of assent. It was duly noted by the good doctor.

"Thank God. We do need help. My husband's getting worse. They decided to move. They left Emerson Hill. I'll show you the way to the other house. It's not far. They moved, said things were going sour, and Thomas got even more crazy. He's ranting and raving about Roosevelt. I hope it's not too late. Maybe you can do something, Doctor. I have a horse and buggy inside the gate. It'll only take a few minutes."

Falconer realized his opponent had outwitted him by changing the location in anticipation of the arrival of outside help. He had to find some way to let Roosevelt and his men know where they had gone. Sergeant Bell could follow a trail, if there was one. As they came toward the carriage, Falconer purposely stumbled, hands in pockets, and fell to the ground. He thrust his clenched fist hand through the coat pocket and lining ripping it open. Clutching the six .45 caliber bullets, he left one on the ground pointing toward the gate. Even in the dark, an experienced tracker would see this. "Careful, Dr. Falconer, you can get seriously injured in the dark," cautioned a gloating Majors, missing the vital clue.

They traveled down the Richmond Road to the Moravian cemetery at the foot of aptly named Todt Hill. There the carriage made a sharp right turn up the hill. As the buggy turned, with the obviously bogus Mrs. Renfield driving, Falconer leaned over the edge and let another bullet drop to the ground. He was sure that Majors had not seen this either, and determined to let each of his six bullets show the trail. It was much like Hansel and Gretel being lost in the forest and dropping bread crumbs along the way. At least birds wouldn't eat these goodies. He had thought of the extra bullets as his insurance. Now they were going to have to underwrite a policy for his life and that of Gaby Irish as well. He had dropped two more cartridges along the road when they reached a walled estate near the top of the hill. Only two .45 slugs remained. He transferred them to his trouser pocket, along with the gold coin which still remained there. With his right hand he clutched the Smith and Wesson, finger on the trigger.

The group alighted from the carriage and approached the house. The large, stone structure had a living room, dining room and kitchen on the ground floor and several bedrooms on a second level. Falconer noted one large entrance at the front and several French windowed openings on both sides. A man with a bristly moustache, pince-nez glasses, and protruding teeth stood on the porch. He wore an army uniform, complete with boots, military jodhpurs, spurs, and a blue campaign jacket topped by a tan felt army fedora. Indeed, he could be Teddy Roosevelt standing atop San Juan Hill savoring his victory. Thomas Renfield had melted into the role of the Rough Rider Colonel so that even he could no longer tell the difference.

"So you've finally come back. It's about time. Brought some fresh recruits? We'll need every one of them. We're getting started soon. I've got to get rid of the phony Roosevelt. That coward Renfield has to be eliminated, and right now. He wants to be vice-president. Probably will kill off McKinley and grab the big prize for himself. He must be stopped."

"Welcome men, we have room for good soldiers. The traitors must be stopped. We're fighting for honor and glory. Don't worry, I will personally lead you."

"Where is my sword? Damned thing is gone. It's here somewhere." He paced about as if to locate a sword under a rocking chair on the porch.

"What's this? Another woman? She'll be another nurse, eh? Bully, we can use the help."

Renfield raved on and on, seemingly without pause concerning how he was going to purge the country of the bogus Roosevelt, and save the republic. He was clearly insane.

He looked at Charles Majors and said, "Haven't I met you before, sir? Weren't you one of my adjutants in the past? You look familiar to me. Have a seat, young man. Come in, have some coffee. The night is still young. We have much to do."

It was abundantly clear to Dr. Falconer that Renfield was suffering from General Paresis, a form of tertiary syphilis. Incurable, it resulted in insanity. At the beginning, a small, red lesion on the genitals. Later a fever, which could mimic any kind of disease, and therefore often misdiagnosed. Finally, the tertiary stage, a gumma, a large, rubbery lesion began to form in the brain, the kidneys, or the liver. When it was in the brain, it caused obvious madness. Most of the victims thought they were famous people. Delusions of grandeur were common. Bismarck, the King of England, Napoleon were favorite targets.

This poor soul had chosen Teddy Roosevelt. He was clearly mad. His charge against Roosevelt was founded in his own delusion. He undoubtedly signed the document which had been shown to Roosevelt, but now had reversed roles and believed himself to be the real T.R.

Majors had somehow met the man, seen the possibilities and taken advantage of the lunatic's delusions. The disease would inevitably be fatal to Renfield, and might be to Roosevelt as well.

CHAPTER THIRTY TWO

As Renfield ranted on, his "wife" slipped out of the room. Falconer noted her absence and suspected the fireworks were about to begin. Clutching his pistol, he positioned himself with his back to the wall.

Majors noted the shift and said, "It's time to end the charade, Professor Falconer. You can see that Renfield is quite mad. The document which I showed you, Gaby, is undeniably phony. I could never hope to prove it now. My only alternative is to get out of this unfortunate situation with as little damage as possible.

"Don't even think about pulling your gun, doctor. You're covered on three sides by my men. One has a rifle aimed at Gaby's head. Any false movement on your part and my men have orders to fire. Both of you will be killed outright, and I don't want that to happen, just yet." Dropping his disguise, he spoke with the soft consonants and broad vowels, more in keeping with his Southern origins. Even his demeanor changed as facial muscles tightened and the jaw thrust forward. The man made a slight bow in the direction of Gaby Irish and said, "Please forgive me, Gaby, I did have dishonorable intentions toward you, I can't deny it. However, I never intended any personal harm just some mutual pleasure. But now, as you can see, we're at the point of no return. Roosevelt's calling in Falconer changed my plan. I have to make the best of it now." An almost regretful smile crossed his face.

Gaby gasped, her mouth open in total shock. "I don't understand. What are you talking about, Charles? I mean, I understand about your intentions. I always knew you weren't the marrying kind. But what is all this other...what are you...I don't," she fumbled for words, totally at sea.

Falconer added, "I'm sorry. I should have let you in on my conclusions, but I wasn't sure if this fanatic had some how involved you in his plot. I now see that isn't so. I'm afraid I've put you in a very bad situation. The man you know as a newspaper reporter only uses his profession as a disguise to further his plans as an empire builder for himself and his friends. He was educated at Yale but this fellow is not a gentleman, are you, Majors?"

"A gentleman? One of your Yankee fantasies. True gentlemen are the product of the old South, destroyed by you and your carpetbagger friends! We have no time for that kind of nicety in the new South. The one we will create in the Caribbean, yes and the Pacific, too." His color grew a bright red, even crimson as he went on.

"A true gentleman needs a gentle woman by his side, not some abolitionist, suffragette copy of a female. Woman's place is in the home. Home and hearth; that is the role of women in our new world, your place, Gaby. This nonsense of being a reporter and an adventuress will get you what you deserve. You'll have your headlines. Someone else will have to write them, I'm afraid. The story will go something like this."

As he spoke, Maguffin, the two Lieder brothers and a fourth man, Small, entered the room. One of the brother's left-side was wounded. It was bandaged and oozing blood, the product of Falconer's bullet two days earlier. All four were armed. Small reached into Falconer's pocket for the Smith and Wesson, and shoved it into his waist band.

Majors went on, "I've devised a story to cover the tragic outcome of our visit to Renfield. I am a pretty good journalist after all. Tell me what you think of it, Gaby. Will Hearst print this? We three came here to interview Renfield. Falconer became increasingly upset as Renfield started raving about his decision to kill Roosevelt, to save the republic, and so on. Falconer lost control."

"His head wound probably was more serious than anyone suspected. He assaulted Renfield. You and I tried to stop him, of course," Majors was enjoying his story.

"You reached out and tried to prevent him from further injuring the poor madman but he swept you aside with one blow, and sent you reeling into the corner of the room. Something like this," and at that moment, Majors swatted his great right hand toward Gaby, struck her on the chin and knocked her to the floor dazed and confused.

"I think that will do for the blow," he said. Meanwhile, the two Lieder brothers held Falconer by the arms to stop his surge forward toward their leader. "Yes, and then I tried, too. The doctor struck me as well, something like this," and he hit himself in the mouth with his own right hand, very sharply.

Falconer was surprised at the force of the blow. It actually staggered Charles Majors himself. He was bleeding from the lip and may have loosened a tooth. "Oh, Lordy, the things one has to do in the service of the cause. I think that will be enough." He spit out some blood and went on. "I was unconscious for some time. It must have been then that the crazed physician took his Smith and Wesson." He reached over to Small's waist band, removed the .45, "and shot poor Renfield dead." He aimed the gun directly at the lunatic's head, pulled the trigger, and blew away the top of the man's cranium.

Blood, pieces of bone and brain splattered all over the ceiling and the wall behind the victim. His gumma would no longer render him insane. His delusions were over, cured by a dose of lead.

Gaby retched and vomited as she viewed the sudden assassination of the madman.

"Having done this in the presence of Miss Irish, you, Falconer, can no longer tolerate her alive, to be a witness against you. You considered shooting her, too, but thought you might have other uses for her before her death. As I said, you're quite mad, from your head wound no doubt."

By this time, Falconer seething with rage, was about to wrench himself loose from the two men holding him. Majors gave instructions to Maguffin and Small.

"You two tie his arms. Make sure he can't move. He won't like what's to come and surely will become very, very angry at us. Don't leave any rope burns on his wrists in case some coroner is as meticulous as he."

Maguffin, large enough to do so, pinioned Falconer's wrists behind him and quickly wrapped adhesive plaster around and around his wrists.

The former sergeant shoved Falconer to the floor in the corner of the room. "Now do I get my chance with this girl? We're going to kill her anyway. Everybody should get his turn." A growing bulge in the front of his trousers suggested more than one dimension to his energy.

"All in good time. We'll each have an opportunity to visit with Miss Irish before the night is over. You see, Falconer, in your madness, you raped this lovely young lady and then slit her throat so she could never give evidence against you. It was only because Mrs. Maguffin, Mrs.

Renfield to you, got away and brought her husband that you were stopped at all."

"Unfortunately, Maguffin arrived too late to save Renfield or even poor Miss Irish who had been raped and killed by you just as Maguffin entered and shot you. You did manage to pull off a few shots, as he came into the room." With this, the would be Filibuster fired one shot through the closed window shattering the glass and another two into the wall opposite Falconer. "Obviously you missed, didn't you? Well, so be it." He placed the half empty weapon on the floor and said, "Now to the festivities of the evening. Let's tie the young lady's arms behind her back so she won't physically object to our amorous advances as much as she would otherwise. I've had enough bleeding tonight."

Gaby, still dazed from Charles' blow, stared in disbelief and shook her head negatively.

"What's going on here. You're going to rape me. You and these gorillas." Her voice got louder as the words came out. She began to scream. "Help! Help! Help!" The screams were rather shrill and even though no one was likely to be nearby, Majors didn't want to take any chances.

Majors said, "Some adhesive across her face might make it a little quieter in here." Maguffin grabbed the sticking plaster and effectively muffled her shrieks.

Falconer was beyond rage. The scene before him was monstrous. The man he had tracked down was about to rape a helpless woman. It was a reprise of the death of his wife. Marjorie and Gaby were merging into one. Would their fate be the same? He had to do something.

When Maguffin had taped his wrists together, Falconer had flexed his muscles to their ultimate expansion. This, he had extrapolated from a conversation he'd had with Harry Houdini, the escape artist. Houdini never revealed his methods. But Alex figured this must be his trick. Flex every muscle to its fullest was the best way to free yourself from ropes, handcuffs, and the like.

Now, relaxing his muscles, he prepared to wrench his hands free from the tapes and leap upon the man closest to him. The fellow's shotgun was pointed to the ground as his attention lewdly focused on the bound Gaby Irish.

Falconer knew it would be better to let the rape begin before he made his move. He could then attain the utmost in surprise in attempting to overcome five armed men. But his rage and unreasoning thirst for revenge allowed for no such delay.

Where was Roosevelt? Had the bullet trail failed? The original plan had been to allow his group to enter the house on Emerson Hill for no more than ten minutes. After that, T.R. would begin an assault. That is, unless Falconer had exited the door and lifted his cap in the air twice as a signal not to attack. They had been here far more than ten minutes. Besides, the shot which killed Renfield and the three other bullets Majors fired would tell anyone outside something was wrong, and badly. Where were the Rough Riders?

CHAPTER THIRTY THREE

Theodore Roosevelt's anger was growing. He had miscalculated the Bayonne crossing. Ferry service stopped at 7:00 p.m. daily. It was nearly 8:00 when they arrived at the dock. He had planned to be at Emerson Hill before Falconer, and quietly get his men in position. This would no longer be possible. Now he worried whether they'd arrive in time at all.

Shaw had gone to the mayor's office in the small New Jersey town to get someone to rouse the boat men. T.R. had asked Bill Vanderbilt to lend him his new Daimler automobile. The fine British machine was capable of forty miles per hour, and had large electric arc lights to pierce the darkness of the rural night. All for naught if he couldn't cross in time.

It was well past 9:00 when the ferry finally got under way. The heavily armed group included Roosevelt, Shaw, Woody Kane, Sherman Bell, Bat Masterson, two six-shooters strapped to his waist whilst cradling a Winchester repeating rifle in loving arms, and even Sudberg, carrying a double-barreled shotgun, were aboard. The six had ample room in the spacious Daimler, and with Sudberg driving, made good time once they crossed the waters of the Kill van Kull.

The late crossing and then the poor roads on the New York side were further delay. They were forced to cut the engine and leave their vehicle a half mile away from Emerson Hill. The motor sounds could easily be detected and give warning to a watcher. It was essential to remain unobserved. Only a few moments late, Roosevelt hoped to still be in time. It was five minutes past ten when they approached Emerson Hill. T.R.

gave orders to the men to spread out and move cautiously in the shadows. He himself, as was the leader's prerogative, approached the gate first.

It was deserted. There was no woman in a yellow polka dot dress, no Irish, Majors, nor Falconer. They must have gone up to the house. He gave the prearranged signal, the trill of a whippoorwill. The men were to scale the wall, and he'd come through the gate, still ajar.

As he entered, he noticed what seemed to be the figure of a man to his right. Drawing his pistol and aiming it toward the shadowy figure, T.R. approached slowly, hoping to remain unobserved. As he came closer, the tall, gaunt figure in the moonlight incredibly looked like the publisher of the New York Journal, William Randolph Hearst. It was no other. "What the hell are you doing here, Bill?" he spoke in half whisper, half expostulation.

The fellow Harvard man jumped and looked as if he'd heard a ghost. "My God, it's you, Ted. I didn't know what to expect. I came here with Winterbottom. We followed Miss Irish. Perhaps it's foolish to get mixed up with this business, but I couldn't let this one go. I wasn't sure I could trust a woman in something this big. I knew if I insisted on coming along with her, the plan would fail. I followed her aboard the ferry boat and took Windy along."

Hearst spoke in his characteristic high-pitched nasal tone. He wasn't whispering any longer. Roosevelt realized they were alone. "You mean to say," he shouted, "that they're not here? They're not up the hill? Where the hell are they?" His agitation increased with every word. "If you've done anything to foul up our plans, you're the one who's going to pay for it. I can't believe you've wrecked this plan. Those young people are in incredible danger. That man Majors, that good old Democrat of yours is a killer! He'll stop at nothing, don't you know that!"

Hearst had regained his composure and shot back. "Hold your horses, Ted. I haven't done anything to foul up anything. I'm here to save your bacon. Winterbottom and I followed them from the ferry terminal. We hired a cab and kept at a discreet distance. When they left the trolley, we got within earshot. Windy crept closer than I. He was an Indian scout during the plains wars, you know. He heard them talk."

"If you know what happened to them, stop wasting time!" insisted the leader of the Rough Riders.

"Windy said they'd changed their plans and were going to another location, a place called Todt Hill nearby. I was sure you couldn't pass this thing up. I told Winterbottom to follow. He said he'd leave signs so one of your cowboys could track him. I imagine some of your rustic friends can do that." Hearst, born in the west, resented T.R.'s plainsman mystique. "If they can't, our friends are in for a rough time." Roosevelt recognizing Hearst had been in the right place at the right time said: "I'm sorry, Bill. Of course, you're right. I may be excitable at times, but I'm in control. I'll get my men together. We'll find the trail." He sounded the whippoorwill call.

Bill was a master at tracking. A cavalry scout prior to becoming a lawman, he quickly found the first bullet. "It looks like someone left a trail. Here's a .45 caliber bullet pointing toward the road. There'll be more of these as we go along."

Along the Richmond Road, the other bullets appeared as predicted plus several broken branches bent in an arrow-like direction, in Indian fashion, left by the old photographer.

It was 10:30 when they met Windy waiting at the entrance to the walled estate.

"I don't know if you're too late or not. I'd sure of gone in myself but, I didn't think to bring iron. I heard three gunshots. One alone, then a few minutes later three more. I've got no idea what's going on. They were very loud, a noise only a .45 would make. Nothing for ten minutes now. There's a few of them in there. Those last three shots, our three friends, I don't know what's happened. Maybe we're too late," the ancient lens man was visibly shaken.

"God forbid, if we are, it's all my fault," added Roosevelt. "I should have had the foresight to know about the ferry. I should have planned more carefully. It'll never happen again. We may still have time to do something right. Do you know anything of the layout of this place, Winterbottom?"

"Yes, Governor. I scouted around while waiting for you. This stone wall goes all around the house. There's only the one entrance a little further up the road, wide enough for your automobile to come through or for a horse and buggy to come out."

"Has there been any movement through the gate since you arrived?" asked Bell, ever the cautious lawman.

"The woman in the yellow dress before I heard the shots, I didn't follow her. She left on foot, probably isn't too far away in this darkness. The only sounds I heard were the gunshots. It's too quiet in there. There's lights, and people moving, I can see that. But I don't like it, there's not enough noise. If I'd only had an iron I'd of gone in myself, believe you me. The house is smack in the center of the property. It sits on a little rise of the hill. The front entrance is smack at the end of the driveway," observed the old man.

Masterson approached Windy, and said, "Here old timer, take this Colt Peacemaker. I've had good use from it for years. It's never misfired. I have another and a rifle too. The Colt's loaded with six rounds. Do your best with 'em." Masterson had uncharacteristically not said one sentence all evening prior to that moment. His tightly sealed lips gave him the deadly look of the killer he was reputed to be, ready to do his business.

Roosevelt spoke to the men, succinctly. "We'll charge up the hill toward the house, just as we did in Cuba. Instead of a horse, I'll take the Daimler. I'll race it directly toward the front entrance of the house, making all the noise I can, and shining those big front arc lights at the entrance. The rest of you will attack in a semi-circular line, the moment I give the word."

"We'll place the vehicle at the entrance to the gate. I'll stand up in the driver's position and shout so they can hear me inside the house. I'll order them to surrender and give them thirty seconds to open the front door and walk out with their hands over their heads. It's not likely they'll respond, but I'll give them a half minute." It was evident the colonel was in full command.

"When they don't respond, I'll gun the engine and start up the hill lights blazing. At that moment, I want every one to start up the hill, firing one or two rounds in the general direction of the house. That'll flush them out, and if our friends are trapped in there, give 'em some hope. I'll stop the Daimler at the entrance, take cover behind it, and fire at targets of opportunity. I want each of you to do the same. We know these men are armed, dangerous and have killed at least four people, God knows how many more." Roosevelt was deadly serious. Although he relished battle, this was one engagement he wished he didn't have to undertake.

The reedy voice of Bill Hearst sounded beside him. "Just a minute, Teddy, don't forget me. I'm no flincher. I never got into the Spanish War because I was too busy running the paper. But I'm here now! I want to be part of this. I know how to use a gun, and I'm not afraid to shoot. What do you say? Let me help. I'll sit in the passenger seat and cover you while you drive. You know, ride shotgun for you." Hearst, his pale complexion now flushed with excitement, smiled for the first time Roosevelt could recall.

"Bully for you, Bill. Woody, can you lend Bill Hearst one of your six-shooters?"

"With pleasure, Ted. Here you are, Mr. Hearst. It's a Colt like Masterson's. You've seen this kind before." He handed the weapon to the newspaper magnate.

The group was in position within two minutes. Driving the Daimler through the gateway, Roosevelt turned on the brilliant head lights of the motor car, raced the engine, and shouted, "You, inside the house, the game is up! This is Governor Theodore Roosevelt. The legally deputized militia of the state of New York has you surrounded. You have thirty seconds to surrender. Leave through the front entrance of the house with your hands up, or we will attack. This is your only warning." Roosevelt's voice now transformed into one of harshness and authority, had the timbre of a lion growling in the summer night, challenging its prey within the house.

Falconer was ready to rip his hands from the sticky encasement of the tape which bound them as he watched Majors preparing to sexually assault the helpless, bound and gagged Gaby Irish. Maguffin held her by the shoulders, with one of the Lieder brothers spread eagling each of her legs. Only Small's gun was trained on Falconer.

If he could rip his hands from the encasing tape quickly enough and dive for Small's legs, the man would be so preoccupied in watching the preparations for the rape of the beautiful captive that Alex could catch him unawares. He'd snatch the pistol and in the ensuing melee, have a chance to shoot, wound or kill the remaining men. At least he'd shake them up so much that they'd stop their attack, even for awhile. Alex realized he couldn't survive a fight with five armed men. Maybe, if he killed one or two of them, the others might give up, especially if he could get Majors first. That was it! Grab the gun from the preoccupied Small, and shoot their leader with his first round. He'd try for Maguffin next, but he couldn't be sure of that. All he knew was that he had to do something. There was no more time to wait for Roosevelt and the Rough Riders.

Gaby's face was swelling. It was hot and painful where Chuck had struck her.

The animal who held her by the shoulders breathed his cigar and whiskey-scented breath into her face. The adhesive over her mouth prevented deep breathing. Her flaring nostrils were sucking in every fetid odor on the creature's body. Her distress, the terror in her eyes, the flush on her skin and even her labored breathing were exciting the man sexually. His grip tightened on her shoulders and the hardness in his crotch as he pressed his groin against her neck was all too apparent. He literally drooled. His face was close to her cheek as they watched the two henchmen pulling her legs apart in preparation for Majors, who was to have the first turn.

It was nothing like her adolescent sexual fantasies. In those adventures, she was captured by Arabian Sheiks, African warriors, red Indians and other exotic and sexually powerful men. They never smelled in her dreams! Besides the tape about her wrists stung and made her hands numbs. The rough hands of the men pulling her legs apart were anything but gentle and erotic. Being raped was real! There was nothing sexually arousing in this, as it had always been in a thousand dreams. It hurt! She was terrified.

The man holding her left leg was giving her a little slack. Maybe she could kick forward and catch him in the testicles. Maybe she should wait a few moments until Chuck began to try and enter. She was no virgin, to be sure. But the others like Blackenck and Billy were gentle and slow. Never terribly exciting, hence the rape fantasies right on through adulthood, but this was real. It was horrible. She closed her eyes as Charles approached her; an aura of lust wreathed his face as he anticipated the next few moments.

Gaby had no idea that Roosevelt and his men were expected, even remotely. She was prepared for her doom, eyes tightly closed, waiting only to strike out one more time with her imprisoned left leg.

CHAPTER THIRTY FOUR

The bright lights of the Daimler shone through the front window of the living room where the captives were held as the rape was about to begin. Roosevelt's shouted warning interrupted the scene. The lust obvious in Maguffin's and Majors' faces swiftly changed to fear.

"He's given us thirty seconds, Mr. Majors, I think maybe we ought to give up, don't you? The militia's out there. We can't fight the state militia. That's his voice, I heard him in Cuba. He's deadly, a real killer. He can't be stopped. He charged the Spanish positions on horseback and never got hurt. Teddy leads a charmed life. We're through." Maguffin, in total panic, was prepared to run for the door to escape.

Majors smacked Maguffin across the face with the back of his hand. He shouted, "You fool, you're panicking. You'll be the death of us all. How could he have the militia out there? Roosevelt hasn't had time to mobilize troops. It's a bluff. He's probably got a couple of his stupid cowboy friends with him. You were a soldier once. Act like one!"

Majors' ability to command was obvious to everyone in the room, as he barked orders with force and authority.

"We're in a perfect defensive position. We can crouch behind the walls and cut him down as he charges up, the fool. Cool heads and marksmanship will stop this nonsense in quick order. If the Spanish had trained professional officers with them in 98, instead of aristocratic dandies, they'd still have their empire. Crazy cowboy tactics won't win the day. We're not red Indians. Of course, we won't surrender. You, Small, go to the kitchen, cover the back entrance! You two Lieder brothers, over to the dining room behind the windows! Keep under cover and wait for the firing to stop. Maguffin get to the right French window in here. I'll cover the left. These two can wait til later," he nodded toward the bound and apparently helpless Irish and Falconer.

Falconer decided to wait until the firing started to reveal he wasn't as helpless as his opponent assumed.

The thirty seconds ended quickly. The roar of the Daimler engine became louder as the vehicle raced up the small hill. Pistol fire crackled from the right side wing of the vehicle.

Other bullets were aimed in the general direction of the house. Each and every slug seemed to find its way through an opening and shattered something inside. The Rough Riders indeed were mobilized. These men, Majors learned quickly, were more than good shots. Within a minute there wasn't a pane of glass in front of the house left intact.

There was no assault from the rear. Had the Filibusterer studied Roosevelt's previous record, he would have recalled the famous attack came straight on from the front. Majors didn't have time to bring Small back however, as Masterson and Bell, on the left wing of the assault force, had gained a position close to the dining room windows.

Masterson with cool precision aimed to the right of the shadow on his side of the window, and fired in that direction. The remaining slivers of glass shattered as his .45 caliber slug rocketed through the opening. The bullet struck the wall behind the shivering Lieder. Glass splinters slashed into his arm. He moved toward the window to return fire. Masterson's second shot caught him squarely between the eyes. He fell like a rock without a sound. His brother, seeing him drop to the floor, panicked and moved toward his body. It was at that moment that Bell's revolver, held in his left hand, barked twice in rapid succession. Each heavy slug caught the moving target, and the second Lieder brother collapsed with wounds through his heart and left lung. He died as quickly as his brother, with only a gurgling sound of air being sucked into the punctured lung as his epitaph.

On the other side of the house, next to the living room window, Charles Majors proved he was indeed a dangerous adversary. He saw the moving shadows of Sudberg, Kane and Shaw, and fired rapidly in their general direction, smiling as Kane stumbled, a bullet in his left shoulder. The Rough Rider captain was wounded, but not fatally. Sudberg stopped to give assistance, but Shaw went on. The wiry little man, with his Winchester repeating rifle, began shooting at the muzzle flashes from Majors' gun. The rapid fire from his weapon caused Majors to back away from the window, and prevented further response in that direction.

In the meantime, Maguffin had regained his composure to some extent, and fired toward the Daimler. He knew Roosevelt was the one at the controls of the automobile even though blazing lights from the vehicle prevented Maguffin from seeing him. The former sergeant realized his old colonel would lead the charge. The car was the centerpiece of the action. Maguffin had an eerie feeling that he'd be unable to wound or kill his erstwhile leader. But he was also terrified that if he didn't try, Majors would shoot him in the back as casually as he had murdered Renfield. The auto had stopped. T.R. emerged with a revolver in each hand, firing at the bedazzled Maguffin. Earl screamed, "He's weird. He's supernatural. He can't be killed." Another man was in the vehicle, armed and firing from the passenger seat. "He'll kill us. We've got to get out," and at that moment Earl Maguffin dropped with a bullet in his throat.

It was never clear, in the aftermath, whether the bullet came from Roosevelt's two blazing six-guns or from the Colt that Hearst had been firing to cover him. In any event, a substantial chunk of lead entered the man's larynx, severed his carotid artery and raced on through the several anatomical structures of the former sergeant's neck to crush his cervical spine. He didn't die immediately. It took at least three minutes for him to exsanguinate. His life's blood poured from the severed carotid artery, while he lay helplessly paralyzed by the overwhelming force of the lump of metal pressing on his spinal cord. Falconer later opined that he died in the agony that he deserved.

Sudberg, not a formidable marksman, decided to fire his weapon straight on through the front door, both barrels simultaneously. The roar was deafening to the inexperienced musketeer. He even thought he heard someone calling to him after the door had been blown off its hinges. He couldn't make out the sounds, so decided to immediately reload and repeat the shot. This time, there was nothing to impede the double load of .12 gauge pellets. It roared through the entryway, disintegrating the stairway banister, shattering a chandelier hanging down into the stair well from the second floor. The shards of glass flew everywhere. Small, acting as rear guard was badly cut. He was bloodied, hurting and scared to death.

The terrified man rushed forward, realizing that the game was up, and raised his hands in an attempt' to surrender. Majors had blood in his eye. His plans had gone up in smoke, his rage enormous. "You useless swine, no wonder they cashiered you from the Rough Riders. You're no trooper, you're a coward and a fool." He fired his two remaining bullets into Small. They were gut shots, calculated to kill him slowly. "Lie there and die. You deserve to die in pain and agony, you yellow dog."

"This isn't the end of the story, not by a long shot." He snatched the fallen Maguffin's weapon and grabbed Gaby by her hair. "Get up, you bitch, in front of me. You'll be my ticket home." He forced her toward the door.

Falconer, freed from the tape, moved toward his own .45 discarded on the floor. He had just reached the weapon when Majors held his pistol to Gaby's head and shouted, "Cease fire, cease fire, you fools. It's over. They're all dead in here but this one and me (in his frenzy, he had forgotten Falconer entirely). If anyone fires another shot, I'll put a bullet through her empty head," and he thrust Gaby forward through the open door.

Roosevelt, both six-guns in his hands, and Hearst, off to his side with his Colt, stared at his helpless reporter, bound and gagged in the grasp of the enraged failed adventurer.

"Get away from that motor, get back. Drop those weapons. Don't come close to me, or she's dead. I'm going to take this automobile back down the hill. Anyone who follows me does so at the risk of this one's life."

He shoved Gaby into the passenger seat, holding the gun on her with his left hand, and releasing the brake of the vehicle with his right. Controlling the wheel with a single hand, Majors allowed it to roll backward down the hill, shouting at the victors of the Todt Hill charge, as he rolled through the gate, "Don't follow me or I'll kill her. I mean it. You know I do!" He forced the gears forward and drove away.

Roosevelt shouted in response, "Stand and fight like a man, Majors!" By this time, Falconer had raced out the door, watching, enraged as the gang's ringleader escaped. "There's a horse and buggy behind the house. That's how we got here. I'll take it and shadow him as closely as possible."

"We'll join you, of course," Roosevelt added.

"Colonel, there's barely room for three men in the rig. We squeezed two men and two women in before. I want to make speed. He's got the Daimler and must be moving like hell! One person with me will have to be enough. I have my gun. I think I know what he plans to do."

"You've been right so far, Alex. I'll defer to your expertise here. I'd love to join the chase, but I'll follow as soon as possible," a disappointed T.R. added.

"I expect the man to head for Manhattan and try to get to a Central American Consulate. Once there he has asylum. We can't arrest him inside their gates. We've got to catch him before then." He thrust the revolver in his belt as he spoke.

"You, if you'll allow me to suggest, Governor, get to the nearest telephone. There must be one in the village below. Instruct the police to surround all of the Latin American Consulates from the outside. Set up a cordon so that if Majors tries to get through, we'll have him. I'd like Masterson to go with me."

Falconer had now reached the rear of the house, harnessed the rig, and hopped in to pursue Majors and his captive. He knew he'd have to apprehend and destroy the man in any way possible. He had his revolver with three bullets remaining in the cylinders, and an unshakable resolve to track down and destroy this twisted man whom Alex equated with the killer of his wife. Here was another ruthless murderer who must be stopped.

CHAPTER THIRTY FIVE

It was well past midnight when Majors cautiously approached the docks at St. George. The ferries had stopped running for the night. It didn't matter, he dared not board a public transport with a captive in hand. There was no sign of pursuers. "Good, there's no one in sight. I think we'll get away with this one, Gaby. I'll take you with me to the Nicaraguan Consulate in Manhattan. You'll have to stay with me for a while longer. You do have beautiful, soulful eyes." He stroked her tangled hair as if to make amends for the horrors of the night she had already endured.

"I should have killed Falconer first. He's the most dangerous of the lot, the one likely to anticipate my plan. There's no telephone at the Todt Hill house. They'll have to find one. That'll take time in this hick town. If we get across the harbor and into the city before dawn, we can make it to the Consulate in the darkness. I'll be safe there. We have friends all over Latin America who understand what's at stake," he informed her.

"I can't even release you once we're inside. You can't testify against me. I'll have diplomatic immunity. They won't be able to touch me. I'll go to Central America and offer my apologies to our sponsors. I can still be of service. Our plans never hinged on just this one operation. Other arrangements have been made."

He was lecturing the bound and gagged hostage. The tape across her mouth was increasingly painful. She was having difficulty breathing because tears clogged her nostrils. She looked at him pleadingly to release the covering over her mouth. "I don't think I should remove the gag yet, Gaby. You might scream for help from these island yokels. All that would achieve is their death with a bullet, and possibly your own. Don't shake your head, I don't believe you. It's best you keep your mouth shut for the time being."

"We should find a boat down here to take us across the harbor." He abandoned the Daimler a few hundred yards from the waterfront, pushed his prisoner in front of him and peered into the darkness towards the wharf. Several fishing boats rode at their moorings, awaiting the morning tide. One steam launch stood among the group of sailing vessels. Steam power was best for his purposes.

"It'll take a while to get the steam up, but once it's ready, we'll make good time across the harbor. Besides, I'm not good with sails and rigging. This will have to do. We can't wait for the morning ferry. You understand that." Amused by his own joke, he shoved her onto the boat and into its wheelhouse.

"You sit here and wait for me to return. Please don't take any walks. You'd have a very difficult time swimming with your arms tied behind you like that." Thrust unceremoniously on the floor, she cried some more and wondered if there were some way to free herself. Perhaps if she rubbed the tapes against the door jamb of the wheelhouse, she might catch them in the door hook and get them loose. The adhesive was starting to loosen a bit through the perspiration of her tormented body, and it began to give way, if only slightly. The same was true for the gag. She was beginning to get her jaws and lips to move a little bit and, hopefully, could shout for help in a few minutes even if she had to tear the skin from her face in doing so.

Meanwhile, Majors found a banked fire in the boiler below, prepared for the morning tide. He began pouring on more and more coal to generate enough power to sail. It would take a half hour to raise adequate steam, loosen the moorings and begin the crossing.

Falconer had come down the Richmond Road in the horse and buggy with Bat Masterson at his side. He told the former lawman he expected Majors to steal a vessel and head for Manhattan.

"This man's clever and probably knows how to handle a boat. I hope he can't manage a sailing ship, so he'll have to get up steam on a launch. If so, we'll be in luck."

"Why's that professor?" Bat asked with the respect of a school boy for his headmaster.

"Because it takes at least thirty minutes to fire up a boiler to get underway. It'll give us time to catch up. We've got to be careful not to alert him and give him a chance to use Gaby as a hostage again."

When they saw the abandoned Daimler at dockside, Falconer knew he was right. He told Masterson, "You take the wharf on the left, I'll go to the right. If either of us sees him, let's signal to warn one another."

"How about the hoot owl? I can do an owl hoot. If I squawk once, that'll mean I've seen him and you come to my wharf. Okay?" the ex-town tamer suggested.

"Fine. With only two wharfs here, there can't be many boats. Whichever one of us is lucky enough will give a hoot, and the other one will come as quickly and quietly as possible."

Falconer moved down the dock. There were three fishing skiffs moored to the wharf with their sails lowered awaiting their dawn departure.

Not a soul stirred on the dock. Alex began to fear that Majors had not acted as he imagined. Gaby was in real danger.

It was then that he heard the owl hoot. Falconer retraced his steps down the wharf toward the sound which told him his quarry had been flushed. "Just as an owl flushes a field rat," thought the doctor.

"It's over there, a steam launch," Bat whispered. "I just saw Majors coming forward from the boilers at the stern. He's in the wheelhouse now. I can't see Miss Irish, but he seemed to be talking to someone. He's probably got her down on the floor. It sounds like he's got steam up. The thing must be ready to leave. What do we do now, Professor? You're in charge here. I'm just an ex-marshal, not even in my own jurisdiction."

Falconer considered for a moment and said, "Our best plan is to catch him on the water. If we jump him now, he'll use Gaby as a hostage again. We'll have a better chance in the harbor when he's busy. I saw a Coast Guard Station a few hundred yards from here. Go there for help. They'll have steam launches available."

"I'll slip aboard Majors' launch before he leaves. I can swim from the blind side of the dock under the boat and climb aboard. With the engine clattering, he won't hear me. If I board at the stern, he won't see me either. I'll hide there until you get the Coast Guard launch going."

"You can distract his attention by hailing him from the Coast Guard vessel and saying he's cut off and can't get away. That's when I'll come out and get to him before he uses Gaby as a hostage again."

Masterson hastened off to the Coast Guard station.

Chuck Majors, now certain that he'd escaped, slipped the moorings on the launch and headed north toward the lights of Manhattan. There was no trouble in finding the right direction. Lady Liberty's torch gleamed brightly in the harbor, and many buildings in the city were ablaze with light in the wee hours of the morning. New York City led the world in electrical illumination, even before dawn.

Falconer crouched behind the boiler and anxiously scanned the horizon for the government boat. There was no movement as the Guard dock grew smaller in the distance. The plan might fail. The only alternative was sabotage the launch. In a half hour, his quarry would be across the lower harbor and into Manhattan still holding the girl hostage. From there it would be a brief trip even if he had to commandeer a hansom cab to any of the Consulates. He could easily get there before dawn, possibly before the police had time to surround the place.

Alex knew he must do something now. Removing his suit jacket, he shoved the Smith & Wesson into his wet trouser waistband. He then used the jacket to protect his hands from the searing heat and began twisting one of the valves at the bottom of the boiler. It was the drainage valve for excess water. The water, according to the immutable laws of physics, had to keep on boiling in order for steam to be maintained. He finally managed to loosen the stubborn handle, and superheated fluid sputtered out. It was scalding hot, and he had to jump backward to avoid being burned as it seethed out of the spigot. Fortunately Majors didn't seem to hear a thing. The man was obsessed with peering forward at the New York skyline and his imminent escape.

It took fifteen minutes before enough water had drained off from the boiler and the steam gave out. Falconer's chance would come when the fellow went back to find out what happened to the power. He'd check the fire first to see if it had gone out, or in what other way the engine had failed. He'd never imagine anyone had opened the tap to drain off the water. Alex planned to get the drop on him then.

The would-be Cortez moved rapidly toward the stern, foully cursing the faulty engineering of the stolen vessel. He got to the boiler itself and saw that the fire was working quite well when Falconer stepped out from the shadows training his revolver on his adversary.

"Hands up! You're under arrest. Don't move a muscle. The boat ride's over old chap. You'll never make it to any Consulate. We'll just sit here and wait for the U.S. Coast Guard, now on its way."

Majors, although shocked at Falconer's unexpected arrival, realized he had to think quickly to escape from this newest trap. "So you swam aboard. You're soaked. You must have snuck aboard while I was putting up steam. I should have expected it. You're like a limpet clinging to the side of a rock. Well, this is one rock that's going to get rid of you. I don't believe your gun is loaded. There may be one or two bullets left and I don't think you're a dead shot like your cowboy friends. Let's see" and he reached into his pocket to remove his own pistol.

Falconer unhesitatingly squeezed the trigger. The boat was rocking in the waves of the inner harbor and his first shot went off to the right. There was only one other bullet left. The second squeeze of the trigger and the damned thing misfired. All Alex heard was a metallic click, as Majors removed his weapon from his pocket. Falconer threw the useless revolver at the man's chest with all the force he could muster. The arm of the ex-big leaguer still had lots of power. The heavy weapon struck Charles Majors in the right shoulder, causing his own pistol to fire wildly off in the direction of the statue and knocking him backward toward the bow of the boat. The gun clattered to the deck and skidded across it.

Majors realized it would be pointless to scramble for the gun in the dark. Actually, Falconer might have a better chance at reaching it than he. The killer turned and ran toward the bow. "I'm not through yet, doctor. Let's see how girl reporters like morning swims." He dashed into the wheelhouse, grabbed Gaby, still bound but struggling to release herself and threw her over the side of the launch. "Maybe you'd like to go for a swim yourself, Falconer. She won't last long out there."

Gaby had been sitting up on the floor of the wheelhouse gradually working her arms loose from the tapes. She suspected that she could by now shout, and when she heard the conversation in the back, her heart skipped a beat. Alex was there! He was alive and he'd come to save her. At first she thought he had the drop on Chuck and then realized that it had gone wrong again. She wasn't quite able to get her arms free when the failed rapist came and grabbed her about the waist and threw her overboard.

She was going down, and managed to force her mouth open against the tape only to swallow a huge amount of salt water, or so it seemed. Her hands were still ensnared in the tape, loose, but not able to propel her above the water as yet. It was at that moment Falconer dove in, grabbed her about the neck and pulled her to the surface. "I've got you,

Gaby. Don't worry. I won't let you drown. You'll be all right. I'm here, it's okay," he shouted, as he pulled her toward the drifting steam launch.

Majors realized that the launch was dead in the water. He saw, at long last, the approaching Coast Guard vessel and leaped off his useless boat to swim toward nearby Bedloe's Island.

By now, Falconer had regained the drifting boat, pulled Gaby up and made sure she was able to breathe. All of the water went into her stomach, none into her lungs.

But the killer had reached the island. He was clambering up the rocks towards the statue. The Coast Guard cutter was still minutes away. Alex told Gaby, "You stay here and tell them what happened. They'll be here in a few minutes. We're drifting toward the rocks, but the boat will just grind against them. It won't go down. I'm going after Majors. He can't get away again." Before she could object, he leaped over the side of the boat and headed for the island.

Majors, having gained shore, desperately reckoned he could hide in the recesses of the monument and later melt in with the crowds bound to turn up the next morning. Thus he could return to Manhattan and plan his next move. He saw Falconer doggedly pursuing him.

"That bastard. He'll never give up. I've got to kill him! That damned Yankee will follow me to Hell!" He headed towards the colossus which loomed in the night sky above him, its beacon gleaming toward the east and the Old World.

The big man rapidly ran to the base of the statue and entered the monument. Falconer was now on shore, relentlessly chasing him. Deciding he could best overcome the doctor in the narrow catwalks above, Majors went up the inside of the Lady of Liberty. At the base of the statue, he looked over the edge and saw Alex Falconer entering the structure. The Coast Guard had still not reached Gaby and the disabled launch. He had plenty of time to dispose of his antagonist. Once rid of him, the others would be easy to evade. They were far less resourceful than the tenacious physician.

The blond giant climbed upward within the statue, up the circular iron stairway higher and higher. His ultimate goal was the torch. He knew that if he could reach it, he could block the stairway and kick down at the clambering Falconer and plunge his opponent to his death.

Alex realized his game, and thought the man might have still another weapon with which he'd attack once he reached the top. He knew both would be exhausted by then, and it would be a struggle to the death. That's as it should be, he thought. It's up to me and me alone to finish him off. He climbed up the spiral stairs towards the base of the lamp.

Majors indeed had a stiletto secreted in the lapel of his black and green coat, now soggy with sea water. It was the last weapon in his arsenal. He removed the six inch, thin steel knife, "good Toledo steel," he thought. "A perfect weapon to skewer a meddling sawbones." He waited, panting, in the darkness at the base of the torch. The villain stood in the shadows just outside the catwalk, as Falconer climbed hand over hand toward the exit of the stairway.

As the forensic physician's head emerged, Majors made his move. He jumped toward him as a great cat would leap from a tree limb to its prey below. His claws held the stiletto in his right hand, and he plunged it down toward the base of Falconer's neck.

Alex, expecting an attack, sprung toward the side as the blade clattered against the iron grill work of the stairs. His assailant was off balance, and Falconer jumped onto the catwalk. The two faced one another, each ready to kill or be killed. Majors' hand, bruised and bleeding from its collision with the ironwork, clutched the stiletto in its grasp. "Now is the time for the final act, Doctor. It'll be my distinct pleasure to end this farce." He vaulted forward once again. Falconer, his only weapon the gold coin, still in his pocket, grasped it between his right thumb and index finger and tried the gambit of his dream. There was no choice. Even if he couldn't, despite his ninety mile per hour fast ball, drive the heavy metal into his adversary's forehead, he could hit the mark.

The oversized medallion flew through the air with such velocity that the big fellow scarcely saw it before it crashed against his forehead just at the bridge of his nose. The serrated edge of the coin bit into his skin, the aurous missile fracturing the nasal bone plate immediately adjacent to the left eye.

The pain was overwhelming. For a moment, the giant was blinded in agony. As his vision returned, Falconer was upon him wresting the blade from his hand.

Majors, caught by surprise, cursed his opponent once again. But he rapidly regained his composure and with a wrenching blow of the left hand, tried to force Falconer off the iron walkway to the rocks below. Alex grabbed the catwalk with one arm and half slipping over the side, managed to keep his balance. He kicked forward with his right leg and managed to catch his opponent in the hip. Still bleeding liberally from his lacerated nose, Chuck Majors winced with the new pain and backed off. His rage was growing. Falconer saw it plainly.

Alex figured his antagonist had reverted to animal instinct. Falconer, too, was filled with hate, but kept telling himself, think, reason, do not let your emotion overcome you.

"You filthy rebel, you crude, stupid beast," he shouted. "You and your absurd cause, Southern gentlemen living a crazy dream of the past. You're all through. The flag of the Confederacy is just an old piece of worthless shit, a tattered rag to wipe the world's ass. You're done. Soon I'll see Teddy Roosevelt dance on the tomb of your lost cause." Alex couldn't think of anything more insulting to say to this maniac, and hoped it would have its effect.

Majors was indeed out of control. Without thinking or reasoning, he must destroy his tormenter immediately. He charged the offending voice as if it were the symbol of those who had destroyed his heritage, defiled his name and ruined his ancestors. Now they were ruining his and his friends' plans for a renaissance of antebellum glory.

Majors would, like a bull, throw the hated representative of the Yankee Roosevelt and all that he stood for off this stupid French statue and down to the rocks below where he belonged. He charged, literally with blood in his eye. Falconer, like a toreador measuring a beast, stepped aside. Charles Majors, too late, realized he had been had, and careened over the statue rail, plunging to his doom below.

Aboard the Coast Guard cutter, which had taken the Governor aboard just as it steamed out, Roosevelt watched the battle unfold. After Majors had fallen to certain death, he saw the victor, apparently Alex

Falconer, inexplicably crouch down on the catwalk and remain so for several minutes. "What the devil is he doing now?" T.R. wondered aloud. "Is he still searching for clues?"

Dr. Alexander Falconer scanned the ironwork catwalk beneath the great torch. Searching for several minutes, at last he saw the golden gleam. He bent over, picked up a large coin shaped object, examined it briefly and slipped it into his trouser pocket.

EPILOGUE

As Roosevelt put it the next day, "Those Boxers in China sure have saved us a lot of complex explanations."

The scare headlines the morning after the charge on Todt Hill and Majors' fall from the Statue dealt not with these matters, but with the Boxer Uprising in China and the lifting of the siege of the Europeans and Americans trapped inside the foreign quarter by the Nationalist killers.

"I persuaded my good friend and former fellow Harvard student, Willie Hearst, to take a new approach to the whole matter. He's got enough sensationalism in the China matter to make our dramatic rescue of his star reporter take second place in the Journal, even including his own active part in the affair." The vice-presidential candidate beamed his toothy smile at the publisher and wrapped his muscular arm over the shoulder of his new comrade in arms.

Indeed, the morning headlines in the Journal occupying the second lead (the Boxers had the first) read: **"JOURNAL REPORTER RESCUED FROM MAD MAN."**

The entire party from the previous night had gathered atop Todt Hill and Winterbottom was composing a group picture, (including the Daimler borrowed from Bill Vanderbilt), before the glassless windows of the house which had been the center point of the rescue.

The sub-head of the newspaper story read: **"PUBLISHER OF JOURNAL AND GOVERNOR ROOSEVELT LEAD RESCUE EFFORT."** It went on to say that a mad man had kidnapped Hearst's reporter and mentioned Bat Masterson, Woody Kane, Al Shaw, and a physician named Alex Falconer, along with Sudberg and Winterbottom, who had taken part in hunting down the villains and saving the day. Unfortunately, the crazed killer had been responsible for the deaths of several Rough Rider veterans, as well as a friend of Miss Irish, Mr. Charles Majors.

It was also determined that the homicidal lunatic had killed Dr. and Mrs. Clifton of Trenton, New Jersey. Apparently, Thomas Renfield had suffered from a brain fever brought on by Yellow Jack while serving with T.R. in the Spanish American War. The Jack had caused him to have an insane delusion that he was Roosevelt and all those who denied it were traitors and had to be killed.

The story with Gaby Irish's byline went on to describe how Dr. Alexander Falconer of Columbia University had ferreted the killer out and eventually had been captured along with the reporter, only to be rescued by the gallant Hearst, Roosevelt, and the others.

"Stand a little closer together folks," the ancient photographer insisted. "Gaby, I want you between the Chief and the governor. Professor, you stand next to the governor," and so on.

When the old man finished his chores, the group headed down the hill toward the new Rubsam and Hormann Brewery located on Staten Island. Hearst had arranged for a banquet at the place to cement his new alliance with Roosevelt and to partake of the beer which was now being produced there. T.R. welcomed any opportunity to speak at a function, shake hands with the R&H workers, and get even more press coverage.

"Governor, there's something unfinished that bothers me about this whole affair," Falconer said as he held the governor's elbow lightly while speaking more softly than usual.

"Bothers you, Alex? I've been under the impression that almost nothing truly bothered you. This was a splendid adventure, bully, and you were the key man. Your skills in crime detection won't go unnoticed in Albany or in Washington for that matter if we prevail in November as I'm sure we will."

"It's the backers of Majors and his scheme, Governor. The ones who put up the funds for the hare brained plot. They're all still at large," Alex reminded the triumphant chief executive of New York State.

"A bunch of *crazy Filibusters?* Alex, we haven't time to *waste* on them. Their *scheme has* failed. We're beginning a national *campaign,* and I'm sure we're going to Washington next spring." The toothy smile emerged in all of its glory.

"But I think, I'm sure, these men had something to do with Vice-President Hobart's so-called heart attack, and worse, they may have plans in motion to assassinate McKinley!"

"Utter nonsense, Alex. If they killed McKinley, Roosevelt takes over. So much the worse for them. They'd be mad fools to even consider it and stupid as well," Roosevelt assured him.

"Well, it's my assumption that they are mad fools, sir, and perhaps their plan is already in motion and can't be stopped," Alex suggested.

"That's a federal matter, Alex. Not in our jurisdiction at all. We have other fish to fry, doctor." TR. was becoming a bit impatient.

"There is no real federal investigatory body capable of dealing with this," Falconer said. "Interesting, Alex, a good point. If and when we come to office, perhaps we can form a commission to look into some kind of Federal Office of Criminal Investigation. Remind me about that next spring will you? Maybe you could serve as chairman? Who knows what kind of possibilities lay ahead in the next century?"

"But….. "Alex began to say.

THE STATUE OF LIBERTY CURSE

Read Chapter One to whet your appetite------

CHAPTER ONE

The tour guide wiped his brow and continued his talk.

"The lady holds a torch aloft in her right hand and in her left a book inscribed July 4, 1776; broken chains of tyranny lay at her feet. Funds were raised by the people of France to pay for the statue and the children of the United States raised money for the pedestal with their pennies and nickels to install the Great Lady here in New York Harbor."

"She rises three hundred six feet eight inches from ground level to the top of the torch," the middle sized pudgy young man went on.

It was hot, even for August, and the refreshment stand boy in the background was shouting: "Get your cold beer and soda pop! Only a nickel! The best buy on the island!"

Two hundred seventy four feet above him, a tall slender very pale young man dressed in a dark suit and sporting a full black beard and mustache removed and uncorked a small flask from his pocket. Instead of the scent of alcohol, Sulfur Dioxide fumes emerged from the silvered container with their noxious and penetrating odor of rotten eggs. The dozen tourists peering through the windows in the lady's crown quickly became aware of it.

"What's that smell?" shouted a young woman, all too aware of the recent fatal accidents at the sixteen year old monument.

"Some kind of gas, I think," answered the bearded-fellow in an upper class British accent, "I think we had all better get out of here. It might be poisonous. Go ahead, I'll stay back here and make certain everyone's gone," he told the three or four people rushing towards the down going stairs. "Not here, this is the up staircase. I'll warn those coming up," he gallantly volunteered to some others.

Every individual in the crown viewing area rapidly departed, leaving the bearded man alone in the great statue's crown. He quickly scanned the area and thumped his heavy ebony walking stick on the steel deck.

The sound resonated throughout the up coming staircase where Mr. Walter O'Brien, his lady friend, the spinster Bridgett Rooney and her charge, the son of wealthy railroad and shipping baron, Arthur J. Haverhill, were climbing upwards. Little Arthur, a somewhat frail child, had tired from the climb and was in the arms of the family chauffeur, Tony Charles.

The grey uniformed Charles led the way. When the clang of the walking stick hit the metal, O'Brien, bringing up the rear, deftly reached up and tripped his new lady friend causing her to fall onto the steps. The narrow stairway was completely blocked by Bridgett and also by the massive bulk of the over-sized Mr. O'Brien.

A lady called from below, "What's the matter?"

"She fell ma'am. The climb is too much for her. I told her so didn't I, Bridgett?" The woman didn't reply.

"Is she well?" asked the chauffeur.

"Bridgett, are you hurt?" inquired the ten year old Arthur.

"'Go ahead Charles," said O'Brien, "don't spoil the boy's good time. I'll take care of Bridgett, she just slipped, she'll be fine."

Tony Charles carried the boy up to the crown while the burly O'Brien ministered to the fallen nanny.

"You'll be fine. It looks like your ankle is twisted. Just a minute, let me see."

"Is she alright?" asked an impatient man, climbing with his family, but glad for the breather provided by the accident. He was getting too old to make this difficult climb, but he didn't want to admit it. Besides he couldn't move past the bulky O'Brien and his injured companion.

His wife chimed in, "Is she dizzy?"

"She might be with child, ma'am. I told her the climb was too much, but she insisted. Being what women are, if you'll beg my pardon," O'Brien said.

Bridgett, at the suggestion she might be pregnant, shrieked, "Oh, jays us, Oh, God forgive me!" The shameless man had revealed the secret of her sexual indiscretion, the only one in her life. A desperate spinster of twenty-eight, Walter was maybe her last
hope. This was too much.

Walter's comment to this stranger was the ultimate betrayal. Bridgett was born and raised in an Irish Catholic family in County Cork. Sex wasn't permitted unless a girl was married and even then, it was only for the purpose of having children. You just didn't talk about sex to anyone, let alone some lady in a stairwell in a monument. Her face had turned beet red and her very ears burned with mortification.

"She'll be alright, folks, in just a little while, I'm sure," O'Brien assured those below, on the steps.

"Just a little dizzy, you unnerstand." He winked at the couple standing on the stairs below.

Bridgett moaned yet again. What was a spinster to do? This man, so late in her life, was certainly her last chance. O'Brien told her he was a lonely widower and had seen her in the park watching young Arthur at play. It was only a month or so ago and by then she had given up all hope of ever connecting with a suitor. This one was a real find. An Irish widow man, retired from the Police Department, and only in his forties, at least he told her that. She kept quiet except for a few sobs as he rubbed her ankle. It did seem sore to her.

Meanwhile, further up the stairs, the chauffeur carried little Arthur to the crown viewing area. The bearded man nodded as Charles lifted the boy towards the large aperture where one could see the harbor.

"No, no, I'm scared, Charles, not so high!" shrieked the little boy. "No, no!"

The bearded man in the black suit reacted swiftly to this alarm. Surely someone below would hear the little brat. Hopefully, O'Brien had kept up his Irish patter to drown out the whines. He raised his cane and shouting "Farewell, misbegotten bastard," struck the child with its heavy brass head directly in the back of the boy's small skull.

There were no more cries from the boy. He never heard a word past "farewell."

"Alright, Charles, throw him through the window. There's no time to waste."

When the gray uniformed man hesitated, his leader insisted. "Hurry up, you fool, we have no time to waste, he can't utter a sound, out the window with him, right now!"

As soon as the child's body began to fall, he ordered Charles: "Alright, raise the alarm. Call them here, say the brat fell, just as we rehearsed." And he quickly descended down the stairway.

Below, the tour guide was completing his pitch and about to send his charges into the building which was the pedestal of the harbor colossus. He could taste the nickel beer or two he'd buy once they went inside. Something came hurtling down barely a foot behind him. Several people screamed. There was a resounding thud as Arthur Haverhill, Jr.'s body impacted the bricks, once the foundation of old Fort Wood, which had guarded the harbor at the beginning of the century.

"Shit," shouted the tour guide rather unprofessionally.

"It's a little boy!" screamed one of the tourists.

"It's the curse of the statue!" added a sailor on leave. "The curse-again," one of his shipmates chimed in.

"It came down, kerplunk. I never saw anything like it. I was at Manila Bay in '98 under fire from Spanish guns, but we never had a shell come anywhere as close as that; poor kid," Yeoman First Class Daniel Bear later told a reporter from the New York World.

"Not a sound, no warning. I never saw anything like it," he repeated to the journalist. "He hit the ground like a sack of small melons," Bear recalled.

The paper printed the story under a huge black headline:

STATUE KILLS AGAIN

IS THERE A CURSE

SON OF PROMINENT RAILROAD MAGNATE

PLUNGES TO HIS DEATH ON BEDLOE'S ISLAND

Other papers followed suit the next morning.

The New York Herald:

SON OF MILLIONAIRE

FALLS TO DEATH AT LIBERTY MONUMENT

The New York Journal:

CURSE OF STATUE

STRIKES AGAIN

OFFICIALS BAFFLED

The New York Sun:

CHILD FALLS TO DEATH

STATUE AUTHORITIES DENY CURSE

The New York Times:

ARTHUR HAVERHILL, JR.

IN FATAL ACCIDENT ON BEDLOE'S ISLAND

Park authorities interviewed the grief stricken, hysterical Bridgett Rooney, who saw nothing. Her would be suitor, former New York City Police Department Sergeant Walter O'Brien, said the child was anxious to get to the top and see the sights of the harbor.

Tony Charles, the chauffeur, described how the child wriggled out of his arms as he held the boy up to the window. "I've got to see it better Charles, I can't see down there, the little chap said and then he squirted right out of my hands and through the opening. It all happened in the twinkling of an eye." Mr. Charles, English born chauffeur to millionaire magnate, Arthur Haverhill, told the park officials.

No one mentioned or noticed the black suited, bearded man. It was as if he never existed.